CRACKED
FOUNDATION

Dorothy,
So nice to meet
you, thank you for
your support!

Enjoy the road!

CRACKED
FOUNDATION

Based on Actual Events

TA'SHE'ANA BANKS

Columbus, Ohio

Cracked Foundation: Book One of the Eruption of Life Series

Published by Gatekeeper Press
2167 Stringtown Rd, Suite 109
Columbus, OH 43123-2989
www.GatekeeperPress.com

Library of Congress Control Number: 2018949543

ISBN (hardcover): 9781642371741
ISBN (paperback): 9781642371772
eISBN: 9781642371765

Printed in the United States of America

DEDICATION

To my mom . . . with all my heart.

CONTENTS

ACKNOWLEDGMENTS

THANK YOU, GOD, for everything. For protecting me, guiding me when I had no sense of direction and drowning out the noise of the countless distractions. Also, for giving me clarity, for teaching me to stand still and to be patient. There is no me without you.

To the family and friends who supported, encouraged, and strengthened me along this journey, I extend the upmost gratitude to you all. Be blessed.

PART I

No More Tea Parties

CHAPTER 1

THE MOANING ECHOED from wall to wall, floor to ceiling, and my teeth chattered a bit as the sound grew distressful. I stood alone at the top of the stairs and attempted to untangle the strap of my backpack. Although my curiosity increased with each passing second, my feet hesitated to move. I was too afraid to look, and even more fearful of the unknown. Slowly, I forced myself to walk down the stairs, and with each step, the low grumbling undertone became louder and louder. My breathing was shallow as panic lodged in my throat.

Finally, I stood at the bottom of the stairs, staring at my brother, Jordan as he sat on the couch watching *Bugs Bunny*. The TV blared throughout the living room; it was distracting, and I wondered if he'd turned up the TV to tune out the moaning. I couldn't blame him. I forced a slight smile at him, and he giggled. Then, a scream rang through my eardrums. The sound of a desperate cry made my bottom lip quiver.

"Help! God, help me!"

I looked slightly to the left. I was stuck in shock. My eyes flooded with tears.

Mama's feet shook rapidly; her legs twitched and her left hand rested on her chest, while the right covered her eyes. A box of Raisin Bran cereal was on the floor next to her, flakes scattered across the linoleum. Milk covered the countertop in a pool as the plastic gallon lay on its side, dripping into a puddle on the floor.

"Tori, come downstairs! Something's wrong with Mama!" I yelled for my sister as my heart beat faster and faster.

"Mama?"

I stooped down beside her. She lay flat on her back with a face full of tears, eyes struck with fear as she attempted to speak. Her lips tightened as if they were holding her tongue hostage. It seemed painful for her to move her mouth.

Her lips trembled. "Give me the phone." She extended her arm, and her hand shook like a tambourine.

I reached for the phone hung on the kitchen wall and stretched the cord as far as it would go. Jordan came running, standing in the doorway, gazing wordlessly with wide eyes.

I heard the operator on the phone as I held Mama's other hand.

"Nine-one-one. What's your emergency?"

"I need help. I'm lying on the kitchen floor. I can't move. My chest hurts. My head hurts. Everything hurts."

"What's your name, sweetheart?"

"Dina. Dina Brooks." Struggling to breathe and gasping for air, she coughed. Blood splattered all over my jacket as it ran from her nose and down the side of her cheek to her ear.

I couldn't breathe. I grabbed the phone from her hand. "Please! Please help my Mama! She's bleeding."

"Who is this? What is your name, sweetheart? What's your address?"

"My name is Talisa. Please hurry. Something's wrong with my mama. Please, come quick. It's 1128 28th Street." I shook all over and the telephone bounced against my chin.

"Okay, honey, hold on. The ambulance should be there in just a few minutes. Stay on the phone with me. Are you able to unlock the door?"

"Yes, ma'am, I can." I set the phone down and ran to unlock the front door.

When I returned, Mama was still shaky and not speaking clearly. Her chest moved up and down, faster and faster, and I screamed into the phone, "Where are they? Where's the ambulance?"

"I promise you, sweetheart. They're coming in just a couple of minutes."

Jordan came running from the living room; his feet skidded around the corner. "I hear the sirens. I see the lights!"

"Talisa, I need you to go open the door for the paramedics, okay?" The voice on the other end of the phone was calm.

"Yes, ma'am."

I set the phone back on the floor and ran to open the front door. I couldn't feel my legs but I could feel a cool breeze against my sweat-beaded face as the door swung open. Two paramedics came up the walkway to the front porch—one white man, one black man—moving fast, and carrying a large black bag with a yellow board. It looked like a surfboard. Jordan grabbed my hand as they ran past us.

A few minutes later, Mrs. Tyler from next door came over.

"Talisa, Jordan, are you guys okay?" Mrs. Tyler's eyes were filled with worry as she kissed us on our foreheads.

"Yes, ma'am."

As she slowly walked toward the kitchen, she placed her hand on her chest as if to still her heart. "Oh dear. Oh, my goodness. Talisa, what happened?"

"I don't know, Mrs. Tyler. I just ran downstairs for school. She was just lying there on the floor."

"Where's your sister?" She raised both eyebrows and put her hands on her hips. "Where's Tori?"

"She's upstairs. I yelled for her to come downstairs, but she didn't come."

"I'll go get her." She stomped up the stairs, mumbling to herself. "This damn girl, I swear."

We sat on the couch, waiting. The white paramedic walked into the living room and kneeled down in front of us.

"Hi, my name's Thomas. What's your name?"

"I'm Talisa, and this is my little brother, Jordan."

"How old are you? What grade are you guys in?"

"I'm eleven. In fifth grade." I was trying to look past him to see what the other paramedic was doing to Mama. All I could see was a flurry of movement, and I felt like he was blocking the view on purpose. I sat up taller but still couldn't see.

"I'm six years old," Jordan smiled. "I'm in kindergarten. My teacher's name is Mrs. Kiplinger. Isn't that a funny name?" Jordan giggled as he wiped away his tears.

"Yeah, little guy," the paramedic agreed, "it *is* a funny name. So, listen, you guys. We're going to have to take your mom to the hospital. She isn't feeling very well and she needs further medical attention beyond what we can assist her with here. Do you understand?" He slightly smiled, but his eyes revealed serious concern.

"Yes, sir." My heart pounded. What did all this mean?

Mrs. Tyler and Tori came back downstairs. Tori walked sullenly over to sit next to me, shrugging away from Mrs. Tyler. Since Tori turned fifteen, it seemed that she constantly had an attitude about everything. She sat and pouted and didn't say a word, as though she was mad for some reason.

Mama had written all of the emergency phone numbers on the marker board on the refrigerator in case of emergencies, so Mrs. Tyler called Grandma. When she hung up, she turned to us.

"You guys aren't going to school today. Your grandmother said for you all to get in the ambulance with your mom, and she'll meet you at the hospital. After I lock the front door, Tori, take these keys. Give them to your grandmother when you get to the hospital. Got it?"

"Yes, I got it." Mrs. Tyler locked the door and handed the keys to Tori. She grabbed them and shoved them into her coat pocket.

The paramedics wheeled Mama down the walkway and

carried her over the four cement steps to the sidewalk. Her nearly lifeless body made my heart beat rapidly, her eyes closed, and once we sat in the ambulance it smelled like bleach. Everything was shiny and clean—too clean. Thomas put a plastic mask over Mama's mouth and nose. A needle in her arm was attached to a long plastic tube, which was connected to a bag of clear liquid that flowed into her arm. I didn't know what it was. What were they putting into her?

Her eyes suddenly opened, and she looked into mine. I took a deep breath and exhaled.

Her voice was gentle and raspy. "Don't cry. It'll be okay."

I tried not to, but I was so confused and lost. It was so hard. I tried to hold back my tears and blinked to stop them from falling. Jordan gripped my hand with his small, clammy fingers and I knew he was scared. Tori's slumped posture leaned against the back door staring out the window. Her headphones blasted music as she watched the traffic go by. She was speechless not acknowledging what was going on, as if she were scared to look at Mama.

While speeding through traffic rushing to get to the hospital, Mama's breathing became faint. Thomas yelled at the other paramedic driving, and he was alarmed, using medical words I didn't understand. The more the machine beeped, the tenser Thomas became as he moved hastily around her. He repeatedly checked her eyes, placed two fingers on her neck, pinched her wrist, and shook her each time she closed her eyes. As her arm hung loosely through the metal railings, her fingers swung back and forth as the ambulance rolled over every bump on the street. The rapid motion of her chest slowly declined before it stopped. Her head limply fell to the side, her eyes rolled back, and she didn't respond.

"Come on, man, we need to get there. I'm starting compressions. Let's go!" Thomas started to sweat as he silently repeated, "Come on, stay with me. Come on, just breathe." He pressed continuously on her chest and with each compression, her body jerked.

The ambulance stopped, the back doors swung open, and four nurses and two other paramedics were waiting to pull her out. They pulled us out first to get us out of the way.

"Why are they here?" one nurse asked as she picked Jordan up and set him on the ground.

"Necessity," Thomas answered.

They pulled Mama out and rolled her through the big, red, swinging doors stamped EMERGENCY. Tori stood behind me with watery eyes and a blank face. Jordan sat on the ground with his backpack still on, knees to his chest, head tucked down and crying. One of the nurses kneeled down in front of me and grabbed my hand.

"Hi, I'm Laura. I'm going to take you guys to the waiting room."

"What's wrong with her?"

"I'm not sure, sweetheart, but we're going to figure it out."

We walked toward the red doors, and I looked up at the nurse. "Can I go with her? I want to see if she's okay."

She grabbed my arm. "No, you can't go back there."

"Please," I begged her, trying to pull away. I didn't want Mama to be alone. She was all by herself back there.

"I know you're scared, but you have to let the doctor figure out what's going on. Please, calm down."

Tori walked over to me, finally awakening to the tragic scene. She slid her arm around my shoulder. "Come on, we're just going to have to sit down and wait."

Jordan wrapped his arms around me and rested his head on my stomach. His hands shook. Grandma and Mama's boyfriend, Samuel—we called him Sam—came twenty minutes later. Sam stood by the nurse's desk, nearly stunned and stared blankly at us. He paced back and forth in the hallway and repeatedly rubbed his left hand over his beard. The longer we waited, the more worry mounted on his face.

"Are you guys hungry?" he asked. I thought of my breakfast covering the kitchen floor back home and nodded. He took us to the cafeteria to eat. He told us that we shouldn't have any fear or be sad.

"The doctors will figure out what's going on with your mom," he assured us as he bit into a piece of toast. His hands were bulky and his fingers were long with a couple strands of hair above each knuckle. He was highly educated, spoke eloquently, and his broad-shouldered demeanor was quite assertive. His typical scholarly approach to things often intrigued me, especially when he helped me study my spelling words or encouraged me to think out of the box. Sam loved to talk. People often said he was quite articulate, and many sought his advice on various topics. So, I decided maybe I should believe him.

Grandma joined us in the cafeteria. She was tiny, but frank. She usually didn't have a lot to say, but her hand gestures and body language spoke loudly. She talked to Sam for a long time, and he listened and nodded his head as if he was agreeing with her.

Sam walked slowly back to the table and hovered over us in silence. He placed his hands in his pants pockets. "Okay, listen closely. Your mom has to stay here because the doctors need more time to examine her. They aren't quite sure yet what's wrong, but it's their job to figure it out. Do you understand?"

Jordan and I nodded while Tori stared without blinking.

"They're going to run some more medical tests and examine her more thoroughly," he continued. "In the meantime, I'm going to take you home, and I'm going to stay with you guys so you're not alone."

We left Mama there, alone. I couldn't comprehend it. I was so confused. Sam said we couldn't stay, so we had no choice but to leave. He firmly held my hand as we walked out the door, and Jordan followed.

"Come on, let's go." His voice was low; a near whisper. One by one, we did as he said because there wasn't anything else we *could* do. We followed him out, and as we drove away, I stared out the back window. Mama was all by herself—alone.

CHAPTER 2

~April 8, 1989~

Dear Diary,

I just couldn't sleep last night. Mama has never been away before. I tossed and turned thinking about her. It was so scary. Jordan slept in my bed last night because he was afraid, too. Sam left this morning to go check on Mama. I don't know why we couldn't go. We stayed home until he came back. He said Mama has to stay in the hospital for a couple more days.

~April 9, 1989~

Dear Diary,

Mama was transferred to a different hospital. They flew her to the University of Iowa Medical Center in a helicopter. We can't even see her now, so something must be really wrong. Sam says he doesn't know what's happening, but the local hospital wasn't equipped to handle Mama's condition. What condition? Jordan was crying. Tori acts like nothing's happening, but I heard her crying in the bathroom. Sam said he'll stay with us, but we'll have to go to Grandma and Grandpa's house if he has to go out of town for work. Sam's a cool guy. He's really nice and always talks to me, but I really wish Daddy was here. I feel helpless. I don't want to go to Grandpa and Grandma's house—not to stay for a long time. I just want Mama to come back home with us.

THE NEXT MORNING, it took a long time to wake Jordan up. I yanked the blankets off of him and watched him kick his feet on the mattress as he rolled around in the bed. He was quite the character. It was more quiet than usual this morning, getting ready for school. We packed strawberry Pop-Tarts in our backpacks for an after-school snack. Tori left me the key to lock the door, then got in a blue car with someone. She didn't even say bye. And she didn't look back. Mama usually dropped us off at school. It wasn't too far to walk, but Mama said we were too young to walk by ourselves. Today, we had no choice. Sam told Tori to walk us to school, but she didn't.

On our way to school, we crossed paths with a big, brown dog walking down an alley. We stood stiffly like mannequins when it stopped by a garbage can and stared at us. Its tongue hung out of its mouth as big drops of drool fell to the ground. My heart raced. I grabbed Jordan's hand and quickly crossed the street. We watched the dog walk in the opposite direction.

"I was scared. I was going to run really fast and leave you."

"Yeah, that's not funny, Jordan. He could have caught me and bit me."

"Then I would have beat him up, jumped on his back, put him in a choke hold, flipped him over, and body slammed him on his head." He showed me all of his moves.

I shook my head at him. "You watch way too much WWF wrestling. Run to class. There's your teacher. I'll come get you after school." We high-fived each other and he ran down the hall.

After school, we walked home and the house lurked of silence it was borderline creepy. We watched TV for a while, then Tori arrived finally just before sunset. Later, the phone rang several times while I sat outside the bathroom door waiting for Jordan to finish his bath. I wasn't sure if I should answer or not. Tori was in our room listening to music. Sam was supposed to come back, and we weren't allowed to answer the phone without Mama's permission. I thought I should just wait for Sam. The ringing stopped, then it rang again, so I answered it.

"Hello?" I whispered.

"Talisa, it's me. It's Mom." Her voice was low.

I was so excited to hear her. "Hi, Mama. Are you okay?"

"No, baby. I'm not okay. I'm sick." Her voice cracked.

I didn't know what to say. "It's okay, Mama; don't cry. Should I go get Tori?"

"Yes, go get her."

"Okay, hold on a minute." I set the phone down on the coffee table and ran back upstairs. She came downstairs, and I wasn't sure what Mama had said to her, but Tori kept repeating, "Yes, ma'am." Not once did she ask a question. After she hung up the phone, she sat quietly with her hands on her head.

"Tori, what's wrong?" I sat next to her on the couch. My mouth watered and a numbing feeling tingled throughout my body.

"Talisa, Mama is really sick." She paused in between each word. She sat in shock and her face froze as if she had just seen a ghost.

"Like the flu or something?"

"No, not like the flu . . . or a cold. Like a sickness that only special doctors can fix with medicine and medical research and stuff."

"So, she's not coming home?"

"Talisa, are you listening to me? She's sick. Like something is wrong with her entire body. It's not functioning right. She's probably not coming home for a long time."

We held hands and our fingers intertwined as doubtfulness draped over our heads. I laid my head on her shoulder and she put her arm around me. I didn't know what to think or how to react.

*   *   *

~April 14, 1989~

Dear Diary,

Tori was supposed to pick me and Jordan up from school today, but she never showed up. Luckily, she gave *me the house keys this morning. We watched the big numbers flash on the bank's clock across the street as we waited thirty minutes for her. We realized she wasn't coming, so we walked home, playing tag along the way, racing from the swings to the water fountain. Jordan was really fast. He almost beat me, and it surprised me. I didn't know he could run that fast. Thankfully, it was nice outside today and the sun was shining. I picked a lot of dandelions from the playground and put them in my hair.*

When we got home, Tori wasn't there. In fact, no one was. It was just us—Jordan and me.

Tori was a straight-A student; witty, smart, confident and determined to do whatever she set her mind to do. Last year, she was a member of the school's band and played the clarinet. She could *really* play, too. She used to laugh and play with me, but lately she was different. Quiet, stayed to herself. I heard Mama tell Grandma she had tried everything to help her, and sometimes she just didn't know what else to do. I didn't know what that meant, or if there was something wrong with Tori.

Tori didn't come home until after dark and Sam was peeved. His patience was running thin and his face said it all.

The following day, Sam went into work to finish a project, but he called often to check on us. Tori told him he didn't have to come over, and that she was going to look after us. Usually on Saturdays, we either ate pizza, hotdogs, or corndogs with potato chips, and we watched a movie from the collection of VHS tapes on the bookshelf. Tori sat in the chair with her feet up on the ottoman. Jordan and I popped popcorn, shared a blanket on the couch, and watched *Beetlejuice*—one of our favorite movies.

We knew all of the words from the beginning to the end, just like *The Color Purple* and *Little Shop of Horrors*, but my favorite was *The Jungle Book*. I fell asleep during the movie and a loud noise woke me up. Jordan was sound asleep next to me, wrapped from head to toe with Mama's favorite brown blanket. I sat still for a minute and waited, trying to listen for Tori because the chair was empty. I darted up the stairs. It was completely dark when I walked into our bedroom and flipped on the light switch. There was no sign of her anywhere. I checked the bathroom, kitchen, and dining room. She was gone. I turned on every light in the house and stood at the front door looking through the glass, hoping she was outside or something. But when I pulled back the sheer curtain, there was only darkness. No sign of her.

The clock read 11:38 p.m. Maybe she went to the store. Something didn't feel right, but I had no other answer. I sat at the bottom of the stairs and waited for her to come back. As the clock continued to turn, the more frightened I became. By 1:18 a.m., I realized we were truly alone. I called Grandma. I could tell from the tone of her voice she was annoyed. She said she was going to call Sam. He came immediately.

*   *   *

~April 17, 1989~

Dear Diary,

It rained all day. I just sat on my bed, looking across the room at Tori's vacant bed. Where was she, and why did she leave us alone? Is she coming back?

Tori finally came home a few days later. I stood on the step stool in the kitchen, fixing breakfast, when I overheard Sam speaking to her.

"Where have you been? Do you know your grandmother called the police?" He pushed his glasses back from the tip of his nose.

She yelled, "It's none of your business!"

I peeked around the corner of the kitchen cabinet. Sam stood still with his hands on his waist, shaking his head left to right in disappointment.

"Get upstairs and pack your clothes. You're going to your grandparents since you don't want to listen to me."

She threw her jacket across the room. "I'm not going anywhere. You can't make me."

We were late for school. Sam's silence during the car ride clearly indicated his frustration with Tori, I could tell; he kept shaking his head. Then, he told her, "Your behavior is unacceptable."

Sam assured me that he would pick us up. We got out of the car and Tori stared at me. I smiled at her, but she just rolled her eyes and crossed her arms. I waved goodbye to Sam, grabbed Jordan's hand, and walked through the playground to the school doors. Jordan's classroom was in the building next to mine, and I usually walked him to class first before I ran to my own.

*   *   *

~April 29, 1989~

Dear Diary,

I'm sorry I threw you against the wall today. It's just that I was so mad. No one's telling us what's wrong with Mama! When will we get to see her? Is she okay? I called Grandma to ask, but she just said the doctors are still trying to figure it out. It's all anyone ever says. Shouldn't they know by now? Sam promised me that he would take us to see her as soon as the doctors give us permission. Don't be offended, but I don't want to write anymore.

~May 6, 1989~

Dear Diary,

Yay! We got to talk to Mama on the phone this morning. It's been almost a month! She sounded so tired. Her voice was really soft, like she just woke up. Jordan and I told her we loved her and missed her, and she said that Sam would bring us to the hospital to visit her soon. I was so glad I got to talk to her. I miss her!

~May 13, 1989~

Dear Diary,

Oh boy, I really messed up today. Tori is back home with us. I wasn't sure if Sam was coming back, and Jordan's hair was getting out of control. I didn't have any money to get his hair cut, so I cut it with Mama's electric leg shaver. Big, big mistake. There were spots everywhere, patches of missing hair. I just couldn't fix it. The more I tried, the worse it got. Jordan was mad . . . really mad. He started crying and he doesn't want to go to school. Honestly, I can't blame him. He's going to get teased. I feel sooo bad. I really thought the shaver would work, but it looks worse than ever.

~May 16, 1989~

Dear Diary,

Jordan's teacher came to my class today because Jordan wouldn't take off his hat in the classroom. I told the teacher what happened and asked her if he could just wear it for a couple of days. She giggled, but she agreed to let him wear it. I must have apologized a million times to him, but Jordan just looks at me with a face of disgust.

~May 19, 1989~

Dear Diary,

We had to stay with Grandma and Grandpa for the last couple days because Sam had to go out of town. Tori was really mad, but Sam said that he didn't trust leaving us alone with her anymore. I didn't blame him. Grandma's house was so much fun, all of my cousins came over, and we played games like Life, Clue, Uno, and Trouble. We dressed up in old clothes from Grandma and Grandpa's attic and made up dances as a group. I wished we could have stayed longer, but Sam came back today. So, we had to go home. I don't know why. All I know is that being home alone without Mama is starting to feel lonely.

~May 20, 1989~

Dear Diary,

Today, drill team practice was hard. We learned a new step routine for the upcoming Memorial Day parade. I joined the team two years ago, and practice is held right down the street from Grandma and Grandpa's house. My best friend, Leslie, only lives a couple of blocks away, so we walk together. Her mom walks with us, too. She treats me like her own daughter. Leslie and I have been friends since the second grade. She was the first person I met when we moved here from Pennsylvania two years ago. Before then, we lived in Wisconsin, where I was born.

But, the day we arrived here in Rock Island, Illinois, everything changed.

I remembered sitting outside on the front steps of Grandma and Grandpa's house while Daddy unpacked boxes of clothes and toys from his black Cadillac. He and Mama set everything on the front porch, and they never spoke one word to each other. Once he finished, he sat next to me and told me to stop crying. He kept repeating that he'd be back to visit us. He kissed me on both cheeks, then picked Jordan up off of his Scooby Doo Big Wheel and hugged him and kissed him all over his face. He got in the car, started to drive away, and we watched his red tail lights fade into the distance. Then, he was gone. I didn't understand why we had to move, or why Mama and Daddy didn't want to live together anymore.

I sat alone outside for a while, hoping Daddy would return. Then, I heard the beating of boisterous drums that awakened the entire neighborhood, and people stood on their porches observing. A large group of kids came marching and dancing down the street. Red and gold flags flew in the air, and white wooden guns were tossed and spun around. There was a line of boys with drums and wooden sticks in their hands, and a group of girls danced behind them. A little group of kids my age led the team. I stopped crying and ran into the house to get Mama. She came out on the front porch, and we watched the group march by.

Leslie's mama, Ms. Rose, walked up to Mama as we stood on the front porch. Ms. Rose asked Mama if she knew about the drill team, and Mama told her we had just moved to Illinois. They introduced themselves, and after a few smiles and a couple of head nods, Ms. Rose invited us to the team's practice the next day. I had begged Mama a million times that night to let me join the drill team, and she repeated, "Hush, girl. Go sit down somewhere." Eventually, she said yes.

Many Sundays had passed and I terribly missed Mama's Sunday dinners. Grandpa cooked, and it smelled awful. Pig's feet and pig ears boiled away on the stove. I sat at the end of the kitchen table and watched him cut the meat into small pieces. I pinched my nose to block the smell, and Grandpa sprinkled hot sauce all over his plate.

"Little girl, what's wrong with your face?" He grinned at me.

"That smells like the sewer. Why are you eating that?"

"You don't know nothin' about good eatin'."

I curled my top lip. "If that's good eatin', I'll just take all the bad eatin' instead."

He chuckled and shook his head. "Go make you a bowl of cereal or a peanut butter and jelly sandwich. Make something for your brother, too."

"Yes, sir." I smiled.

Mama said Grandpa was a very authoritative man, which meant that when he talked, you just listened, and when you answered him, you said "sir." We tried to stay outside and out of his way as much as possible, but sometimes he'd sit on the porch humming and watching us playing in the yard.

* * *

~May 25, 1989~

Dear Diary,

I'm ready to go home. To our own house. I don't like using the bathroom upstairs here. You have to flush the toilet with a bucket of water because someone broke the handle.

Mama says Grandpa's really cheap. He's always looking for ways to fix things himself, just so he doesn't have to spend any money. There's a hole in the roof of the house, and Grandpa refuses to get it fixed. Instead, he just stapled plastic over the hole. When it rains, the water runs down the plastic into buckets in the attic, which we all have to empty, no matter what time it is, day or night. It's just insane to me. Just fix it, Grandpa.

Tori and Aunt Nita, Mama's baby sister, got in a big argument. Tori grabbed her bag and bolted out the door. Aunt Nita loved to boss us around and always yelled at everyone. Grandma demanded that Tori come back, and Grandpa quickly got in his car to try to catch her. Her frequent disappearances puzzled me and left me clueless. When Grandpa returned, Tori wasn't with him. We had to stay with our grandparents because Sam was out of town for work again. He said he had to go for a training class or something and wouldn't be back for a few weeks. Jordan and I slept upstairs and shared a twin bed in the bedroom next to Aunt Nita's room.

"Pssst . . . Talisa," Jordan whispered.

I rolled over. "Oh, is that your feet smelling like that? Did you wash 'em?"

"I did." He giggled and wrestled to hide his feet under the cover.

"No, you didn't. I'm getting the powder." I tiptoed to the dresser to get the powder and sprinkled a little on his feet. "Why aren't you sleeping?"

Jordan shrugged, and his face was grieved—even in the dark. "Mama's never coming back, is she?"

"Don't say that," I frowned. "She'll come back. You'll see."

"How do you know?" He crossed his arms.

I really hoped he was wrong because that would mean we'd have to live with our grandparents forever. Not that I didn't like Grandpa and Grandma; I just wanted to be with Mama.

"Because the doctors will figure it out; it's their job. And then she'll come home. That's why they took her to a different hospital . . . because she needs special doctors."

"I hope you're right. I really miss her."

"Yeah, me too."

"If y'all don't take y'all's little asses to sleep right now, I'm gonna whip both of you! Stop all that talking and go to bed." Aunt Nita's voice projected through the wall. She was just mean for no reason. We covered our mouths, giggled, and rested our heads on the pillows.

*   *   *

~June 1, 1989~

Dear Diary,

Tori didn't come back last night. Grandma called the police again. Tori is always so mad. One morning, she just kept yelling at me and saying that I get on her nerves and that everyone's against her. I hate it because we used to do everything together.

~June 3, 1989~

Dear Diary,

Today is the last day of school. Summer break! I'm so excited! We get to ride our bikes. Sam is coming to pick us up on Sunday. I hope this means we get to see Mama. In September, I start sixth grade. Jordan will be in first grade, and Tori will be in tenth grade. I can't wait. One more year, then I'll be in junior high. If we have to stay here with Grandma and Grandpa, I may have to go back to my old school, Grant Elementary. All of my friends go there. I made a lot of friends at my current school, Lincoln Elementary. It was different though. There were black kids, white kids, and Mexican kids. At Grant, there were a whole lot of black kids, and most of them were part of the drill team, too.

Sam didn't pick us up. Grandma said we had to stay longer. We were running out of clean clothes, and Grandma taught me how to use the washing machine and how to hang the clothes on the line outside to dry. The washing machine was old, not nearly resembling the ones at the laundromat Mama went to. This one was ancient. In order to wring out the water in the clothes, you had to slide them through two rollers that looked like rolling pins you used to roll out pie crust. The socks, especially Jordan's small socks, were the hardest. I tried to put them on the bottom roller so they would just catch and roll through. But my fingers were too close and the rollers caught them. Before I knew it, my whole arm was in between the washer's rollers.

The pain was indescribable. The entire family circled around me. Uncle Darren, Mama's baby brother, pulled the plug out of the socket. I screamed and screamed. Grandpa and Uncle Darren used tools to take the roller apart and get my arm out. For once, Aunt Nita was nice. She actually gave me a hug and wrapped my arm with a cold cloth. My whole arm throbbed that entire night.

*   *   *

~June 5, 1989~

Dear Diary,

Daddy called today. He talked to Grandma for a long time. I heard Grandma tell him Mama wasn't doing good, and she had no clue when Mama was coming home. Grandma called us in the living room to talk to him. I asked Daddy when he was coming to visit us. He said he was working really hard and would come as soon as he could. He lives in Tennessee now, and I've never been there. Maybe we can live with him until Mama's better. I really miss him, too.

~June 6, 1989~

Dear Diary,

We had to move. Mama always said the neighborhood isn't what it used to be because now it's full of drugs and gangs. Well, my aunts and uncles moved all of our things from *our old house to a different house two blocks away from our grandparents. I can't wait to tell Leslie I won't have to miss so many drill team practices anymore. Grandma says we have to stay here for the summer, which means Mama isn't coming home anytime soon.*

~June 7, 1989~

Dear Diary,

Sam came by Grandma's today, and we sat on the front porch and talked. We're going to see Mama on Saturday. Jordan jumped up and down, and I gave Sam a big hug. We haven't seen her in two months. I can't wait to tell Mama that I've been doing my own hair and that Jordan knows how to write a lot of words now.

CHAPTER 3

I WOKE UP BURSTING with excitement and somewhat relieved. Jordan smiled from ear to ear as he danced around the bedroom.

"We're going to see Mama today, right, Talisa?" He smiled.

"Yes, we are. Go brush your teeth and finish getting dressed. I'll get our jackets, then we can go sit on the front porch and wait for Sam."

I would have to miss drill team practice, and I told Ms. Rose that we were going to visit Mama. Sam drove me, Jordan, Grandma, and Aunt Joi to the hospital. Aunt Joi was another one of Mama's younger sisters. She was quite knowledgeable like Sam and always wore business clothes like the people on TV. The hospital was in Iowa City, Iowa, which was a forty-five-minute drive. On the way there, we passed by a lot of semi-trucks. I wondered if Daddy was in one of them. He was a truck driver.

When we arrived at the hospital, a lot of fast-walking people crowded the hallways and wheelchairs lined up along the walls. As we walked past each hospital room, machines beeped, people coughed constantly, and nurses ran around like roaches after someone turned the light on.

Jordan squeezed my fingers and whispered, "Are all of these people sick like Mama?"

I whispered back, "I don't know."

We stood in the hallway leaning against the wall, anxiously waiting to see her. Then, Sam opened the door and waved for us to enter. Grandma and Aunt Joi were standing by Mama's bed, and the room smelled like the mothballs in Grandma's closet. It was cold, but clean. Sam pulled back the curtain, and Mama's eyes were barely open. Her skin was dark, and countless light spots freckled her face, arms, and hands. Her eyes were sunken with thick, shadowy rings around them. Only a couple of strands of hair laid on the top of her head but the majority was just bare skin. She looked like a real-life skeleton. I almost didn't recognize her. Disbelief made it difficult to continue to observe but I couldn't stop looking at her. Could this be her? What happened to her?

I inched to her bedside and softly touched her hand. Jordan attempted to climb up on the bed, and when Mama looked at us, in the moment it was such a relief. We were finally with her, and everything would soon go back to normal.

Mama looked at Grandma. "Who are they?"

"Talisa and Jordan. Your children," Sam answered.

Why did she say that?

"I don't have any children," she firmly responded. Mama then pulled her hand away from me and waved her other at Jordan to get off the bed.

"It's me, Mama . . . Talisa." I reached for her hand again, and she pulled back as though I'd hurt her.

"Just go away," she insisted.

"It's me, Mama. It's Jordan." He tried to convince her too, but she wouldn't listen. She yelled for Aunt Joi to take us away.

Aunt Joi took my hand and pulled me back into the hallway. Jordan cried, kicked, and screamed as Sam picked him up and struggled to set him in the chair in the hallway. I was astonished. Aunt Joi sat next to me. Jordan's loud cry, made me cry.

"Aunt Joi, why doesn't Mama want us? Did we do something wrong?" I asked. My heart felt frozen. This couldn't be happening.

"No, sweetheart. You guys didn't do anything wrong. Your mom is *very* sick. She just doesn't remember right now. But she will when the doctors figure out how to help her." Aunt Joi put her arm around me as assurance.

I pushed her arm away. "She wasn't sick like that at home. The hospital is making her sicker. The doctors are making her worse!" I yelled.

Two nurses hurried over to Aunt Joi. "Do you need our help?"

"No, she's only eleven. She doesn't understand, and I'm trying to explain it to her." Aunt Joi nodded at them. She kneeled in front of me. "Talisa, listen to me. Your mom is very, very ill, and the doctors are only here to help her. They're trying really hard, sweetheart. They have to figure out what's wrong with her first, then they can help her get better. Do you understand?"

"No, I don't understand. Why does she look like that? What

happened to all of her hair? Why is her skin so dark? Why? Why doesn't she remember us? We're her kids! She pushed me away like she doesn't like me anymore. She remembered you and Sam and Grandma. Why doesn't she want us?"

"Oh, niece." She placed her hand on her chest. "You're too young to understand. I'm going to try to help you understand once the doctors figure it out. I promise."

I wrapped my arms around Aunt Joi and laid my head on her shoulder. It felt like someone took my favorite toy and smashed it into tiny pieces. My heart ached.

"I just miss her so much, and now she doesn't want to see me."

Aunt Joi kept saying that it was the sickness causing Mama's memory loss.

"Talisa, can you please do me a favor?"

"What?" I looked in Aunt Joi's eyes.

"Go sit with your brother for a little while and calm him down. I need to go check on your mom. Can you do that?" Aunt Joi smiled at me. "Remember, you have to be a big girl now."

Jordan was still kicking and screaming; his arms were extended as he tried to reach for the door of Mama's room. If I didn't understand, I knew he didn't either. I grabbed his hand and he settled down. He hugged me, and I picked him up and set him on my lap. I patted his back until he fell asleep, and we waited in the hall for a long time until Sam returned.

I felt lightheaded, and my mind yearned for answers. We didn't get to say goodbye. A doctor came up to Sam, Aunt Joi, and Grandma before we left the hospital. I heard the doctor say that they would keep searching through the blood work and call if they found anything. I didn't know what blood work meant, but I hoped for a solution. The awkwardly silent ride home allowed me too much time to think. More than I wanted to as images of Mama's frail body flashed in my mind like a projector. Jordan fell asleep on my shoulder and I leaned my head against his, wondering what do we do now.

* * *

~June 13, 1989~

Dear Diary,

Today is Tori's sixteenth birthday. I don't know where she is. She never came back to Grandma and Grandpa's house. Uncle Ted, Mama's other brother, is a police officer. He's been looking for Tori but hasn't found her. Happy birthday, Tori. Wherever you are . . . I love you!

~June 14, 1989~

Dear Diary,

I walked to drill team practice with Leslie today, and I told her about Mama. She gave me a big hug. She didn't know. No one really does. We had a good practice today. We learned a new step routine. It was really challenging at first, but our group's captain made us do it over and over until we got it right. It was a slight relief and a good distraction being able to think about something other than my worry for Mama.

Sam and Grandma talked for a while; each time I walked through the living room, they became mute. Jordan was asleep on the couch and Tori was still out in the world somewhere. At times, I wished I could rewind time and go back to having fun like we did when we lived in Milwaukee. I wondered what Mama would think if she knew about Tori or did she even remember her.

My cousin Sharae and I played hopscotch and tic-tac-toe outside until Sam asked me to sit on the steps with him.

"How are you doing?" he asked as he patted the cracked concrete step for me to sit.

"I'm fine. We were trying to draw straight lines to play hopscotch. There isn't enough chalk left, though. Grandma said we can't be in the house playing board games all day, so we rode our bikes around the block a couple of times. Then we helped Grandpa pick up the sticks in the yard."

"That's good. Sounds like you're having fun. I have to talk to you about your mom. If you don't understand anything I say, just say you don't understand, okay? And I'll try to explain it better."

"Okay." I was nervous. Mama had been gone for so long, I thought it couldn't be good news.

"So, the doctors have run a lot of different tests on your mom's blood. At first, they diagnosed her with HIV, but they were wrong. Some special doctors have been testing her for months now. They did a spinal biopsy, and they thought it was cancer."

"What's a spinal biopsy?" I grabbed my notebook. "How do you spell that?"

"S-p-i-n-a-l and b-i-o-p-s-y. See, everyone has red and white blood cells. If the doctor takes some blood from your body, it's called blood work. They can then determine if something's wrong with you. So, they took a long needle and put it in your mom's lower back to take a sample of her blood cells to see if it's cancer."

"Well, is it cancer? I thought cancer happens to people who smoke cigarettes. That's what they say on TV. Mama doesn't smoke."

"You're right. It can happen to people who smoke. But the test came back negative, so it's not cancer."

I stared at him. "If it's not HIV or cancer, then what is it? Then what's wrong with her?"

"Well, she's been diagnosed with something called lupus. Umm, a type of disease where the body attacks itself. It's called SLE, which means systemic lupus erythematosus. Now, I know you don't know what that means, but that's the name of it. The doctors don't have a lot of information on this disease, but that's what they think it is."

I threw my hands in the air. "All these big words, Sam. How do you spell them?" I prepared to write.

He smiled at me, "Are you ready?"

"Yep."

"Lupus is l-u-p-u-s. Systemic is s-y-s-t-e-m-i-c and erythematosus is e-r-y-t-h-e-m-a-t-o-s-u-s. Got it?"

"Got it. Sam, is Mama going to die?" I hesitated. "If there isn't any information, how do they know it's this thing called lupus?"

He grabbed my hand. "Hey, little one. But don't cry. Let's just talk about what it is first and let's think positive, okay?"

"Okay, what is it?"

"It's an autoimmune disease. The body's immune system is supposed to protect our bodies from things like sickness, germs, and viruses. But, for some reason your mom's system has turned against her."

"Say what? Again, Sam. All these big words. Spell autoimmune." I looked at him, completely confused.

"Are you going to ask me to spell every word?"

"Are you going to keep using big words?"

"Probably."

"Well, then, yep. What does all this mean?"

"Look at it this way. Your mom's blood cells have started fighting each other, which is causing more problems to other parts of her body."

"That sounds stupid. Why would your body fight itself? Just tell me if Mama's going to be all right. Will the doctors at the hospital help her?"

"The doctors are doing the best they can to help her. So, don't worry."

"Okay."

"Do you have any questions?"

"Nope. Just let me know when Mama's coming home."

He gave me a hug, walked to his car, and drove away.

*   *   *

~June 23, 1989~

Dear Diary,

Today is Jordan's birthday. He's seven years old now. I woke him up singing "Happy Birthday." He put the pillow over his head, then I tickled him until he fell out of the bed.

Grandpa moved us down the hall away from Aunt Nita's room, where we slept on bunk beds with metal rails. We giggled all morning in bed telling knock-knock jokes. Jordan stopped laughing and grew alarmingly quiet.

"What's wrong, Jordan?" I leaned my head over the railing.

"Do you think Mama remembers my birthday?"

I jumped off the top bunk. "Yes, she remembers. Of course, she remembers your birthday."

I snatched his sock off his foot and zoomed down the hallway. He ran after me, laughing. I didn't know what Mama remembered, but I didn't want him to be sad on his birthday. Obviously, he didn't get a cake from Mama like he usually did but he negotiated a handful of assorted candy from Grandpa. Jordan loved candy.

*   *   *

~July 4, 1989~

Dear Diary,

Happy Independence Day! I love this holiday. Every year Uncle Ted and Grandpa give us sparklers, snap poppers, and confetti poppers. Uncle Ted goes out of town to get really big fireworks, and after we eat, we all walk to the big field across the street to watch him light them. They're always so pretty, lighting the sky with different bright colors. Holidays at Grandpa and Grandma's house are the best! They have sixteen children, so I have a lot of cousins!

~July 6, 1989~

Dear Diary,

I took Jordan for a ride on the back of my bike today. Grandma said we can only ride our bikes around the block. I keep telling him to tie his shoestrings, but he never listens. His foot got caught in the bike spokes, and he has two small cuts on his ankle now. I told him so.

~July 8, 1989~

Dear Diary,

Sam, Aunt Joi, Uncle Darren, Aunt Nita, and Aunt Denise are going to see Mama tomorrow. Grandma says we have to stay here this time. Aunt Denise is another one of Mama's younger sisters. She's pretty and funny—a really cool auntie. I really want to go to see if Mama remembers us now. But, then I'll be sad if she doesn't. I just want to hug her and give her a kiss.

~July 11, 1989~

Dear Diary,

A lot of people are living in Grandma and Grandpa's house: Aunt Nita and her son Jacob, my cousin; Uncle Darren, who always dresses really nice in a suit and tie (I think he works at a bank); and Aunt Denise who's home from the Army. Mama has a lot of brothers and sisters: Uncle Buck, Uncle Mitch, Aunt Bertha, Aunt Carol, and Uncle Reggie. Mama's younger brothers and sisters are Uncle Ted, Aunt Victoria, Uncle Troy, Aunt Denise, Aunt Joi, Aunt Bernice, Uncle Byron, Uncle Darren and Aunt Juanita. There are a lot of people.

Aunt Joi, Sam, Grandma and Grandpa gathered at the kitchen table. I sat on the back steps coloring in Jordan's Ghostbusters II coloring book, but when Aunt Joi started talking about Mama, I tiptoed down the stairs to get closer to the door. I turned the knob and cracked it just a little so I could peek in.

"She isn't doing any better. I'm not sure where to start." Aunt Joi's wavering tone was full of emotion.

Grandma said, "Just take your time and be straightforward." She crossed her hands and tapped two fingers nervously on the table.

"Her memory's been affected—they said her long-term memory, specifically. Her level of mobility has decreased, and they think the disease may have attacked her entire neural system somehow. They want to try a couple of electric shock treatments to see if it'll help balance out her nervous system and maybe even help with the memory loss as well."

Sam kept clearing his throat as if he had something stuck in it.

"Mom, Dad, should we tell them to do this? It just seems like such a risk, especially when they aren't sure if this treatment will even help her. This could cause more damage to her body, or even her brain. What should we do?"

Then Grandpa cleared his throat. "So, Sam, do you think this'll help her?"

"I'm not sure, sir. But they made it seem as if this is her only option at the moment. Without treatment, she probably won't remember the kids—or any of us eventually. When we all went to visit her this past Sunday, we had to remind her who we were."

"Oh, Lord, help my child. When do you plan to go back to the hospital?" Grandpa stood up and rubbed his hands together.

"I was planning on going back after work on Friday. You're more than welcome to come along, sir." Sam extended his arm to shake Grandpa's hand.

"Well, we'll decide when we get there. I need to speak with these doctors and get a full understanding of this treatment process." Grandpa's startled demeanor caused a slight imbalance as he walked away from the table.

Sam adjusted his shirt. "There's one more thing before you go, Mr. Brooks. They said her kidney function is decreasing and recommended starting dialysis treatments."

Grandpa paused, grunted, shook his head, and continued to walk into the living room.

I didn't know what the nervous system or electric shock treatment was. Dialysis. Like an electric socket plug shock? I got shocked once and it burned my finger. Is that what they're talking about? Are they going to do that to Mama's body? To her brain?

CHAPTER 4

~July 23, 1989~

Dear Diary,

*We went swimming today. It was so much fun! Aunt Nita
and Uncle Darren took us to the park's swimming pool.
There were a lot of kids and a huge slide. Jordan had to
go to the kiddie pool. I don't know how to swim. Uncle
Darren taught me how to hold my breath under water. It
wasn't bad until the water went up my nose and it burned.*

WE USED TO go to the pool all the time when we
lived in Pennsylvania—just me and Tori. We'd
walk to the pool near our apartment building,
and we always had the best time. Jordan and I once got in big
trouble. We really wanted a Slip-N-Slide, but Mama said it was
too expensive. So, Jordan and I waited until Mama went to the
grocery store and Tori was in our bedroom listening to music.
We got the furniture plastic cover from the closet and laid it
down on the hallway floor and in the living room. We filled

Mama's mixing bowls with water and poured it on the plastic. We ran from Mama and Daddy's room, sliding on the plastic all the way to the living room. It was a blast until Mama returned earlier than expected. Mama turned into Taz the Tasmanian devil within a matter of seconds.

"Have you two lost your damn minds?" she shouted. "I swear, you two are always plotting something. Talisa, I bet this was your idea." She scrunched her face at me and her nostrils flared like a dragon.

"I'm going to beat both of your asses. Look at all of this water everywhere. On the TV, the walls, on the side of the couch! Oh, you two are mine." Her face turned even redder. "You two stay right here; you better not move an inch."

When she turned around, we took off running. I hid under my bed, and Jordan hid behind the curtains in the living room. I told him to follow me, but it was too late.

Mama got the belt. I heard Jordan yelling my name from the living room, and I knew she'd eventually find me, but I hoped her energy was drained by the time she got to me. We were soaking wet, the whipping stung, and we had to clean up everything. Later, we laughed into our pillows.

After riding my bike around the block, the next day, I heard Grandma whispering on the phone. "One minute we think she's making progress; the next, something else happens. The electric shock treatments helped her to move better, but her memory's still a bit shaky. The treatment caused a lot of fluid to go to her brain, which caused her to go blind. They aren't sure if it's temporary or permanent. Only time will tell. We're all praying for her, too. Talk to you soon." She hung up the phone and sat back in her chair.

I didn't know who she was talking to but I heard her loud and clear. I frowned with anger and stomped through the kitchen to the back porch bottling my tears. Mama was blind? Why was this happening?

* * *

~July 26, 1989~

Dear Diary,

Daddy called today. He said he's coming to see us. I'm so excited. I haven't seen him since he dropped us off at Grandma and Grandpa's house three years ago.

~August 1, 1989~

Dear Diary,

Daddy never showed up. He promised. Sigh.

Aunt Nita woke us up before the birds chirped to get ready to go visit Mama. Once we got to the hospital, I tried to shake the nerves rattling my hands. What if she still didn't remember us?

Jordan whispered in my ear, "I'm going to give Mama a really big hug and kiss. It'll make her remember us."

I threw my arm around his shoulders. "I hope you're right."

Like before, we sat outside Mama's hospital room. Sam waved for us to come in. The room was full of flowers and balloons sitting along the window sill. Mama sat up, slightly grinned, and opened her arms to hug us. Relief flooded through me at the sight of her familiar smile. She remembered us. We climbed up on the bed and hugged her tightly. She kissed us all over our faces.

I waved my hand in front of her face. "Mama, can you see me?"

She giggled. "Yes, I can see you. The blindness was temporary."

"Were you scared?"

"A little. Scared I wouldn't see your little faces again." Tears ran down her cheeks.

Jordan kissed her on the cheek. "Don't be sad, Mama."

"I'm not sad. I'm happy." Her pretty dimples shined like stars. "I just missed you guys so much."

"See, Talisa? I told you the hugs and kisses would work."

Mama's underweight frame made us cautious as we snuggled beside her. Her skin dimly brighter than before, but her narrow eyes darkened like a raccoon. Short strands of hair sprouted on top of her head but thicker this time. Her skeletal hands shook nonstop. Since Uncle Darren sang in the choir at church, he sang a song for Mama. After, he continued to hum as they held each other closely.

Sam took us to the hospital cafeteria to have lunch, and when we returned, a doctor stood at the foot of Mama's bed. He was a tall white man with blonde hair, a blonde beard, and a blonde mustache.

"You all have come back just in time. I'm Dr. Kurten. You must be Talisa and Jordan."

"Yes, sir, that's us."

He shook our hands. "Nice to meet you." He turned to Sam. "Should they sit in the hallway while I give you all an update?"

"No, let them stay," Aunt Joi told him.

"Well, she was very responsive to the electric shock treatment—as you can see. It's helped her slowly regain some of her long-term memory. However, her short-term memory is questionable at this time due to some slight nerve damage." He touched Mama's trembling hand.

"What do you mean by slight nerve damage? Will she have difficulty with her memory going forward?" Uncle Darren sat on the edge of his chair, face flushed, and his right leg nervously shaking.

"The short-term memory will more than likely be a temporary challenge. We believe, or hope, that the neural system will balance itself, eventually. Because the lupus is active, her immune system is extremely suppressed, which is causing her other internal organs to be vulnerable and at risk. We're trying different medications to reduce the inflammation right now. We have a team here trying to figure out what works best. Lupus is new to us as well. But she's in good hands. The slight nerve damage means she'll have to learn to be self-sufficient again, to learn to brush her teeth, to comb her hair, walk, run, and cook. We'll provide her with some strengthening rehab that will help her with all of her motor skills. Also, she'll have some speech therapy to ensure her cognitive thinking is where it should be." He looked at Mama and smiled.

"I don't know what you just said, or the meaning of a lot of the big words, but does this mean Mama will be here for a really long time?" I walked closer to Mama's bed and stood next to the doctor. I looked up at his face for an answer.

He kneeled down in front of me. "Well, it really depends on your mom. If she works really hard, does the exercises, and gets stronger, she'll probably be able to recover quickly. But, we don't know enough about lupus to say for sure." He patted me on my shoulder.

She still wasn't going home.

A couple of weeks later, Grandma, Grandpa, Jordan, and Sam and I went to visit Mama again. She was still very weak, but her sun-kissed complexion was starting to glow again. She shook all over as if she had constant chills racing through her body. She couldn't hold a cup to drink water without spilling it on herself, and it was hard for her to eat with utensils.

She threw a fork across the room and shoved her plate onto the floor. We jumped back from her bedside, and Grandpa stood up.

He wrapped his arms around her and patted her on the back. "Now, come on. You stop acting like that. You just have to keep trying. God will see you through this, but you have to let Him help you."

She clenched her hands onto his shirt and whispered, "Dad, I can't. This is too hard. I feel like a child having to learn to use

00046481386

the bathroom again. Wetting the bed like I'm a baby. I can't even wipe myself. Why would God do this to me?" She cried and dove into his arms.

It was hard to see Mama like that . . . so I closed my eyes.

PART II

Loose Marbles

CHAPTER 5

~September 4, 1989~

Dear Diary,

Last night, Aunt Denise was my savior. She pressed my hair, the back and edges; it was beyond nappy. I was so afraid I'd have to go to school looking ridiculous. I couldn't go to school like that, especially since I'm going back to my old school. I'd be setting myself up to be the main joke at the lunch table. My hair was screaming for a perm relaxer, but the hot comb made my hair straight and shiny.

~September 5, 1989~

Dear Diary,

This is it! The last year of elementary school—sixth grade! The main goal this year is to learn as many new words as possible and keep an A+ average in math. My teacher, Mrs. Nelson, is a tall, white lady with a bad smoking habit, and although she seems nice, her breath is not nice at all. Jordan's in first grade. We walked to school by ourselves today since it's only a block away from Grandpa and Grandma's house. Leslie met us across the street from the school next to the crossing guard. I'm so glad we're back together again at the same school.

N O APPETITE TODAY as I sat at the lunch table thinking about Mama. The thought of her never coming home made me sick to my stomach. I didn't eat. Instead, I sat in the cafeteria listening to other kids laugh and joke around. By the time the last bell rang to dismiss school, I was starving, my stomach roaring like a lion. Jordan and I speed-walked home. I headed straight towards the kitchen to fix a bologna sandwich with mayonnaise, a handful of potato chips, three slices of pickles, and one circle of yellow mustard on white bread. I smashed the sandwich together and took a huge bite.

Soon after finishing, Grandma called me into the living room. She said Mama was coming home in a few days. I took a deep breath in, then out, and then a smile struck my face. Grandma smiled back at me. Mama was coming home, finally. I wanted to dance, then run up and down the street screaming, "My Mama's all better! She's coming home!"

We called Daddy since it was his birthday.

"Happy birthday, Daddy!"

"Why, thank you, darling. I really do appreciate it. How was school today?"

"School was fine. Grandma said Mama's coming home tomorrow. I can't wait."

"That's good. I'm sure she misses you guys a lot. Let me speak to your grandma for a second."

"Wait . . . Jordan wants to talk to you."

"Okay."

"Happy birthday, Daddy. When are you coming?" Jordan sprung out his seat.

"Not sure, son. Real soon, though. Maybe in a couple of weeks, okay?"

"Okay, Daddy. Have a happy birthday." He handed Grandma the phone. "Daddy wants to talk to you."

"Y'all go outside and play."

Jordan turned to me. "He's coming to see us soon."

I wanted to believe that, but he'd been saying he was coming for a long time. The most important thing was that Mama was coming home. Nothing else mattered. When the day arrived, I skipped to Sam's car. I was excited to be going home . . . to our own home. The ride home was short. The dull, rusting fence surrounded the house and there was a tall, skinny, black dog chained to a large tree along the side of the house. Uncle Ted had given us a dog.

We walked through the door. Mama was slowly unpacking clothes from her black suitcase. Jordan pampered her with hugs. The closer I walked toward her, the smaller she appeared; slender, thinner, with such a slim face. Her eyes were pinkish-red with thick black circles underneath, and she looked weary. Her hand shook as she wiped away the falling tear from her right eye. I hugged her. I missed her.

"Mama, are you all right now?" I waited eagerly for a response.

"No, I'm not. But in time, I hope it'll get better."

Sam interrupted, "Hey guys, let's go upstairs and unpack some things. Let's give your mom some time to get situated."

Sam took us upstairs where we each had our own rooms. When Tori came back, I guessed we'd have to share a room like we did at the other house.

* * *

~September 17, 1989~

Dear Diary,

Today's my twelfth birthday, and everyone celebrates their birthdays at Grandma and Grandpa's house. I went bike riding with Leslie. Mama stayed in her room all day. Jordan couldn't come because he doesn't have a bike yet. Daddy promised he would buy him one for his birthday and bring it when he comes to visit us. But, he never comes.

Fall arrived, and multi-colored leaves were scattered across the backyard—tons of them stuck in between the wire fence. Every fall, we would help Mama rake them into large piles. Jordan always ran through them as Mama chased him through the yard. Our house was older, and although the warm heat comforted each room, a cool breeze still found its way through my window.

I walked across my bedroom and felt a cold chill race through my bare feet. I slightly opened the door and glanced in Mama's room. She sat in a daze on the edge of the bed, staring out the window. I had no clue as to what was actually going on with her; it remained a mystery. But the dialysis treatments seemed to greatly affect her.

As I walked across the room, I noticed the left sleeve of her pajama top was covered with blood. It dripped from the outside of her arm to her elbow. She took off her shirt, sat on the side of the bed, and rocked back and forth. She screamed and threw her shirt at the wall, and blood continued to trail down her arm and dripped onto the white flower-printed bed sheets. I eased down to sit next to her, then placed my hand on top of hers. Jordan woke up and ran in the room. He stood in front of her, his hand on her knee. Mama continued to rock and her body shivered; her teeth chattered like she was trapped in a freezer.

"Mama, are you okay?" Jordan tapped her knee.

I darted down the stairs to the bathroom and grabbed a hand cloth from the cabinet. I wet it with cold water and ran back upstairs. She and I locked eyes for several seconds. I didn't move, and she half-smiled as I handed her the wet cloth. She burst into tears as she wrapped the cloth around her upper arm while taking deep breaths. She scrunched her face in pain as she attempted to reach for the phone, knocking over the magazines on the nightstand.

"Who are you trying to call, Mama? I'll dial the number for you."

"Call Sam. The number's right there."

Her hands gripped the edge of the mattress and I held the phone to her ear.

I heard Sam answer. "Hello?"

"Sam, something's wrong with the graft placement. My arm's bleeding. It's hurting. It feels like my arms on fire."

"Okay, I'll be there in a few minutes."

I hung up the phone. I wanted to ask what a graft placement was, but she was so upset already. She screamed again and pushed all of the papers on her nightstand to the floor. Jordan jumped off the bed and hid behind me, clinging to the back of my pajama top.

"Go downstairs," she requested, her saddened eyes glazed with ache. "Wait for Sam."

Jordan whispered, "Talisa, what's wrong with Mama?"

"Shhh, I don't know," I said. "Let's just wait for Sam."

He grabbed my hand.

Mama threw a temper tantrum as we listened from downstairs. We were rescued by Sam's knock on the door, and I rushed to unlock it.

"Are you guys okay?"

"Yes, sir. Mama's arm's bleeding, and I don't know what's wrong."

He patted me on the shoulder. "You guys go put some clothes on. Get some clothes for school, too. I'll drop you off at your grandparents. I'm going to take her to the hospital, okay?"

My shoulders slumped forward. Back to the hospital again.

After school, we found Mama at home sleeping on the couch. Her whole arm was wrapped with big, white bandages and white tape. Sam sat at the dining room table looking through work papers. Shortly after we settled in, Sam left. No one said anything about what was going on, and I didn't want to disturb Mama while she slept.

* * *

~October 28, 1989~

Dear Diary,

Today is Mama's birthday, but she wasn't feeling up to celebrating, so no birthday party. Tori is still nowhere to be found. I thought surely, she would come back for Mama's birthday, but no one has said anything about her lately. We sat in the living room on the couch with Mama, watching movies. Aunt Denise came over and we cooked three Totino's pizzas, opened a liter of strawberry soda, and had nachos with cheese. Although Mama could barely stay awake, she found enough strength to laugh at all of our jokes.

~October 31, 1989~

Dear Diary,

Happy Halloween! I got second place in the costume contest this year. Mama stood along the wall of the gym, not far from the stage, and waved when I walked across. Her face was lit up with happiness. She'd made my Diana Ross costume. Before the contest, Aunt Denise had put her hand on her hips and pranced around the living room, teaching me how to walk in high heels. After practicing and practicing, I got the hang of it.

She kept saying, "Come on, Niece. You gotta show 'em what you're working with. Move those hips."

I sighed. "I don't have any hips . . . just bones."

"Well, I guess you better just work them bones then. Move it."

Why do women wear these things in the first place? Mama laughed at us as she watched from the couch. She looked defeated as if she'd lost today's battle.

Mama's room remained dark, uninviting, and noiseless. The entire day spent in bed completely motionless, TV off, and she never got up to use the bathroom or to eat. I tiptoed into her room a couple times just to make sure she was still breathing, and she hadn't moved—not even an inch. She seemed so sad all the time. It made us sad, but we didn't say anything. We just left her alone.

Jordan and I occupied our time by finding other things to get into, like playing games, watching TV, or listening to music. Just us.

Later, we sat at the kitchen table by ourselves, and I studied my spelling words. Jordan worked on addition and subtraction math problems. He didn't like math at all, but I helped him.

* * *

~November 24, 1989~

Dear Diary,

Thanksgiving Day! Sam's been staying over a lot lately and helping Mama, especially on the days when she can barely move. We went to Grandma and Grandpa's house for dinner and there was a lot of food, but never enough space for everyone to eat. Food, food, food, everywhere there was food: two turkeys, two hams, collard greens, corn, candied yams, green beans, spaghetti and fried chicken. The list was endless. Sweet potato pie with whipped cream is the best. I just wanted to eat the whole pie by myself.

It's the best. All of my cousins and I play games, but someone broke the plastic bubble on the Trouble board, so we were down to two board games. Mama was in a good mood, and everyone looked like they were having a good time.

Early one morning, I heard Mama talking to Daddy on the phone.

"Listen, stop telling them that you're coming when you know damn well that you're not. Stop lying to them." She wasn't yelling, but when I snooped around the corner, her face was beet red.

Mama called for me to come to the phone. I paused before moving so she didn't know I was listening. I took the phone.

"Hey, how's Daddy's baby girl?" He sounded so excited.

"Hi, Daddy, I'm fine. I got a ninety-two on my spelling test yesterday." I was happy to hear his voice.

"That's good, baby girl. Keep up the good work. Listen, I know that I told you that I was coming over the summer, but I just couldn't make it." His voice lowered.

"I know. Grandma said you had a lot to do. It's okay, Daddy." I was just happy to hear him.

"My baby girl, you are such a joy. Where's your brother? Let me holler at him for a minute."

I reached out to hand Jordan the phone. "Jordan, Daddy wants to talk to you."

Jordan jumped up so fast he almost knocked me down. "Hi, Daddy, when are you coming? Can we go fishing?" Jordan stood still, smiling.

He handed me the phone back and jumped around in the living room, "Daddy's going to come. He said he's going to take me fishing, Mama, when it gets warmer outside."

Mama nodded with a disbelieving expression. Jordan didn't understand how long it would be before it got warm outside.

"Daddy, you there?" I asked into the phone.

"Yes, baby girl. That boy sure is something else. I'm going to come for Christmas this year so I can give you guys your gifts. What do you want for Christmas?"

"Um, we would really like a Nintendo with the Track & Field pad."

"With the gun, Talisa." Jordan was still jumping. "Tell him with the Duck Hunt game and gun."

"Okay, calm down." I placed my hand on top of his head to halt the bouncing. "Daddy, did you hear him?"

"I heard him loud and clear. I have to go. I'll talk to you guys soon. I love you."

"I love you, too, Daddy."

I told Mama what Daddy said. She stopped flipping the pages of her Ebony magazine and looked at me. Her face was absolutely blank as if she wanted to say something, but she didn't. Not a word.

*　*　*

~December 7, 1989~

Dear Diary,

I didn't do well on my science test today. I studied a lot, too.

~December 10, 1989~

Dear Diary,

We had drill team practice today in the school's gym. It's getting too cold to practice outside. We practiced for the Christmas performance. We're performing at the Quad City Thunder basketball game this year. The dancing and laughing is nonstop, but the minute we step foot on the floor, it's magic. Everyone in the stands cheers us on. We always put on the best show, and people can't wait to see us do our thing.

Daddy said he was going to call this week, but he didn't. Mama's exhaustion keeps her in the house, in her room. Sometimes she can't even stand for long periods of time. Some days, she gets up and right out of bed with no problem. Other days she lies still in bed with the covers over her head. On those days, I take care of Jordan.

~December 22, 1989~

Dear Diary,

Winter break, no school, and fun in the snow today. Jordan and I made snow angels and the weirdest looking snowman you've ever seen. We unchained our dog, Max, from the tree and let him run wild. He helped Jordan find some tree sticks in the yard to use as the arms. We found some rocks in the alley for its eyes and mouth. Mama's smile today was refreshing. She made us hot cocoa with marshmallows. She sat on the couch with us bundled up with blankets and we watched The Christmas Story. *It was a good day.*

CHAPTER 6

CHRISTMAS MORNING.

"Talisa, look. Daddy got us the Nintendo! See? I told you he would." Mama looked at me but quickly looked away.

"I see, Jordan." My throat felt thick.

I didn't have the heart to tell him that I saw the Nintendo mixed in with all of the other shopping bags when Mama went shopping the other day. Mama bought it. We gave Mama a Christmas card that we made at school. She was overjoyed. Sam gave Mama a sparkling necklace.

Weeks ago, Daddy said he would be here but never showed up. I guess he had to work.

A week later, New Year's Eve wasn't the same, not at home at least and Mama was sick again. She'd been yelling at Jordan all day for no reason. He was chastised for the slightest movement. We walked to Grandpa and Grandma's house, and Mama continued to imprison herself within the walls of her room. All of the grown-ups clapped and danced with us, bouncing around with glittered party hats and noise makers. It was memorable. Grandma always made nasty black-eyed peas on New Year's, lining us up to eat a spoonful. She said they were for good luck for the new year. Luck, my foot!

Although the cold, blistering weather kept us in the house, nothing was better than a good old-fashioned snow day. Three feet of snow had fallen within twenty-four hours, so no school today. Again, Mama was taken hostage by her bed. I poured Fruit Loops into a bowl, peeled an orange and placed the slices on a napkin on the food tray. I tiptoed up the stairs, avoiding the creaks and groans of certain steps. I opened the bedroom door and slid the tray on the bed next to her.

"Mama, I made you breakfast. Maybe you should eat. It might help you feel better," I whispered. She pushed the blanket off her head, sat up, and her hair stood up like Don King's.

"Why are you wasting food? Did I tell you to get me anything? No, I didn't. I'm going to ask you one more time. Why are you wasting food?"

"I just thought you might be hungry, Mama. That's all."

"I don't need you to think for me. If I wanted something to eat, I would get it my damn self." She shoved the TV tray onto the floor and milk splattered everywhere. "Now, clean it up."

"Sorry, Mama." I picked up the mess from the floor. I was stricken by her temper. Confused. What in the world was that? She plunged back into multiple pillows and pulled the blanket over her head. I didn't know what I'd done wrong. I got paper towels to clean up the milk, and Jordan ran in the kitchen.

"Are you okay, Talisa? I heard Mama yelling at you." His eyes saddened as he whispered.

"Something is wrong. That's not Mama. But, it'll be okay." I swallowed my tears.

*   *   *

~January 6, 1990~

Dear Diary,

Sam came over today, I wanted to tell him about Mama, but I don't want her to be mad at me. Mama and Aunt Denise spent all day looking for Tori. Sam stayed with us. When they finally got back, Tori wasn't with them. I saw Mama kneeling down and praying at the side of her bed. She was mumbling and shaking her head. She looked scared and worried.

It was Martin Luther King Day, and Mama's spirits seemed to have lifted. We watched Dr. King give his speech on TV. The phone rang. Mama placed her hand over her mouth, hung up the phone, and slowly sat on the arm of the couch. There was a knock on the door. It was the police . . . and Tori. Tori stood silently next to the officer. Her head hung down as if she were too embarrassed to look up.

"Ms. Brooks, is this your daughter?"

"Yes." Mama's voice was waspish.

"She was reported missing a couple of months ago."

"Yes, that's correct. I have called and called."

"We understand, ma'am, and we've done our best to locate

her. She was at the mall with a group of girls when a teacher from the high school recognized her. We're pleased to bring her home. Just give us a call if you need us again."

Mama stared at the officers. "Thank you. You can leave now."

She snatched Tori by the arm and pulled her in the house, slamming the front door in the policemen's faces. She dragged Tori up the stairs. I was excited to see her and wanted to hug her, but Mama didn't give us the chance to even speak to her. We ran to the bottom of the stairs and listened to Mama yelling at the top of her lungs.

"I want to beat your ass right now, but I don't even have the strength. Where have you been? Do you even understand how worried I've been?" Mama's voice cracked. "I need you to stop running. Let me help you. I'm not the enemy. Help me to help you. Please."

Tori never spoke.

The Saturday morning ritual following the first of each month was mandatory grocery shopping at Food-4-Less. It was Mama's favorite grocery store, and she stayed there for hours, especially when she brought her coupon envelope. When it was one coupon per customer, we'd buy items in different lines. She'd hand Tori, me and Jordan some food stamps, and we'd go through the checkout line by ourselves. The cashier would look at Jordan and then look pointedly at Mama in the next line. We weren't fooling anyone. Mama's "mind your own damn business" facial expression was furious and the cashier could never deny Jordan's infectious smile. But this particular morning, Mama became tired as she placed the groceries on the conveyor belt. Each time she leaned in the basket for another item, her eyes squinted and she'd rock back and forth unbalanced. She placed one hand on her head, then pulled up the sleeves of her sweater.

The cashier was concerned. "Ma'am, are you, all right?" she asked Mama.

Mama unwrapped a paper plate before she paid for it and fanned her face. "Yes, I'm just a bit tired, that's all." She smiled a little, but it was unpersuasive.

"Ma'am, your right arm," the cashier pointed.

Mama glanced down, and I pushed the cart to the side to see. The majority of her arm was bruised black, blue, and purple. I looked at Mama, and she shy fully looked away, as if she were ashamed. Another cashier came to finish bagging the groceries and helped us load them into the car. The car jetted and jerked as Mama swerved around the idling shopping carts in the parking lot. The car skirted onto the street; moments later it lurched suddenly to a stop and sat on the side of the road. As she gripped the steering wheel, Mama dropped her head and unexpectedly screamed. Her high-pitched squeal arrested us as Jordan and I reached for each other's hand.

"Mama, are you okay?" Jordan unfastened his seat belt to lean up to the front seat.

A vein pulsed in her forehead and Mama shouted, "Sit down, boy! Didn't nobody tell you to get up. SIT DOWN!"

She slapped his hands, and I yanked on Jordan's jacket to pull him back into his seat as quickly as I could.

"Mama, stop it! Don't hit him." I didn't mean to yell at her. It just came out.

Mama turned around and grabbed the front of my jacket. "Who in the hell do you think you're talking to? Don't you ever talk to me like that. Ever."

Our eyes locked and I just didn't recognize her, not anymore. I grabbed Jordan's hand and whispered, "Shhh, don't cry."

When we got home, Tori came outside to help us with the groceries. Mama went up to her room and slammed the door. As we stood in the kitchen putting the groceries away, she screamed again and burst into tears. Those days created false hope, rejecting the encouraging thoughts of her getting back to her normal self—the Mama I used to know. When she got upset like she did in the car, everything always came crashing down again.

*   *   *

~January 26, 1990~

Dear Diary,

Tori and I are back to sharing a room. I'm glad she's back, although she doesn't talk to me at all. She doesn't even smile. She and Mama barely speak to each other.

Our house was a war zone. Tori never stayed long. She and Mama screamed at each other until they both cried. Then Tori would run away. Mama would call the police, and the cycle repeated itself. I didn't understand any of it. At all.

The house was a disaster and the wreckage was awful.

Couch pillows were tossed and furniture was displaced. Silence chilled the air throughout the house as Jordan's sweaty palm settled in the center of my hand. I thought burglars must have struck our house. We turned toward the stairs and found Mama sitting on the bottom step. Her face was flushed, eyes full of fire. I pushed Jordan behind me. If she had done all of this herself, she was unstable.

"Mama, are you okay?"

"Yes, I'm fine. Y'all go upstairs and change out of your school clothes. I'll call you down when dinner is ready." She slowly got up and walked past us.

"Why is the house so messed up? Where's Tori?"

She turned around. "Talisa, stop asking me fifty thousand damn questions. When I tell you to do something, just do it. Now get upstairs."

Our bedroom was a mess, as if a tornado touched down and damaged everything in sight. All of my teddy bears were on the floor. My coloring books were scattered in the corner of the room. Tori's clothes on her side of the closet were gone. Shoes, jackets, socks, even her curling irons, all gone. A big fight this time, apparently. I cleaned up the room, hoping she'd left something behind so she'd have to come back. So I could talk to her, see her again. But deep down in the pit of my stomach something told me she wasn't ever coming back.

A couple nights before, Tori was sitting on the edge of her bed, looking out the window. Dreaming, I assumed. She'd wiped tears from her cheeks. I got out of bed to sit next to her, hugged her, and her head fell on my shoulder. We rocked back and forth and eventually she rested her head on my lap. I stroked her hair until she closed her eyes, but then she started to cry again.

"Tori, what's wrong? You can tell me. I won't tell anyone."

"I can't." She'd grabbed my hand and buried her face in my lap, shaking her head. "I couldn't stop it, I just couldn't stop it."

"You couldn't stop what? What are you talking about?" I hugged her, but she never answered, and eventually, she fell asleep.

Why did everything have to change? Tori was once so funny and happy, and she always knew all the answers. She was full of so much anger, but what was she angry about?

*   *   *

~February 14, 1990~

Dear Diary,

Happy Valentine's Day! I made Mama a card. Mrs. Nelson, my teacher, brought rose petals to class today and passed them around the room for students to use. I glued the petals to the pink construction paper, sprinkling the front with glitter. Mama's card was so pretty that when I gave it to her, she glowed from the inside out. Sam gave Mama really pretty flowers. They were really colorful in a pink glass vase with a yellow ribbon wrapped around the middle. Tori is still gone; I guess she's not coming back. I heard Mama talking to Uncle Ted on the phone, asking him to please help find Tori.

Mama was having one of those days again, staying all to herself downstairs, cleaning everything in sight and not speaking to us. There was a knock on the door. It was Mama's friend, Miss Jacqueline. Tall, black woman, with a weird accent, she was always bringing Mama herbs and oils. She was a spiritual lady with a purse full of cures, blessed oil, and a pocket knife. It was never a short conversation between the two. It was always loud energetic laughter. It was definitely what Mama needed.

"Hey, girl, how are you? Have a seat." Mama's tone was cheery, upbeat.

"Oh, I'm doing. I came over here to see how you were doing. You ain't got no business being worried about my well-being. Where are the babies?"

They sat at the kitchen table. "They're upstairs."

She yelled for us to come down to speak to Miss Jacqueline. Jordan's room was right above the kitchen. We could hear every word.

"Girl, they are so big. Those tall, beautiful babies. And Tori, where is she?"

Mama took a deep breath. "I don't know. I don't know what to do with her. The moment I think I'm helping her, she runs away. Just like now; she's gone again."

"Oh, Lord. What about going back to therapy?"

Mama sighed. "She fights me each time I try to help her. She's so lost. She's so hurt. She runs and I chase her, searching day and night for her. My heart breaks wondering what's happening to her or what's she getting into out there in the streets."

"I'm going to pray for you both. How are you doing, though?"

"I don't know." Mama's voice became shallow.

"What do you mean you don't know?"

"Some days I'm full of energy, other days I'm exhausted. Some days I'm happy. Others I'm angry, sad, can't get out of bed."

"Come on now. You have to do better than that. You still have other babies to tend to."

"I know. I have never had these types of days. I take twenty-seven pills a day. Twenty-seven! Dialysis treatments three times a week for three to four hours each session. It's so hard. I just don't know what to do. I don't know why this is happening to me."

"Hey, hey, hey. Listen, you will get through this. What happened to your arm?"

We paused the video game and listened because we wanted to know, too.

"They had to insert a graft in my right arm for dialysis back in October, then it stopped working in January. So, they inserted a new graft in my left arm, and that didn't work either. Blood clots started to form. The left one stopped working, too."

"Oh, my. I had no idea. Don't worry about these cuts or scars. I'll rub a little blessed oil on them and they'll just fade away. So, if the grafts aren't working, how are you supposed to receive dialysis treatments?"

"Well, they cut my right thigh and inserted another graft into my leg, which seems to be working so far."

"Come here. You need a hug—like a big hug. Why didn't you call me?"

"I don't know. I don't want to bother anyone."

"You call me, night or day, for whatever. Do the kids know what's going on?"

"They don't know all of this. They're too young to even understand. They're both probably up there listening now, though. I swear, they're always up to something. Those two, they just should've been twins."

Miss Jacqueline helped Mama cook and then she stayed and had dinner with us. It was a relief knowing what had happened to Mama's arm, but scary at the same time. What if her leg graft stopped working, too?

I woke up on Easter Sunday to screaming and yelling. Terrified, I hopped out of bed and ran down the stairs to the kitchen. Mama was blasting the radio, listening to Shirley Caesar on the Sunday gospel hour. Mama was singing, cooking breakfast, clapping her hands, and stomping her right foot on the floor. Everything was okay. I exhaled. I'd learned to coach myself into calmness. I'd realized things could change at the drop of a dime. I'd repeat to myself: "Breathe, just breathe. Relax." Then, hope would rise again. Mama turned around and caught me staring at her. She grabbed my hands, spun me around, and she danced.

"It's Easter! The day Jesus rose from the dead and showed all those suckers He is the Messiah."

I didn't know what she was talking about. But as long as she was smiling and happy, Jesus could do anything He wanted to do.

"So, Jesus is a mummy, Mama?"

"No, child. Jesus is not a mummy. He's the Son of God, almighty and powerful."

She was so full of spunk and vibrant energy; now that's the Mama I remember. As she floated around the kitchen, I internally smiled, shocked and scared at the same time. These moments had only become occasional like the groundhog waiting to see its shadow. No more questions for Mama. I thought perhaps one of her new medications was a happy pill and hoped it would keep her smiling. But as long as she was happy, I was happy.

The next day, I sat outside on the front steps reading *Charlotte's Web* for the second time. Jordan was in the front yard playing with his friend Eric from across the street. Eric was a chunky and sweet little boy, cute, always smiling, and walked like Fred Sanford. He was an old soul trapped in a little boy's body. He was never in a rush to go anywhere, and it was funny to watch him act like he was in a rush, especially when his Mama called him home. The front door and porch windows were wide open, and I overheard Mama and Aunt Denise having a conversation inside. It was a bit scary.

"How are you holding up, Sis?"

"I feel weird. Not myself sometimes. It sounds crazy, I know."

"It doesn't sound crazy. You have some medical challenges that even the doctors don't know what to do about. You just have to relax, Sis. Take some time to adjust to a new way of living."

"Adjust? I don't want to adjust. I don't want this disease." Her voice was full of anger. "I keep asking God what I did wrong. Why am I being cursed like this? Yet, I receive no answer. Sometimes, Sis, I can't do anything without getting extremely tired. My body temperature is constantly changing. One minute I'm hot, wanting to rip off my clothes. The next I'm wrapping myself in two to three blankets to stop from shaking. I just don't know what to do."

"What about the psychiatrist sessions? Are they helping?

"Those things are a joke. I only get five sessions, that's all the state will cover."

"When's your next doctor's appointment? I want to go with you this time so you're not alone."

"Not until next month. I have to go back to the University of Iowa Medical Center to meet my new rheumatologist. Thank you, Sis."

"Plus, you have two other children. I'm not saying to forget about Tori, but I *am* saying that they're here and she's not. When Tori comes around, make the best effort to help her. Until then, leave it in God's hands. Stop stressing."

"I understand what you're saying. This world is full of crazy, deranged people. My baby is out doing God-knows-what with God-knows-who, and I don't even know where she's sleeping. What is she eating? How is she eating? Is someone taking advantage of her? My greatest fear is waiting for a policeman to show up at my door telling me that my child is hospitalized, or worse, dead. No mother wants to lose their child."

"Don't think that way. We'll keep praying for her."

"I pray for her all day long. I just want her to come home." They stood in the doorway and hugged before Aunt Denise left.

I was scared for Tori.

On my way home from drill team practice, I saw Tori in a car with another girl and a guy. Their music was loud, and the guy was driving. He had a huge tattoo on his neck and was wearing an all-black baseball hat with a green leaf on the front. He waved for me to cross the street. I just stared at Tori. She didn't smile, didn't wave. She put her head down and leaned back in the seat. I watched the green car drive down the block and turn right.

I wanted to tell Mama I saw Tori, but I didn't want anyone to get mad at me. So, I didn't say anything.

CHAPTER 7

MY FRIENDS AND I got second place in the school talent show. We should've gotten first place because we were precise, on beat, and our routine was flawless. We walked home, and Mama smiled at me and stopped me on the front steps.

"You got up on that stage, fearless. Stay confident in yourself. Hold on to that." She patted me on the back.

"You guys were jamming. Good job!" Jordan jumped on my back.

"You think so? Thanks, Brother."

For a moment, I thought Mama was back to being herself, but that relief was short lived. When Jordan and I stood on the front porch, Mama's voice blared through the door. I had convinced myself that she'd lost her mind and on any particular day she would transform into someone I didn't even know. Sadly, the memories of who she used to be continued to fade. In fact, they seemed hidden behind the shadows of what once existed. The yelling and shouting from inside froze us in our tracks. We stared at each other, then I grabbed his hand.

"Come on; let's just go to Grandpa and Grandma's." Just when we turned around, the front door swung open.

"Get in here, now."

Mama's hair looked like a bird's nest. Sweat dripped down her face. Her eyes were puffy. We were scared to move, but she demanded we enter the house.

Jordan's little fingers tightly held on to the pocket of my backpack. No one was in the house—just Mama. She was shrieking, mumbling, and cursing. From outside, it sounded as if she were having a conversation with someone, but no one was there. Broken glass crackled underneath my thinly layered shoe sole as we stepped onto the kitchen floor and food decorated the wall with a variation of colors. The cabinets, oven door, and refrigerator and freezer doors were all wide open. The whole scene was astounding as we tiptoed through the kitchen and headed toward the stairs to our rooms.

"Wait!" Mama screeched. Her eyes bucked with wildness. "Where do you two think you're going?"

I took a deep breath and my tongue pressed against the roof of my mouth. No matter what I said it would be the wrong thing.

I mumbled, "Upstairs, so we can change out of our school clothes."

"Sit down." We set the kitchen chairs upright, prepared to sit down, and took off our backpacks.

She yelled, "No! Sit down on the floor. Now! Right now. Now!" Her faltering speech continued as she paced back and forth.

We pushed the food and dishes on the floor to the side and we sat cross-legged. We tried to avoid looking directly at her, but she kneeled down in front of us.

"What are you two supposed to do when you wake up in the morning?" Using the sleeve of her shirt she wiped the sweat from her forehead.

"Umm, make our beds?" I muttered my response.

"Speak up, little girl."

I cleared my throat and answered loudly. "We're supposed to make our beds before we go to school."

Jordan interrupted and leaned over to whisper in my ear. "No, Talisa. That's the wrong answer. We have to say our prayers first."

"Both answers are correct. So, why didn't you make your beds this morning?" I repeatedly glanced at her seemingly uncontrollable shaking hands.

"We did, Mama," I tried to assure her.

"Talisa, what did I tell you about talking back? No, you didn't. Now go make up your beds now."

We *had* made our beds. We always did.

She stood up and continued to pace again like a lion in a cage roaring to be set free. We grabbed our bags, ran up the stairs, and saw that our mattresses were flipped and tossed. The pillows and blankets were thrown to the floor, our box springs hung halfway off the metal rail bed frames. The entire house was unreal, and I couldn't believe she had done such a thing. Something was frighteningly wrong. The house was normally spotless, and nothing was ever out of place. This was all so bizarre—pure insanity.

"Jordan, come on." I pulled him in Mama's room to use the phone. "I'm calling Sam."

He didn't answer, so I called Grandma.

I whispered as low as possible, and I spoke quickly. "Grandma, something is really wrong with Mama. She's gone crazy."

"What do you mean?"

"She tore the whole house apart and she's downstairs talking to herself. She's sweating all over and her hands are shaking like crazy. Can someone come over here? Please?"

Mama picked up the phone downstairs. "Who's on this phone? Talisa, get off the phone. I didn't give you permission to use it." She screamed, "Get off the phone now!"

A loud bang echoed in my ear as she slammed down the receiver. The stomping of her loud and heavy footsteps caused me to panic and her outrageous behavior actually forced me to react. The closer her steps became; the more frightened Jordan and I became. We dashed into my bedroom, closed the door, and pushed the dresser against it to keep her out. There was no way she'd ever hurt us; I didn't want to believe she ever would. I felt guilty for blocking her out, but she just wasn't herself. We sat in the closet and covered ourselves with clothes. Jordan cried, and I covered his mouth with my hand. I wrapped my arm around him, and we waited.

"Y'all better open this damn door." She pounded on the door continually. "Right now, damn it."

The banging grew louder and louder, then . . . .

Silence.

The eerie silence was almost more chilling than the banging because we didn't know where she was.

"Shhh, it's going to be all right, Brother." I tried to not cry.

"What's wrong with her? Why's she acting like this?" He stuttered with fear.

"I don't know. I don't know. We'll just sit here until somebody comes." He leaned his head on my shoulder.

We sat in the closet for what seemed like forever. A siren blared through the thin wooden closet door.

I thought I would collapse from relief. Strange voices resounded throughout the house. I heard a knock on my bedroom door. We sat still and waited.

"Talisa, it's Uncle Darren. Y'all open the door. It's okay." We jumped up and pushed the dresser away from the door. He hugged us. I was so happy to see him.

"Uncle Darren, something's really wrong with Mama."

He patted me on the back. "I know, Niece. She's getting help now. Come on downstairs. Y'all are safe."

* * *

~June 1, 1990~

Dear Diary,

According to Sam, some of Mama's medications make her act crazy. Something called prednisone. It causes her rapid mood swings and personality changes. I don't understand why the doctors would give her something that changes her

so much. They are supposed to help her and not make it
worse.

We were prepared for summer break. It was the last day
of school, and there were a lot of performances scheduled
that summer for the drill team. It was the end of elementary
school and I was nervous about attending junior high school
in the fall. But going to a new school was exciting. Mama
continued to isolate herself, staying detached and distant. She'd
changed into someone else—someone no one recognized.
Judging from the crying I heard coming from her room
at night, I wasn't sure if she even recognized herself anymore.
Either.

Sigh. The next morning, my heart broke in two pieces.

Mama sat in the corner of her room biting her fingernails,
humming, hiding beside her dresser. Her knees were to her
chest, and her toes curled into the carpet then she wrapped her
arms around her legs. With her head tilted back, she stared up
at the ceiling. I waited for her to notice me, but she didn't. She
shivered and shook and sweated nonstop. I kneeled down to
the floor and crawled towards her.

"Mama, what's wrong?" I slowly reached to touch her hand.

She continued to hum and shook her head left to right.

"Mama, are you hurt? Is something wrong?"

She whispered, "They were on the ceiling. They were everywhere. Even in the bed."

I turned to look up, but nothing was there. I walked over to
her bed and pulled back the comforter. Nothing. She continued

to hide in the corner like a kid playing hide-n-seek. So, I went back and sat beside her.

"Mama, there's nothing there. What did you see?" She leaned her head against the dresser and closed her eyes. Mama was losing her mind.

PART III

Tested Waters

CHAPTER 8

IRST DAY OF junior high school!

I escorted Jordan to school. It was his first day of second grade. His teacher's name was Mrs. Brighton—a short, white lady with thick glasses and fuzzy red hair. After, I ran three blocks to meet Leslie and Ms. Rose for the bus ride. Ms. Rose was quite particular about being punctual. So, being late meant eventually we'd have a lengthy conversation about time management. The ride only took twenty minutes tops.

The school had a striking resemblance of a small castle with large bay windows. Leslie and I walked side by side, laughing, joking around, and singing. We high fived each other before going our separate ways. Big girl status. Seventh grade. We were finally walking into the next level—Edison Junior High School. Tori had also attended this same school.

It felt awkward going to a different school than Jordan. During the bus ride, I worried if he would be scared without me near. But, when he released my hand and mingled with the other kids, it was a smooth transition. Oh, how I wished Mama was there that day. I fought the water build-up behind my eyelids, and I slowly took a deep breath to calm myself. Ms. Rose's firm voice urged positivity as she encouraged me to be strong-willed.

*   *   *

~September 6, 1990~

Dear Diary,

Junior high school has a different atmosphere than elementary school, where I had one teacher pretty much all day. Here, we switch classes every hour and the bell rings continuously throughout the day. At the end of each class, we're only allowed a few minutes to get to our next class. I'm so lost. I have seven different teachers for all seven different classes, and it's confusing. There are hall monitors who help us when we get lost. Leslie and I only have one class together. So many new faces; how do people remember everyone's names? It's like joining drill team for the first time, but here the faces are a collection of different skin colors.

I grew a lot over the summer—taller, that is. Mama says my rawboned frame was inherited from Daddy. He's quite lanky, but thin, just like me and Jordan. Ms. Rose bought me some new white shoes over the summer. I needed some in order to perform with the drill team, but I didn't have any money.

This past summer, loneliness struck like lightning during a thunderstorm. Jordan and I remained home alone while

Mama was in the hospital. I missed Tori, and I yearned to see her face. Sam occasionally appeared at the house. I pretended to hide the fear rumbling in my stomach and repeatedly assured Jordan that, "We'll be all right." As the days grew longer, the more eager I became, praying that this time Mama would be better, that this time she'd return to being her old self again.

I hoped.

* * *

~September 8, 1990~

Dear Diary,

I made pancakes this morning all by myself. It wasn't hard to grasp, but it took practice. That's all I can cook for breakfast. I don't know how to cook eggs yet. We are almost out of food. There was one box of strawberry Jell-O left in the cabinet, so I used some of the powder to make juice. It didn't taste horrible after adding sugar. I scraped the patches of hardened sugar from the corners of the canister with a butter knife. It was better than drinking plain water from the faucet. Our water tastes nasty plain.

Jordan made me laugh until my stomach hurt. We took turns singing to different songs as we watched Video Soul. He put on his baseball hat and stood on the couch singing "Poison" by BBD. He sang so loud I think the neighbors heard every word.

Later, he went outside with his friend Eric and some other neighborhood kids to play kickball. I sat on the porch thumbing through Mama's old JET magazines. Sam told me the more you read, the more you increase your vocabulary, so I try to read as much as possible. Hopefully, when Mama comes home I can get a public library card and get more books to read.

The nearly bare refrigerator didn't provide many options for us. We strolled to Grandma and Grandpa's house this morning for some food. The box we brought home contained a big bag of French fries, a box of fish sticks, two boxes of Corn Flakes cereal, a gallon of milk, a jar of applesauce, two cans of corn, two cans of peas, a pack of hotdogs, a loaf of bread, peanut butter and grape jelly, a box of frozen chicken nuggets, and a small bag of gumdrops.

We weren't allowed to make long distance calls from home, so we walked to Grandma and Grandpa's house to call Mama.

"Hi, Mama."

"Hey, you sound like you've grown a bit." She giggled.

"I did. Just taller, though. Still sticks and bones. I wear a size eight shoe now. Jordan's a lot taller, too. He almost comes up to my shoulder."

"Oh my, you guys are growing fast. I guess I have to get out of here so I can see it with my own eyes."

"Yeah, when are you coming home?"

"I'm not sure."

"I was really hoping you'd be here for my birthday. I'm going to officially be a teenager."

"I know, I know." She sighed as her emotions escaped, then

wept. I gave the phone to Grandma and she told us to walk home before it got too dark outside.

* * *

~September 17, 1990~

Dear Diary,

Today is my thirteenth birthday, and it sucks. No party, no cake, no gifts, no Tori, and no Mama. Daddy called after school today. He sang "Happy Birthday" to me and said he'd been planning to come up for my birthday but had an emergency.

We raced to Grandma's house to call Mama, and her slurred speech was incoherent. She whispered happy birthday to me as each word faded into gibberish sentences. As she struggled to speak, my emotions heightened to the one hundredth degree and then I hung up the phone. Jordan held my hand all the way home. He took a shower, then we picked out his clothes for school and changed his bed sheets. He flopped down onto his bed, closed his eyes and placed his hands together to pray. I gently rose up from the edge of his bed assuming he was sound asleep. As soon as I turned off the light, he popped his little head up from under the blanket and jumped up out of the bed.

"Surprise!" Through his big smile, I could see all of his teeth except for the two in front that had recently fallen out.

"What are you doing? Go to bed. No clowning around." He ran across the room and shuffled around in his backpack, hiding a piece of paper behind him. Rocking from his heels to his toes.

"What's that?"

He handed me the piece of paper. "It's a birthday card. I made it at school. My teacher helped me. Do you like it?"

I bent over to give him a hug. "I love it. Thank you, Jordan. This is a really cool card, and it's the best birthday card ever."

"Did I spell birthday right?"

"Yes, you did." He'd been working really hard on his spelling words. "Now, you have to go to sleep." I kissed him on the cheek.

"Good night."

I watched him jump back into bed, and I turned off the light. I walked downstairs to wedge a chair under the knob of the front and back doors, then double-checked the locks on all the windows. I was scared someone would try to break into the house, so I always left all the lights on downstairs. I set my alarm clock and sat in the center of my bed and opened Jordan's card again.

Happy birthday to the best sister. Love, Jordan.

He knew my favorite color was purple and had drawn thirteen purple hearts on the front—a heart for each of my years. I loved my little brother. He just made my birthday a special one.

After school the next day, I walked to Leslie's house, and I called Grandma to see if I could stay over for a couple hours. Grandma granted me permission. Jordan had walked to Grandma's house after school with some of the neighborhood kids. She said he was outside playing. Ms. Rose took Leslie and me to get pizza. The afternoon was engaged with laughter, school gossip and a practice session of the latest dance moves learned from our drill team captain. They dropped me off at Grandma's house just before the street lights came on.

When I opened the door, Mama was sitting in Grandma's favorite wooden chair, wrapped in a blue blanket. Her smile relieved me of any worry, of any concerning questions. I stood staring at her, not knowing how to react. Part of me wanted to run and jump in her arms to take the loneliness away. The other part hesitated, awaiting to for a reaction from her to see if she had changed.

She struggled to stand and I insisted she remain seated. But when she wrapped her arms around me, my face became a flowing river on a sunny day. She looked healthier, rejuvenated. As I sat next to her holding her hand, I hoped and dreamt . . . no more episodes and no more bad days.

Mama woke us up early for Saturday morning grocery shopping. Her feeble body moved haltingly as if all of her energy had been depleted. She wrestled to put on her jacket, barely able to lift her arms. Although she continued to smile, finding the strength to maneuver throughout the day became challenging. As we drove away from the store, Mama stopped and turned to face me.

"What's wrong, Mama? Does something hurt? Are you in pain?" I unfastened my seat belt and placed my hand on top of hers.

"No, nothing's wrong." She shook her head and took a deep breath. "I'm so sorry."

"What do you mean? Sorry why?"

"I'm sorry I missed your big birthday. I know you love music. So, let's go to Kmart and you can pick out a new cassette tape. I don't have a lot of money right now, but you can pick one out. How does that sound?"

"It wasn't your fault. We don't have to go if you're tired, Mama."

"Oh, really? You're passing up the opportunity for new music?" She glanced around the car as if I were missing. "Where's my child? Who kidnapped her?" She giggled. "Let's go get you some new music."

School had just become even more interesting. Oh, my goodness, after third period English class today, I rushed to put a note in Leslie's locker to tell her to meet me after school at the bus stop.

A boy passed me in the hallway. He was breathtaking, and his smile sent chills up and down my spine. He was slender, like me, with a heart-crushing smile, brown eyes, and a cocoa complexion. I was detained by his presence with tingling sensations that pricked my face. What was this feeling? The pulse in my neck beat rapidly. I couldn't speak, couldn't move, couldn't even smile back at him.

The bus was slowly approaching, and Leslie was nowhere in sight. The front door of the school flung open, and a loud bang made everyone in line turn around. It was Leslie, finally. She'd almost missed the bus.

"What took you so long?"

"I had to get the instruction sheet for my home economic

project. Girl, I can't slip in my grades. You know my mama don't play." She leaned her head back to catch her breath.

"So, listen. I have to tell you what happened today."

"What? Why are you smiling like that?" She turned up her top lip and squinted at me. "What did you do?"

"Before you jump to assumptions, I didn't do anything. Are you going to ask me a hundred questions or can I just tell you what happened?"

"Go ahead. What is it?" She crossed her arms.

I told her about the boy and she laughed.

"I felt like I was Samantha and he was Jake from *Sixteen Candles*. He's so cute."

"I'm going to need you to come down to Earth with the rest of us, okay, love struck? What's his name anyway?" Leslie grinned at me.

"I don't know."

"You don't know." She laughed hysterically and placed her hand on her head. "You don't even know his name and you're all in love."

"No, but I'm going to find out. You're laughing just a little too hard. Stop."

* * *

~October 3, 1990~

Dear Diary,

Yes! Today, there was a flyer posted in the cafeteria for basketball tryouts for the Edison Eagle boys' and girls' basketball teams. I'm going to try out. I've never played, but I ran track last year in sixth grade. I really want to learn how to play, and I think it would be exciting. Leslie wants to try out, too. Now, I just have to ask Mama for permission.

Mama's inconsistent moods varied by the day—like unpredictable rainy weather after you've gotten your hair done and you're stuck at the bus stop with no umbrella. When I got home from school, Jordan was lying on the floor. He turned around to look at me with dreary eyes—a warning sign.

"Jordan, what's wrong?" I kneeled down next to him.

"Mama's sad again. She picked me up from school. She's mad because I was late coming out of the building. But I couldn't find my jacket."

"Then what happened?"

"She grabbed me by my shirt and pulled me all the way home in front of everybody. She didn't say anything. She just looked really mad."

"Where is she?"

"Upstairs, lying down with her door closed. I asked her if I could have some cereal and she told me to leave her alone. So, I just shut the door."

"Okay, come on." I grabbed his hand and we walked in the kitchen. "Go get a bowl. Don't overfill it with cereal. I'll pour the milk for you."

"Okay," he whispered. "I was really hungry."

"Sit here and eat. I'm going upstairs."

"No, Talisa. Just stay here. She's going to yell at you. You can't go up there. Not right now. That's not a good idea." He shook his head.

"Calm down. It'll be fine."

I couldn't get to my bedroom unless I went through Mama's bedroom, so I quietly opened the door. She sat straight up in the bed and stared at me. I paused, my lips were sealed.

"Why did you open my door? Did I call your name?" Her narrowed eyes and piercing voice froze my entire body.

I mumbled, "No ma'am."

"Then, close it." She pointed for me to go back downstairs.

I just couldn't comprehend the frequent alternating changes; it was like she'd transformed into two completely different people.

Later, Sam came over. He brought pizza, soda, ice cream, and some movies from Blockbuster. Not long after, Mama complained of back pain.

Sam assisted as she tried to stand, but with each movement, she cried and yelled in agony.

I sprinted to grab her purse from upstairs. Sam grabbed her jacket, wrapped it around her, and carried her out to the car. Jordan and I hurried to put on our shoes and coats, and then hopped in the back seat of Sam's car. I stared out the window until we got to the hospital. When we arrived, Mama's skin had turned dull and tinted grayish. The nurses surrounded the car, and one yanked the door open. They lifted her into a wheelchair, and another nurse guided us to the waiting room. Jordan lay his head in my lap and we waited for Sam. An hour had gone by before Sam returned. He said she had to stay the night, but deep down in the pit of my stomach, I knew it probably wouldn't be for just one night. It never was.

Two days in the hospital that time, unaware of the reason but she was home. Mama's grayish, discolored skin tone made her look ashy. In her bedroom, barricaded, and isolated under countless blankets and pillows again. There was a sense of dreary absence floating around the house that left me and Jordan by ourselves. We kept quiet in order not to disrupt her in any way. Sam said the doctors had lowered her prednisone dosage again, but not significantly. Going forward, she'd have to continue taking that stupid medication. Why couldn't they see that it's damaging and torturing her mentally? Mama was lost, internally in shambles, physically challenged by this unjust disease. It was completely out of her control.

At school, sad to say, I felt free. Leslie and I were in the girl's locker room changing for basketball tryouts. I had some worn-out shorts Mama gave me and my favorite purple t-shirt. The season didn't officially start for a couple months, but we were antsy, jumping up and down as we stood along the baseline of the court. The coaches waited with their arms crossed, staring as we positioned ourselves—girls on one side of the gym and boys on the other. I scanned the line across from us, and there he was again. The mystery boy. I yanked on Leslie's arm.

"Ouch! What is wrong with you?"

"That's him! The boy in the hallway I was telling you about."

"Which one?"

"The green shorts and white t-shirt with the apple on the front."

He looked at me and smiled. This time, I smiled back.

CHAPTER 9

~November 1, 1990~

Dear Diary,

It's official! I made the basketball team. Leslie did, too. I want to question Mama to see what's going on with her. Her feet and legs swell up all the time, and she still can't stand up for too long. I remain optimistic, apprehended by hopefulness. I continue to witness the battle she fights daily, but it doesn't seem like she's ever on the winning side.

~November 13, 1990~

Dear Diary,

Basketball is a lot tougher than I anticipated, but I've grasped the basics of the game. It's a lot of running, jumping, bending down, and moving all at once. My shoes should be here in a couple days. Daddy promised to buy me some supportive ones. These flat shoes are starting to hurt my feet and they will not last the season.

FTER SCHOOL, JORDAN and I played around on his Nerf basketball hoop hung on his closet door. His moves and maneuvers made him look like a natural.

"Who taught you how to play?"

"Umm, Michael Jordan." He ran to the hoop and dunked the ball.

"Whatever, Jordan. Michael Jordan didn't teach you that."

"Uh-huh, he did. On TV. Just watch his moves. He's cold. My moves are going to be cold and smooth, just like his."

Before I went to bed, I walked downstairs to check on Mama. Sam had hauled her bed into the dining room being that the only bathroom in the house was downstairs. At the time, it was too difficult for her to constantly hike up and down the stairs.

"Hey, Mama." I peeked around the corner nervously.

"Hey. Why are you standing around the corner like you're scared or something?" She giggled a little like it was a crazy notion. I hesitated to answer.

"Because sometimes you seem highly agitated," I managed to say. "So, I don't bother you."

"Yeah, there are a lot of things you don't know. They're hard for me to explain. I'm not sure if I told you I'd even explain it correctly. Heck, the majority of it I don't even understand myself. Can you come help me to the bathroom? My right leg's been throbbing since I came from dialysis," she exhaled.

"Mama, what exactly *is* dialysis?"

"Lord, help me with this inquisitive child. You ask a million and one questions—always have. Right out the womb, fast-

talking, like your mind runs two times faster than your mouth."
She put her arm around my shoulders.

"Inquisitive. I'll have to look that up. I don't know what that
means either. Is it a bad thing?"

"See what I mean? All the questions in the world, and no,
it's not a bad thing. Just remember this: sometimes you don't
need to know all the answers to everything. But, then there are
some things you must question in order to get an answer. Life
just works that way."

I pretended to know exactly what she was talking about.
"Yes, ma'am." Then, I insisted, "But, can you please tell me
what dialysis is?"

"I'll tell you when I'm done using the bathroom. Or are you
going to question me some more through the door?" We both
chuckled.

"No, ma'am. I'll just wait."

She took forever using the bathroom, and the Sandman's
hypnosis began to hold me captive as I sunk into the couch.
Maybe she was avoiding the conversation or perhaps she
assumed I wouldn't understand. I spoke through the door,
anxious to know, but not wanting to irritate her either by
asking again.

"Mama, are you all right in there?"

"Yes. I'm fine. You go to bed. We'll talk tomorrow." At least
she wasn't upset. I wondered if that was an affirmation that she
was finally bouncing back from the countless trials of lupus.

Although the conversation was delayed by a few days,
Mama remembered. She requested I come downstairs while

she and Jordan were lying on the couch watching *The Color Purple* for the umpteenth time. Jordan had fallen asleep, lying next to her as she rubbed his back. It was unusual to see her so calm, relaxed. Due to the constant, random mood swings that surfaced, we just never knew which direction she was headed each day.

"Have a seat. Let's talk. You can ask as many questions as you want. If you don't understand what I'm saying, just say so. Do you remember about a month ago when I had to go to the hospital because my back was hurting really bad?"

"Yes, ma'am."

"Well, the pain was because of the dialysis treatments. You know I have to get these treatments because my kidneys aren't functioning properly."

"Wait, what?" I was confused because no one had actually told us what the dialysis was for. "Mama, what's going on?"

"Sit back and relax. You can't fully comprehend this if you become too emotional. So, take a deep breath."

"Mama, just tell me this—does any of this mean you're going to die?"

"No, I'm not worried about death, and neither should you. God is my protector."

I nodded.

"So, let's talk about kidney function. Do you know what your kidneys are and how they operate in your body?"

"No, ma'am."

"Your kidneys help to flush out the waste, fluid, and toxins from your body. If your kidneys don't work properly, that can eventually lead to more health problems. When your body retains too much fluid, it will cause areas of your body to swell. Do you understand?"

"Somewhat. So, kidneys get rid of all of the bad stuff. Like bad foods or something?"

"Yeah, to a certain point. Your immune system really fights all of the bad stuff in your body. Other organs like your kidney, liver, and stomach help to get rid of waste and toxins."

"Waste and toxins?"

"Yes, when you pee and poop. That's waste and toxins."

"Got it." I giggled. "So, how does dialysis help?"

"Dialysis helps the kidneys by acting like a flushing system. The machines pretty much cleans the blood in my body to balance it out. So, the times when my legs swell, it's because my body's trying to adjust to the process. Sometimes too much fluid is released from my body and it makes me extremely tired."

"Mama, that sucks. Like really sucks."

"Yeah, I know. They put these grafts in my arms in order for me to receive treatments, but they stopped working. But, the one in my leg works just fine. You want to feel it?"

"Sure, what is it?" I reached over to touch it. It was a long, hard tube and it protruded under her skin.

"The graft is a thick, plastic tube. It's connected to one of my veins, which is coupled to my heart artery. Your arteries are where blood circulates from your heart to all parts of your body. The graft is where the flushing process takes place."

"Mama, that sounds painful."

"Yeah, I know. When the grafts in my arms stopped working months ago, I was scared of what might happen next." I glanced at her arms and saw at least two inches of scars on each arm.

"Sam told me that you have lupus. He told me that it's like your body attacks itself, right?"

"Well, yes. They diagnosed me with SLE. This is new to a lot of doctors and researchers, so there isn't a lot of information about it just yet."

"Yeah, Sam said that, too. If there isn't a lot of research information to help you, how do they know how to help you?"

"They don't. This is all trial and error. They're treating and monitoring me according to my symptoms and episodes, which sometimes includes prescribing me additional medication to my already long daily intake."

After lunch the next day, I went to Leslie's locker to get a marker, and when I shut the locker and turned around, *he* stood there, less than five feet away with goggling eyes. Again, his smile captured me.

"Hi," he softly mumbled. It seemed like he was nervous, too.

My tongue felt thick, and my lips were holding it hostage.

"I'm Kevin. Kevin Miles. What's your name?"

"Talisa. Talisa Brooks," I smirked.

"I really like your dimples."

I glanced at the hallway clock and stammered, "Sorry, I have to go to class. I can't be late." I was overcome with shyness like a kitten hidden behind a curtain. But, at least, finally, I knew his name!

Each year, usually the day after Thanksgiving, we all gather in the living room and decorate the Christmas tree. This particular year, the tree stood in the corner of the living room—stripped of bliss, empty and bare. Jordan and I unpacked the box of ornaments and lights, turned on some music, danced, and decorated the tree ourselves. It took some time to untangle the lights balled up in the bottom of the box, but we enjoyed doing it together.

I sorted the lights, checking for blown bulbs, and Jordan separated the ornaments by color. Mama relaxed in bed the majority of the day but later joined us in the living room. She made us Rice Krispies treats and hot cocoa with marshmallows, and we all watched *Mickey's Christmas Carol*. It was a classic annual holiday cartoon, and we were elated as we curled up next to her on the couch. She was inspired by the moment as her face glowed with glee.

*   *   *

~November 26, 1990~

Dear Diary,

The weekends always seem to fly by. Back to school. My gym teacher, Mrs. Pinkly, announced that the class would learn how to square dance over the next couple of weeks. It sounded like some white-people stuff. She demonstrated a couple of moves and blasted music that would make dogs cover their ears. The class was full of scattered laughter as many mocked Mrs. Pinkly. She blushed as she tried to maintain her composure. She divided us into groups forming several squares. Country music. I had never heard it before; black folks didn't listen to it. Was this even serious? Was this a real thing? Was this the white people's electric slide?

We all had dance partners, and it turned out to be a good time.

I loved school, and my classes were pretty easy except for my advanced math class. It was challenging, but I learned a lot: mathematical applications, operative problems, and problem-solving. It made my head spin, but the challenge was intriguing. We received our basketball season schedules. Of course, I was eager to play and anxious to get on the court and see what it was like. On the other hand, I was pissed at Daddy. He never sent the shoes and hadn't mentioned anything about them ever since I asked.

*   *   *

~December 16, 1990~

Dear Diary,

Two more days of school, then winter break begins. Finally, a chance to escape this bitter, arctic cold weather for a while. I'm tired of walking in the snow and catching the bus. My toes feel like icicles, and I have to put my shoes in front of the heating vent to thaw. We usually get three pairs of shoes for the school year. Mama doesn't have a lot of money. If we're lucky, sometimes we can get another pair or two if we find them at the Goodwill or Salvation Army.

~December 24, 1990~

Dear Diary,

It's Christmas Eve, and Tori has been on my mind all day. Wondering where she is and is she coming home for Christmas? I can't even call her.

~December 25, 1990~

Dear Diary,

Merry Christmas! Mama asked for us to list one item we desired for Christmas. I really want a radio or stereo, but I know we don't have a lot of money, so I asked for a Discman. Cassette tapes are played out. CDs are what's new in the stores, although they cost more than tapes. When I opened my gift, it was a brand-new Sony Discman and three CDs: Bell Biv Devoe's album Poison, *En Vogue's album* Born to Sing, *and Tony Toni Tone's album* The Revival. *I waited for Jordan to finish opening his gifts. He got more WWF wrestlers and Transformers, and he ran upstairs afterwards to line them up along his wall.*

After I installed the batteries in my Discman, I danced and pranced around my room listening to BBD's new CD. Jordan kicked open my door and started dancing with me. He's such a goofball.

*   *   *

~January 1, 1991~

Dear Diary,

Happy New Year! Mama says she used to believe in New Year's resolutions, but no one ever really sticks to their plan, so I thought long and hard about mine. This year I want to be better at sports, in both basketball and track. I think I can do that . . . because I won't quit.

Last year, I went to the skating rink with Leslie and my cousin, Sharae. It was the New Year's Eve all-night party from 7:00 p.m. to 7:00 a.m. A lot of kids were there, along with plenty of chaperones, and they locked the doors. No one could come in or out until our parents come to pick us up. Jordan couldn't come. Mama said he was still too young.

I never knew the great importance of Martin Luther King Day until I really listened to Dr. King's famous "I Have a Dream" speech. After absorbing each spoken word, it became clear to me why black people were so enraged about the actions of the police. Dr. King fought for equal rights, and in his attempt to effect change in the world, he died. Mama told us exactly how and why his life ended so abruptly. The speech touched me and provided insight to an underlining issue I didn't know existed: racism. Most of all, I would never allow anyone to disrespect or belittle me based on the color of my skin.

The documentary following the speech revealed the mind-blowing aftermath of his death. He was fighting for civil rights, and he stood in the face of danger while uncounted threats targeted him and his family. Bound and determined to make a difference, he stood for what he believed to be right, regardless of the consequences. No fear. Without a shadow of a doubt, as I continued to watch, I became angrier but determined to be the same—to be fearless.

Just as I placed my headphones on my head, the banging on the door startled me and everyone. Sam had moved Mama's bed back upstairs months before. I heard Mama stumble before she reached the stairs, and her footsteps heavily resonated through the house. I wondered who was at the door. Then, I heard Tori's voice. I became instantly energized and longed to run downstairs to see her, but I didn't want Mama to yell at me. Mama always said no matter how old a child gets, a mother never stops loving, worrying, or aching for that child. Tori's bed had sat vacant and bare across the bedroom, and I hoped she would stay. When Tori came upstairs, Jordan gave her a big hug. He asked if she was going to stay. I heard her said yes, and then she stood in the doorway of our room.

"Hey, baby sis!" She opened her arms wide. "Dang, are you just going to sit there?"

Part of me wanted to run and hug her; the other part of me felt a need to punch her in the face for leaving.

"Tori, where have you been?" I hugged her and closed the door.

"Oh, my goodness, you're so tall. I had some things to do." She sat on her bed.

"Things? You were gone for quite some time. Mama went back into the hospital, and it was just me and Jordan here by ourselves, like all summer." I couldn't help the accusation in my voice.

"Sorry. I didn't know."

"You *would* know if you had ever come home or even called to see if we were all right."

She sat on the bed, just staring at me.

"Why are you being so sensitive?" she asked harshly.

"I'm not sensitive. Why do you act like you don't care?" I snapped back.

"I do care. I just had some things I had to do."

"You keep saying 'things'? Like what?" I waited, and she was silent.

Finally, she sighed. "Fine, I wanted to hang out with my friends and my boyfriend. Mama didn't want me to, so I left. I was tired of her always yelling at me for stupid reasons." She leaned back to lie on the bed.

"You could have gotten hurt, you know?"

She rolled her eyes. "Talisa, loosen up. Damn, you're starting to sound like Mama. Anyway, how's junior high? Are you still a part of the drill team?"

"Yes, I'm still with the drill team. I met a lot of older girls since I've become a Stepper. Some of them know you, too. They seem to be a little overprotective. Did you do something? Are you in trouble? In danger?"

She ignored my question and sat straight up on the bed. "You need to let me know if someone's bothering you. You hear me?" She stared, sternly.

"How am I supposed to tell you? You're never around. It's not like I can call you."

"Here's my pager number. Just call the number, wait for the tone, enter our home phone number, press pound, then push one-seven-one-seven. That'll be your special code."

I looked at the pager then noticed a mark on her hand. It was a tattoo. I couldn't tell what it said, but the first letter was an L.

"Tori, what's that?"

"Nothing." She hid her hand behind her back. "Can you promise me something?"

"Promise you what?"

"Promise you'll be yourself, Talisa. Don't let anyone take advantage of you. Promise that you won't be a follower. You don't have to be like anyone else. And stay away from boys. They're just trouble."

"I have no idea what you're talking about, but fine. I don't have a boyfriend." I tried to not grin.

"Whoa, what's that? You better start talking right now."

"Well, his name is Kevin Miles. He's so, so, so cute. He smiled at me a couple of times then asked me my name last month. It's like I can't move when he comes around. I freeze, and my heart beats so fast."

"Aw, little sister. I think you have your first true crush. Leave it at a crush. It's all right to talk to him, but nothing else. You hear me? Boys will only shit on you and leave you to clean up their mess." She stared out the window.

"Have you had sex?" I asked.

"Yeah, why? You better not have, Talisa, or I'll punch you in the face right now."

"No, I haven't. I was just asking. There are a couple girls at my school that say they've had sex before."

"You stay away from those fast-ass girls. You don't need to have sex, Talisa. Trust me, you can wait. You only get one coochie. Don't go damaging your goods. Wait until you're older and you meet the guy who really wants to be with you, and only you, and no other girls. Got it?"

"Got it. I don't want to have sex. I don't know what all the hype's about at school."

"Because you guys are a bunch of hormonal crazy-ass kids right now. You . . . just don't do it. You don't want to end up pregnant or with an STD or something stupid."

"What's an STD?"

"Oh, my goodness." She pretended to faint onto her bed. "What are they teaching you guys at school? STDs are sexually transmitted diseases. They're nasty things you get from having sex with nasty-ass boys. With their nasty, sex germ-infected penises. They get all up in your coochie and make it smell bad and itchy, and it'll burn when you pee. It'll make your stomach hurt and some even give you all types of bumps on your coochie. Girl, you better keep your coochie to yourself."

"I'm about to throw up. Geez, Tori. Do you have to say it like that?" I scrunched my face.

"I got your attention, didn't I? And I have to say it, because Lord knows Mama hasn't. Keep your coochie to yourself. I don't care how cute this Kevin boy is. Tell him he can't have it."

Listening to the possible consequences made my stomach turn, but I was happy she was finally home. I prayed she'd stay so we could chitchat more often.

* * *

~January 22, 1991~

Dear Diary,

My first seventh-grade basketball game, and I was jittery from the beginning to the end. Although practices had made me sore beyond measure, once I stood on the court, the soreness and tiredness immediately disappeared. We played as a team—cheering each other on, encouraging and supportive. Although we didn't win the game, it was close, and we only lost by three points. Mama, Sam, and Ms. Rose sat in the stands, charged with energy and clapping. Kevin sat a couple of bleachers behind our bench. Each time I got up, I tried to not look at him, but I couldn't help it.

He smiled at me and nodded his head. He played on the Edison Eagles boys' basketball team. I looked forward to attending one of his games. When he smiled at me, it made me forget how bad my feet hurt from my flat shoes.

Tori walked me to drill team practice, and she gossiped with some of the older girls. I loved being with my big sister. I walked across the street to talk to Leslie. Since we'd become Steppers over the summer, we had to set an example for the girls in the younger group. The president of the drill team focused not only on the perfection of the routines and performances, but he demanded that we keep good grades as well. He constantly repeated the importance of conducting ourselves in a respectable manner, because we were the positivity inspiring our community.

We were not to get in trouble at school: no fighting, arguing, or disobeying any leader, parent, or teacher. A lot of parents from the neighbor devoted their time to helping us with fundraisers, car washes in the summertime, and bake sales. The community supported our mission and we were the largest positive youth group in the city.

Valentine's Day this year was the best ever, as I found a note wedged in the crack of my locker. I opened it, and on it was drawn a heart with an arrow, and a note:

I LIKE YOU! —K.M.

Oh boy, my heart overflowed with excitement. It felt like someone glued a huge smile to my face.

The school counselor walked up to me. "Don't be late for class. I'm not handing out any excuse slips today."

"Yes, ma'am. I'm going."

"Hold on. Wait a minute. What's this?" She took the note from my hand. "Hmm, seems like someone likes you." She winked at me and stuck the note in my notebook. "Get going."

I couldn't wait to show Leslie and Tori.

During our walk home from school, Leslie and I talked about our daddies. I'd never met hers and she'd never met mine. Her daddy lived somewhere in Georgia, and she really missed him.

"Do you talk to him often?" I asked.

"Not a whole lot, but he calls like on the important days, ya know. Birthdays, holidays—stuff like that."

"Yeah, same here. Mine's been promising to come and visit us or send us things that he never puts in the mail."

"Girl, does that make you mad? Upset?"

"It used to," I said. "I want to believe that he's really coming or that he misses us enough and will just come to see how we're doing. But he never does. So, I'm not sure what I feel, but I still miss him though."

"Yeah, I hear you. Same here."

When I got home, Mama was sitting on the couch with her feet up watching *The Jeffersons*. Jordan was playing Super Mario on the Nintendo. My legs were worn out from walking, and I flopped face down on my bed. When I rolled over, Tori's things were gone. I checked the closet: no clothes, no shoes, no curling iron, no fingernail polish, no earrings, no necklaces—nothing. She was gone, again. I pondered her absence as I sat on the floor and leaned my back against of my bed. My head fell backwards and my eyes stared at the ceiling as my arms wrapped snuggly around my pillow. I felt utterly abandoned. Why did she always leave?

*   *   *

~March 17, 1991~

Dear Diary,

Daddy called today. His mother died. Subconsciously, I want to be remorseful, but I feel nothing. I wish I had had the opportunity to know her. I have no memories of her, my grandmother, who I know nothing about. What was she like? What did she look like? She lived in Memphis, Tennessee. I want to cry, but I can't. My thoughts and heart are with Daddy. Sadness is beginning to settle only because I feel like I should be gravely affected by this news. All I can think is how I never want Mama to die.

I couldn't recall the last time we'd attended church services. We used to go to church on Sundays when we lived at Grandpa and Grandma's house. We would be there all day long. People danced, sang, and shouted really loudly, and the choir sang from sunup to sundown. The pastor always patted his forehead with a cloth, but I never saw any sweat, and when he preached, it sounded like one of Grandpa's old lawnmowers starting up.

Mama started attending some church called The Seventh-day Adventist Church, and we would go on Saturdays, not Sundays. It seemed weird at first, but all of the people were cordial and welcoming. Grandpa said the Sabbath was on a Sunday, but this church believed the Sabbath was on Saturday. It was all baffling to me, but we had to do as Mama instructed.

* * *

~March 31, 1991~

Dear Diary,

Happy Easter! The night before Easter, Mama usually watches The Ten Commandments. *It's a really long movie; we always end up falling asleep until Mama shakes us to wake up and pay attention. Some years ago, we had to recite the Ten Commandments out loud, or we couldn't open our Christmas gifts. After memorizing them year after year, she stopped demanding we repeat them because they were ingrained into our brains.*

Without a shadow of a doubt, hands down our drill team was the saving grace for many of its members. The beat of the drums amplified the magnetic energy stored within the crowd before we even stepped foot on the gym's floor. The fieldhouse was saturated with fans screaming and cheering as we strutted into position and prepared to deliver an epic halftime show. The performance for the Quad City Thunder Basketball Conference Finals halftime show was electrifying. Mr. Moore, the president of the drill team, boastfully stood as many spectators circled, showering him with compliments.

We huddled near the concession stands after the show, and Mr. Moore stood with his arms open, ready to embrace us. "I can't tell you all how well you just did. You exceeded my expectations . . . you have just outshined even yourselves. I wish you could see yourselves and what I just witnessed you do out there." He paused and placed his hand on his head. "Did you hear that crowd? Give yourselves a round of applause. I'm proud of you . . . all of you."

Being a Stepper was challenging. The moves were more complex, but my group's captain believed repetition led to perfection. During practices, if you messed up, you did push-ups and you got back up and tried the step or dance move again. There wasn't any room for errors. All breaks were earned through hard work and consistency. Ms. Rose was always there, at every performance, every practice. I knew Mama didn't have the energy most days to participate, but I wished she would come and see us more often.

Since we did exceptionally well at the performance, our team captain was a bit lenient at the next practice. Afterwards Jordan, Mama, and I went to the laundromat to wash clothes. The baskets were extremely heavy; Jordan and I struggled to carry each one. Jordan's love for sweets sent him on a scavenger hunt for quarters. He searched the floor for coins around the candy machines, hoping someone had accidently dropped one. Mama's behavior was erratic and caused me to pause several times. The whole time she paced from one side of the laundromat to the other, biting her fingernails, shaking her head side to side, and sweating profusely.

We tried not to stare, but her actions were blatantly noticeable. So, we sat, waiting for something to happen. Obviously, something was wrong again.

A few nights had passed; I couldn't sleep through the groaning and sniveling. I placed a pillow over my head in an attempt to dream of a place beyond the walls of my bedroom. I glanced at the clock: 2:45 a.m. I wandered sleeplessly to my bedroom door and pressed my ear against it. The murmuring continued as the sound vibrated my hollow wooden door. I slowly opened it and rubbed the sleep crud from my eyes. I found Mama sitting at the foot of her bed, and I sat next to her and touched her hand. She squeezed mine.

"Mama, what's wrong? Why are you crying?"

"My legs hurt." She clenched her teeth as her face crinkled in pain.

"What do you want me to do?"

"You should go back to bed. You have school tomorrow. I'll be fine." She waved for me to go back to my room.

"Mama, I can't sleep while you're crying. I can hear you. Just tell me what to do."

"Just rub my legs for a little while. They're both cramping." She covered her face with her hands.

"I'll help you slide back in the bed." It was discouraging seeing her like that.

She sat for a minute in a daze. After thirty minutes of rubbing, she fell asleep. I covered her with a blanket and went back to bed. But my mind would not allow me to rest. I couldn't sleep.

Things were changing, and I was changing, too.

PART IV

Troubled Waters

CHAPTER 10

THE SUMMER DAYS were long and full of sizzling heat. Plus, the performance schedule for the drill team was extensive. We marched and danced until the soles of our white shoes melted and turned black. We performed nonstop; eventually I began to question what we were marching for. The team was an organized family, bonded by our core principles, unified to function as one, but it seemed we were losing people by the day. I wasn't sure if these team members were quitting, getting older, venturing off to college, or journeying down a different path.

Mama appeared to be in high spirits, although her mood swings continued to interchange between hot and cold. Sad to say, to us it had become the norm. There was not one hospital emergency room episode that entire summer, but the disease still seemed to have taken an emotional and mental toll on her. While refilling her weekly medication container, she threw a temper tantrum and flung the container across the room. I couldn't even remember to take my daily vitamin, so I could only imagine how frustrated this must be for her to sort out all these different medications. Perhaps the medication had finally stabilized the disease. I knocked on wood and assumed the worst had come to an end.

Kevin and I became close over the summer. Mama gave him permission to call the house phone, with stipulations of course. We could only talk for an hour a day and no phone calls after 8:00 p.m. During the summer, he rode his bike to come see me. We'd sit on the front steps, but only for an hour or so until Mama would tell him he had to go. My heart smiled when I saw him and when he smiled at me. I couldn't help but to blush.

*   *   *

~September 9, 1991~

Dear Diary,

Daddy's birthday is today, but I didn't call him. I'm unsure of my feelings at the moment because all summer he continued to promise to be here and spend time with us, and he never showed up. Not once.

My heart ached for Jordan. All summer he'd waited for Daddy to take him fishing. He sat on the front steps of the porch with his tackle box, lunch bag, and two small fishing poles. So many days he waited. I wanted to go out there, to tell him the truth, but the aftermath would be devastating and would crush his little heart. So, I never said a word. Mama noticed, too. She'd watch him sit there all day, from sunup to sundown. Throughout the day, she'd bring him water and food. After a couple weeks, I think he finally understood.

"Jordan, baby, you should come in the house now. It's getting late," Mama spoke softly.

"But Daddy said he was coming this weekend. Can I just wait a little while longer?"

"Just a little while longer." Mama stood with her hands on her hips. Her cheeks turned rosy red. He continued sitting on the steps, as he bounced his legs. He began to sob, and Mama sat beside him.

"He's not coming, is he, Mama?" His face crumpled as he sagged into her lap.

"No, Jordan, he isn't." She was delicate and patted him on the back.

"But he promised we would go."

He stood up, glared at Mama with melancholy eyes, and picked up his tackle box. He drug his fishing poles behind him. He walked past me with his head hung down. I followed him up the stairs, not saying a word. He flopped down onto his bed and wailed. I became internally enraged with protectiveness. I didn't know what to say or do, so I sat on his bed and took off his shoes. He was disappointed and crushed by the false hope Daddy had instilled in his little heart. I rubbed his back until he fell asleep. That's when I heard Mama yelling. From the language she was using, I assumed she was talking to Daddy.

"I don't give a shit. They have feelings, too. They are your children, or did you forget? You are selfish. Don't call this phone unless you plan on sticking to your worthless-ass promises."

The sound of the phone slamming down echoed through the house. I had never heard her speak to him like that before, but deep down, a part of me was relieved that she did. Finally.

The challenging days seemed to be followed by brighter ones, so I was thankful. I was lying across my bed listening to music when Mama barged into my room, grabbed my hand, and pulled me downstairs into the kitchen. Jordan, Sam, Ms. Rose, Leslie, and Tori were standing around the table. On the table was a strawberry cake with real strawberries on top. It was lit up with fourteen candles. One purple and white birthday balloon was tied to the back of the chair, floating in the air, slightly dancing from side to side.

"Happy birthday!" they shouted.

I was shocked and happy to see that Tori stopped by. Her face glowed with happiness. Leslie gave me a nice birthday card.

Happy birthday, Sis. I wish you a very happy birthday. I'm so glad you're my sister. I'm here for you always.

Love, your sister #2,

Leslie.

Mama handed me a purple gift bag with a white and silver ribbon on the side. Inside, there was a Reebok box with basketball shoes covered with white tissue paper. I couldn't believe it. I hugged her so firmly and kissed her on the cheek.

"I wanted to get you something I know you really wanted . . . but also really needed." She patted me on the shoulder.

"Does this mean I get to play basketball this year?"

"Girl, yes. You better do something with these shoes. They weren't cheap."

"Thank you, Mama. I really want to play this year. I have a feeling this year will be better than last year."

"Keep your spirits up," Mama said as she turned away.

Mama stood on the other side of the table before I blew out the candles. "Talisa, I wasn't here for your last birthday, so I'm just a bit emotional. I'm glad I'm blessed with the opportunity to see you turn fourteen."

They all sang to me, and it truly was an unforgettable moment. Daddy called, but I didn't feel like talking.

"Happy birthday. I love you," he said.

I handed the phone to Jordan.

* * *

~October 15, 1991~

Dear Diary,

My advanced math class is thought-provoking, ranging from complex to near insanity. But I'm not going to give up. It's just a lot of new formulas to learn. My teacher is always available for after-school tutoring. I can't always stay after school because the bus only runs at certain times. Missing the bus means a long walk home, and an even longer walk when it's cold outside. My teacher gives me good examples to follow with detailed explanations, which helps a lot. I just have to keep practicing.

After school, I found Jordan sitting on the couch watching cartoons. Mama had settled in her room, turning the pages of some cookbook in pure stillness. I walked through her room to get a shirt for drill team practice, and her eyes were glued to me with such a bewildered expression—her lips were pressed together airtight.

When I returned from practice later that evening, all hell had broken loose.

"What is your problem? Do you think you're that grown to just walk in and out of this house as you please? Answer me." Mama was pissed off, and ready to explode.

"No, ma'am. You didn't say anything when I came in from school. I had to go to practice. I didn't want to bother you." I mumbled under my breath.

"Like I said . . . who gave you permission to walk out of this house?" She walked toward me until we were nose to nose.

"Nobody, but—"

"But, nothing. Walk out of this house again without asking and see what happens. Get in the kitchen, do the dishes, and mop the floor."

"But, Mama, I have homework. I have to go to bed at nine o'clock. I won't have enough time to finish my homework."

"Girl, say something else. Keep talking," she practically dared me. Her eyes snapped. "When I tell you to do something, just do it. You should've thought about your homework before you decided to walk out this house like you were grown or something." She walked away, tapping her fingers on her upper outer thigh.

After a while, I just blocked her out. Those days were tough to withstand her presence. Sam once said that Mama was taking a lot of medication that caused her to be moody sometimes. But, it was difficult to differentiate between the effects of the medication and if the malformation of lupus had permanently altered her personality.

* * *

~October 28, 1991~

Dear Diary,

Happy birthday, Mama! She was in high spirits today. We celebrated at Grandma and Grandpa's house.

A night I could never forget, I closed my eyes and silently repeated, "God if you are there, if you truly do exist . . . could you please stop all of this?"

I swear, it was always something. Mama screamed as she ran in my room in the middle of the night, trembling all over—her eyes bucked with terror and apprehension. The clock read 4:34 a.m. I struggled to wake up as drowsiness anchored my feet like a ton of bricks. Sleep clouded my vision.

"Mama, what's wrong now?" I grabbed her arms and forced them to her side.

"Your sister," she panicked. Then, a ball of fear bounced in my gut. Her eyes wandered unfocused. "I have to go. Watch your brother." She turned and dashed down the stairs.

I followed. "Mama, wait! Please! What's wrong with Tori?"

Whatever had happened caused her such disorientation that

Mama fumbled as she attempted to put on her shoes. There was a knock at the door, and I didn't want to open it. My breathing had become uncontrollable. Mama always said her greatest fear was the police standing at her door to deliver a message—a message that Tori was hurt, or even worse, dead. I took a deep breath, my hands shook, and I turned the knob. It was Sam. He and Mama rushed out the door and left without giving me any explanation.

Multiple chills shook my body like a winter breeze grazing the back of my neck. My body temperature rose as sweat pooled under my arms. Anxiety traveled from my stomach to my throat, making it hard to speak. Jordan ran down the stairs with a million questions, searching for answers that I didn't have. I sat and worried. Where was Tori? Was she dead? Had someone hurt her? Were Mama and Sam going to save her? What had happened?

Another sleepless night crept in my room as I watched the digits on my clock change by the minute. Just before my alarm clock went off, the phone rang, and I inhaled tiny breaths of air before answering.

"Hello?"

"Talisa, are you up and moving? Get your brother up, too." Mama's voice cracked as though she'd been crying all night.

"Mama, what's wrong? What happened to Tori?" My words tumbled out.

"Talisa, I need you to focus. Get up, and you and your brother get ready for school. I should be there when you get home. The spare house key is in the kitchen drawer by the window. Got it?"

"But, Mama . . . what about Tori?"

"I don't have time to explain right now. I'll talk to you and your brother when I get home. Now, get up and get going."

"Yes, ma'am." I sighed and hung up.

We ate cereal and packed our backpacks. I walked Jordan to school and then ran to catch the bus. I thought about Tori the entire day, wondering if she was all right. Why wouldn't Mama tell me? Was it so horrifying that Jordan and I couldn't know about it? I couldn't focus in any of my classes. I prayed.

"Please, don't let my sister be dead."

CHAPTER 11

I T WAS AN accident. A really, really bad car accident.
Every vertebra in Tori's neck had been broken. Her head and neck were connected by a single nerve. The doctors had installed a metal halo to support and stabilize her head and neck and to give the bones an opportunity to heal properly. She was alive. That was all that mattered to me.

The doctors didn't know exactly how long she'd have to wear the halo, but she would be going home. She wasn't drinking or on any drugs or anything. Another car had run her off the road. I wondered why. Mama said she didn't know why someone would do that and just leave her in the dark, in a deep ditch, cold and alone. The more details revealed, the more anger shifted through me.

Mama took pictures of the car she was driving. They were terrifying. She was driving alone, traveling back to Rock Island from Chicago. The driver's side of the car was completely smashed flat like a pancake. Each picture was breathtaking and made me furious. I thought about how scared she must've been, run off the road into a huge tree and into a deep ditch. It was so unreal that my eighteen-year-old sister was almost killed.

From the moment Tori shuffled through the door, my eyes were stuck to her every movement. Sam had brought the bed from upstairs and set it up in the dining room since Tori was unable to walk up and down the stairs. It was surreal. Sharp metal screws punctured her skin and were embedded slightly into her skull—two metal bars in the front and two in the back. It was like something out of a movie, and she was in excruciating pain. How in the world was she supposed to sleep in this thing? How was she supposed to take a shower?

I sat next to her and held her hand. "Tori. Hi. You okay?" I whispered.

"No. No, I'm not. My head hurts really bad." She squeezed my hand.

I looked at Mama. "Can she take a Tylenol or something to make her head stop hurting?"

"She has pain medication, but she has to eat first. I'm going to make her some soup."

Mama headed to the kitchen to fix the soup, and I gently helped Tori lie back in the bed. She couldn't lie flat, so we attempted to prop her up slightly by placing multiple pillows behind her back. Tori ate all of the soup, and that was the first time in a long time she and Mama weren't yelling at each other. Tori stayed quiet, and Mama fed her.

*   *   *

~November 28, 1991~

Dear Diary,

Happy Thanksgiving! One day I'll have a family of my own, and I can cook for them just like Mama. Her peach cobbler is the best ever—made from scratch. I eat it until my stomach hurts. Tori even went with us to Grandpa and Grandma's house for dinner. She talked to everyone. It felt like old times. I'm glad she's home and I'm happy that she and Mama aren't mad at each other anymore.

    Now, if it would only remain this way.

~December 2, 1991~

Dear Diary,

Tori threw a fit today. One minute she was crying, the next she was throwing pillows across the room. I guess I wouldn't like it either if I was stuck in that metal thing— that weird-looking halo. It sure doesn't look like the halos I've seen on the heads of angels in the movies.

"Tori, what's wrong?" I asked.

"I hate this thing!" she screamed. "I hate this stupid thing!"

At that point, I believed she'd snapped and was completely fed up with being restrained and confined by that contraption. We used to play a lot of games when we were younger, so I thought maybe she needed a distraction. Something to occupy her idle mind.

"Hey, let's play Uno. You want to play?" I slightly smiled at her, break dancing in front of her just to make her laugh.

"You're so silly. Sure, Sis, I'll play with you." She sighed deeply and leaned back on the pillows that I'd picked up from the floor.

We played a couple of games. She beat me badly, and quickly, too. The entire time we played, my curiosity toggled between whether to ask or not ask about the night of the accident. I was anxious to hear her version of the story. Why had she become so upset all the time? Why did she run away so often? Last week during dinner, she nibbled here and there as she picked over her food. Then, she suddenly burst into tears, pushing her plate to the side.

I took a deep breath as my curiosity took over. "Tori, what happened to you in the car? Did someone do this to you on purpose?"

She stared at me. "I'm not sure. It just happened so fast. I was driving back from Chicago after hanging out with this guy. The snow was falling so heavy. I could barely see the road or even the cars ahead of me."

"Then what?"

"A car pulled up beside me, speeding fast as hell. I heard a loud noise on my side, like someone bumped me. The car shook. I hit the brakes. I tried to get control of the car, but it kept spinning like three or four times." She sniffed.

"You don't have to tell me anymore. I wasn't trying to make you cry, Sis."

"There was a loud crash," Tori continued. "I saw the tree

coming closer, and closer, and closer. I couldn't stop it. The glass from the windshield shattered. I tried to cover my face, but it was too late. My head hit the steering wheel. I tried to lift my head, but shit, it hurt. My face was covered with blood, then I passed out. I don't know for how long, but when I woke up, I was in the hospital."

"Oh, my goodness, Tori. That's really scary. I'm so glad that you're all right now."

"It's like it keeps replaying in my mind, over and over. I just want it to stop."

I wanted to hug her, but I couldn't with the halo in the way.

"Do you want to use my Discman? Maybe listening to music or something will help you not think about it?"

"Sis, it's in my mind. It'll never leave my mind. No matter what I do, I just have to deal with it."

Mama came downstairs to check on Tori and clean around the screws in her head. I always left the room because it hurt her. Mama took her time cleaning around each one; the dried, built-up blood surrounding each screw caused Tori discomfort. Although they took short breaks, Tori still moaned.

Although the accident had happened, life continued as usual. Each dialysis session for Mama was unalike and potentially high risk. For the last few years, I'd watched her fight herself, lose herself, and forget herself. After observing from the sideline, I learned that no expectation was the best expectation. It was my form of self-protection. With no expectations there was no false hope, and with no false hope, there were no more tears to shed. I was once filled with so much optimism, clinging to what once was, and battling to accept the present.

We had a long night. Once again, she blubbered and complained as her legs cramped. I filled up the mop bucket with piping hot water, threw two towels over my shoulder, and kneeled by her bedside. After soaking the towels and barely wringing the water out, I wrapped them around her legs. The heat helped to relax the muscles. The dialysis treatment aftermath was sporadic: one day it was leg cramping, one day dizziness with migraine headaches, another day leg and feet swelling. The most common, the most frequent, were the damn mood swings. Those were problematic for me and Jordan because we had to live with her. We never knew what her responses, actions, or reactions would be.

*   *   *

~December 31, 1991~

Dear Diary,

New Year's Eve was pretty quiet because once again, Mama lay in bed all day. Tori was bound and determined to go out to a party. She begged me to find her something to wear, but nothing would fit over the halo. After going through my closet, I realized I didn't have any fashionable clothes—at least nothing she wanted to wear. Finally, she managed to squeeze into my silk button-up shirt. We were only able to fasten the last three buttons from the bottom. One foot at a time, I helped her slide her feet into her knee-high black boots, and then, persistent as ever, she walked down the street in the snow with her halo on.

When Mama finally woke up, I told her about Tori.

"That girl will always do exactly what she sets her mind to do. There's no stopping your sister," she chuckled.

Jordan and I enjoyed ourselves. It was just us downstairs, watching the *Video Soul* countdown until midnight. We played music on the stereo, and Jordan thought he was a rapper. He grabbed his baseball hat and stood on the sofa like it was a stage, rapping into an old, rolled-up newspaper like it was a microphone. He could dance, too. If he could've just stopped laughing, maybe we could've gotten through a whole song.

* * *

~January 1, 1992~

Dear Diary,

Happy New Year's Day! Tori came back this morning. Mama and I were just laughing at her. Tori said she was getting down in the club with her halo on.

"Girl, I was dancing in this thing. Ain't nothing going stop me. I've been in this house for almost two months lying in this bed. I'd had enough."

"I can't believe you walked out of this house to go to a party with this thing on your head. Looking like R2D2. Show us how you were dancing," Mama grinned.

Tori got up off the couch and danced and shook her butt.

She was so stiff, I was sure she was going to lose her balance as she tried to rock back and forth.

Later, I helped Mama cook, and she taught me how to fry chicken. Jordan played video games all morning, and after a while, he brought the Nintendo downstairs, and he and Tori played games. Sam came over this evening. Overall, the day was surprisingly pleasant with no mishaps. Perhaps the start of a new year is a new beginning for us all.

~January 11, 1992~

Dear Diary,

Winter school break is almost over, and its brutally cold outside. Once the holidays pass, I wish there was a button to melt all this snow. After a while, it looks messy outside, and the sun doesn't shine much during the winter. One day I'm going to move to a place where the sun always shines. No more of this treacherous, cold snow. Even with our snow boots on, two pairs of socks, and long thermals under our clothes, the wind still cuts through our clothes and pierces our skin. Jordan's always losing his gloves, so I let him borrow mine until he gets into the school building. I take them back so my fingers don't become frostbitten while I wait to catch the city bus for school.

The first day back to school from winter break, and the Edison Eagle Girls' basketball season was about to start. My shoes were laced, stretched, and sitting outside of my closet door. I just had to remind Mama. When I got home from school, asking her was the top priority on my agenda. I took a deep breath and walked into her bedroom. She was reading the newspaper.

"Excuse me, Mama. I wanted to ask—"

She put her hand up in the air. "Before you ask me anything, go get out of your school clothes. Go wash your hands. Go eat. Finish your homework and see if your brother needs help with his. Don't come ask me anything until you're done." She eyed me over the top of the newspaper.

I sighed. "Yes, ma'am."

"Little girl, do you have an attitude?"

"No, ma'am."

Well, obviously, that day was not the right day to ask.

*   *   *

~January 13, 1992~

Dear Diary,

My phone curfew. On school nights, no calls after eight, and on weekends, no calls after nine. But I don't care about the time restraint. Kevin and I don't have to just talk at school—we can talk all the time. Especially on the weekends. I have to admit, I sneaked on the phone a couple times after curfew just to talk to him. Sometimes, I can't think when I'm talking to him. I like him. I really like him. Like, a lot.

I told a lie. A big, fat lie. After school, I had run to the corner gas station and begged the clerk to let me use the phone because I didn't have any change. I had five dollars, but I didn't know if I'd need it to catch the bus later. The clerk allowed me to use the phone, and I called Mama.

"Mama, I have to stay after school to retake a test for my math class," I said.

I probably shouldn't have said math because she knew it was one class I never had a lot of trouble with.

"Fine, go retake your test. Make sure you get home before it gets dark." Before I could even answer, she hung up the phone.

I darted back to the school's locker room to change into my clothes that I stuffed in the bottom of my bag. Leslie was already dressed, waiting on the court with her hands on her hips. I stood next to her. Coach Mills was there. He was the eighth-grade girls' basketball coach and also the woodshop teacher.

"Hey, girl. So, your mama said yes?" Leslie asked.

"Well, not quite." I squinted my eyes.

"Ooh-wee, you're going to get in big trouble if she finds out. So, she didn't sign the permission form for you to play either, did she?"

"Stop panicking. She won't find out."

"Don't say I didn't tell you so."

"It'll be fine. I'm just going to ask her tonight when I get home. I know she's going to say yes." In the meantime, I hoped she didn't find out.

I got home seconds before the street lights came on. I hopped in the shower, put on my pajamas, finished eating, and did my homework. Our bedtime was 9:00 p.m. depending on the amount of homework assigned. I finished two English assignments. Afterwards, it was sink or swim, and I prepared myself to ask for permission to play basketball. Leslie was right—I should have asked beforehand. But, with Mama's moods, the window of opportunity some days seemed to not be open. Right then, I felt I didn't have a choice. If I didn't ask, I'd fall into a deeper hole of continuous lies.

"Mama, can I ask you something?" She was hemming up a pair of Sam's work pants.

"What is it?" She kept her eyes on the pants.

"Can I play basketball this year? You said on my birthday that I could play. I'll keep my grades up and do all of my chores, go to drill team practice, and help Jordan, too," I finished, anxious to hear her response.

She stopped hemming. "That is what I said. You're right. So, I guess you're playing then."

I turned to walk into Jordan's room to tell him. Jordan loved basketball and couldn't wait until sixth grade so he could play at the elementary school.

"Stop. Hold it right there." Mama's icy voice froze me. I had just one foot out of her room.

"Get your narrow behind back in here. Did you really think you were going to just walk in here like you haven't done anything wrong?" She set the pants on the bed and walked over to me. We were eye to eye and she was not pleased.

"No, ma'am." I didn't know whether to just tell the truth or act like I didn't know what she was talking about. Either way, I was dead.

"Ms. Rose called me earlier and told me that you and Leslie were going to catch the bus together today after basketball practice. Now, who gave you permission to play?"

"You did," I mumbled as I leaned back, away from her face.

"Stand up straight. Speak up, little girl."

I cleared my throat. "You did. On my birthday. So, I just went."

"You're right. I did say that, but you still have to ask when the time comes around so I know where you are. And, you didn't just go . . . you called me, then lied. Then, you lied to the coach, and *then* you walked in here lying again to my face like you did nothing wrong."

"Sorry, Mama."

"Sorry? Talisa, nothing good comes from lying. You tell one lie, and you end up telling seven more just to cover the first lie. What's your reason for not telling the truth?"

"I tried to ask you yesterday, but you told me to go eat, change my clothes, do my homework, help Jordan, and then come talk to you. But, once I was done with everything, you were asleep. I just really wanted to play."

"Just because you really want to do something doesn't mean you start telling lies or lying to me about anything. You are not an adult."

I thought, So, it's okay for adults to lie? But I knew if I said that out loud my next journal entry would be a rough draft of my own eulogy.

"Yes, ma'am." I knew I should have just told the truth.

"Now, go get ready for bed." She walked back to her bed. "I went to the school this afternoon and signed your permission slip. You lie to me again and you'll be grounded. You understand?"

"Yes ma'am." I was so relieved. I thought she was going to kill me. When she walked up to me, I instantly had a flashback of Mama and Tori going rounds like two heavyweight champs fighting for the title.

*   *   *

~January 31, 1992~

Dear Diary,

Today is Sam's birthday. Leslie and I walked to Walgreens after school today, and I used my five-dollar weekly allowance money to buy him a birthday card. He deserves it. He's always there for Mama.

~February 1, 1992~

Dear Diary,

We had a basketball game today. We played well as a team, but we lost by six points. 41–35. We were all so excited and happy to just be playing, but even more hyped that we got the plays right. Hopefully, with more practice, we'll do even better. It was a great day!

It was Valentine's Day. Kevin gave me a pink and purple card with hearts all over it. It was really sweet. Mama said no boys allowed in the house. But over the summer, we had spent some time outside on the steps, just chitchatting and laughing. Our phone conversations had become lengthy, and Mama swiftly interceded, reducing our allowed talking time.

I smiled from ear to ear, shut the front door, and attempted to speed-walk through the dining room.

"Umm, where are you going so fast?" Tori asked. "Wait a minute!"

I shyly grinned, and I turned toward her. "What?"

"What do you mean, *what*? Why are you smiling so hard?"

"No reason. I can't be happy?"

"Uh-huh. You know that I know that you're lying, right?"

"Fine. Kevin gave me a Valentine's card today. I was shocked. That's all. I didn't know if he really liked me like that, but I guess he does."

"Aww, how cute. Did you keep your coochie to yourself?"

"Geez. Yes, Tori. I've been at school all day."

"Why didn't you think he liked you like that? He calls here like he's a damn bill collector."

"I don't know. I just didn't think boys would find my gap cute or pretty."

"Girl, please. It's different. It's who you are. It doesn't make you ugly. Anyway, at your age, or hell, at any age, they aren't focused on your teeth anyway. I'm glad he made you smile, though."

I had a gap in between my front, top teeth. It wasn't noticeably different in my eyes until we moved here and I attended elementary school. Kids teased me. The jokes told behind my back cut like razor blades, and I became ashamed to even smile. I tried to convince Mama and Daddy of my desperate need for braces, but Mama said they were too expensive. Daddy asked why. I told him that the gap in between my front teeth was ugly. He said it was unique—that it was what made me standout. But they don't see what I see; the way people look at me doesn't make me feel pretty.

After dinner, we all adjourned in the living room after Mama called our names. She sat on the arm of the couch while we all situated ourselves. Tori sat next to me on the couch, and Jordan plopped down on the cushion next to Mama. She swiftly examined each one of our faces and shifted her sitting position to lean back. This made us uneasy until Jordan broke the silence.

"Umm, what are we doing? Are we playing a game or something?"

"No. Listen up. I know a lot has happened in the past few months . . . past few years."

"Mama, what's wrong?" Jordan touched her hand.

"Umm, well . . . umm, I'm pregnant."

We were stunned. It was so quiet. Tori and I looked at each other in disbelief and I put my hand over my mouth.

"Well, I guess Sam likes you a whole lot. He's been helping you heal and every thang, making it all betta." Tori burst out laughing.

"Tori, don't be nasty. Maybe it was an accident." Our laughter echoed off the walls.

"No, Mama's nasty. She's the one pregnant. Go 'head, girl," Tori giggled.

Mama just shook her head.

"Are you two comedians done over there? I know you two are teenagers, but don't be disrespectful. So, stop it." Mama tried to hide her smile as she reddened.

"Wait. Mama, what about the disease? The lupus? Dialysis? Will this hurt the baby?" I asked. My smile and laughter turned into worry.

Mama put her arm around Jordan and kissed him on the forehead.

"That's what I need to talk to you all about." The tone of her voice intensified. "So, the doctor told me I probably won't survive if I have the baby. They also believe the baby possibly wouldn't survive either, and if the baby does make it to full term, it could possibly be deformed or have some mental defects." She halted. "When I was first diagnosed with lupus, they said I couldn't even get pregnant, but now I am."

"Umm, no. Mama, you can't do this." Tori's authoritative tone rose.

I stuttered, "Mama, this doesn't make sense. You can't have this baby. It's just too risky." I pleaded for her to reconsider, and my heart pounded. It seemed dangerous and nearly suicidal.

"I have to believe that God will see me through this. I know that it's risky, but I can't see me aborting or killing a baby. I didn't abort any of you. I don't expect any of you to fully understand right now, but—"

"But, what?" I stood up and fumed with frustration. "You do this . . . and you die. Then what? What happens to us? Why would you even think about doing this? This isn't fair."

"Oh, damn." Tori slid towards me and whispered, "Girl, you better shut up. She isn't laughing."

Mama's calm demeanor led me to believe she had already made her decision. "Talisa, you always push for answers and reasons. Well, sometimes there are no answers. You just have to pray and have faith that everything will work out the way God intended for it to."

Jordan touched Mama's stomach. "So, there's a baby in there . . . right now?"

"Yes. It's not that big right now, but it's in there."

Tori grabbed my arm to pull herself up from the couch. "Mama, we can't make you do anything, but please think about us before you actually go through with this."

"Tori, I understand, but I have prayed about this and I've decided to leave it in God's hands. Just like I prayed for your neck to be healed. Or like I pray every day for God to help me battle this lupus. I'm not trying to hurt you guys—I just can't abort it. I don't know how I would live with myself. I'm just as scared as you guys look right now."

"Scared." I looked at Tori, and then Jordan. "Mama, you just told us that you could die doing this. Of course, we're all scared."

"Talisa, it's just a possibility."

"Just a possibility. Just a possibility. Mama, a possibility is a maybe. A possibility is a nine out of ten. A possibility is a strong possible chance of something happening."

Tori grabbed my hand. "Talisa, we can't make her. We just have to wait and see."

I started to perspire. "Do you hear yourselves? Possibility. Wait and see. For what? For her to die, Tori? Dead. Gone. Do you hear what she's saying? This isn't fair."

"We just hope everything goes well. If this is what Mama wants, Talisa, let's just leave it at that." Tori placed her hand on my shoulder.

I turned to face Tori. "She dies, and then what? Nobody is answering that question. Who's going to take care of me and Jordan? Tori, you never stay. You're always running off somewhere." I pulled away and stormed up to my room to put on my headphones. I buried my face in my pillow and I cried myself to sleep.

*   *   *

~February 23, 1992~

Dear Diary,

I apologized to Mama for my behavior and she said she understood. The possibility of her dying is overwhelming to absorb. It's all I can focus on right now. I just don't want her to die. Not now. Not ever.

CHAPTER 12

~March 17, 1992~

Dear Diary,

With track season about to start, I have no time to go to drill team practice during the week. After speaking with my captain and the team's president, they understood. So, I'll just go on the weekends. I'm so excited. In two months, I'll graduate from eighth grade, then I'll be on my way to high school. I can't wait. I've met a lot of people from our rival junior high school during basketball season. The majority of them seem pretty sociable.

I THIRSTED FOR INFORMATION in order to grasp a better understanding of what was about to happen with Mama and the baby. Since the dialysis treatment had such an effect on her body, I was curious as to how this would affect the baby.

"Will you still have the dialysis treatments? Is the baby going to be okay? Will the dialysis harm the baby?"

"Girl, when you grow up, you're going to have to get into some profession that'll allow you to express and inquire without restraint."

"I don't know what I want to be, but since you told us you're pregnant, all I can think about is you possibly dying. Mama, I have to admit, I was upset. My feelings were crushed because I thought you weren't thinking about us."

"Of course, I was thinking about you all. My rheumatologist has given me a list of precautions and recommendations to increase the possibility of me carrying to full term. In the meantime, I'm taking prenatal vitamins, eating nutritious food, and relaxing as much as I can."

"Umm, prenatal vitamins are what?" My eyes were wide open.

"Vitamins specifically for pregnant women to help the development of the baby's eyes, brain, healthy bones, the baby's limbs, hand, arms, toes, and fingers." Her light glow beamed.

"Are you scared?"

She sat up on the bed. "Get that pillow in the corner and put it behind my back." She leaned forward just a little and continued, "I was scared at first, but I don't know what I'd do without each one of you. Even your sister—although she can be difficult at times. I love you all. So, I have to believe that God's plan is bigger than any plan of mine."

"But, will the baby have lupus just like you?"

"Lupus is a very complicated disease. So, we'll just keep praying, okay?"

"Yes, ma'am."

* * *

~April 18, 1992~

Dear Diary,

I'm not sure why or if something has happened, but Mama was sighing and sobbing in her room. Tori has no idea what's wrong with her either, but she said Sam came over and she heard them talking. Then he left, slamming the door behind him. I've never seen Sam upset, so it's hard for me to believe.

Spring had sprung and more people were parading the streets, enjoying the warmth of the sun. I chilled outside on the front steps listening to music on my Discman. Jordan and his friend Eric were playing in the alley, picking up rocks.

"Talisa, look what I found! It's a bullet for a gun," Jordan said as he opened his hand to show me.

"Jordan! Put that down! Where'd you get that from?"

"It was in the alley behind a really big rock by the garbage can."

"Give it to me."

"No, I want to keep it. I found it."

"Jordan, stop playing around and give it to me before I go tell Mama."

"Fine. Here!" He slammed it into the palm of my hand.

There was always some mischief going on at the house on the corner, evident from the shiny rims on the cars, to the gold chains dangling from the necks of the corner boys, to the banging trunk subwoofers shaking house windows as they drove by. Spring also sprung up chaos. Empty Colt .45 beer bottles were scattered from the corner to the alley. Our neighborhood quite often attracted the attention of the police. Sirens constantly whistled through the air day and night.

The rumor was that one of the well-known leaders of the Gangsta Disciples (also known as the gang GDs) resided at the house on the corner. Because of that, Mama told us to stay on this end of the block and to never go in that direction. I'd strolled past numerous times, but no one ever bothered me. The bus stop was right in front of the projects, just a block away. But to put Mama's mind at ease, I always walked four blocks in the opposite direction to meet Leslie to catch the bus. I didn't think our neighborhood was dangerous, but then I overheard other kids talking at school about "the kids from the west end of the city." They made my neighborhood sound like a battlefield. I wasn't scared, though. The projects were the place to be—the place where everyone hung out.

*   *   *

~April 19, 1992~

Dear Diary,

Happy Easter! I could smell the neighbors' food floating through the neighborhood and it made my stomach growl. Our dog, Max, whimpered as he scratched at the side door, attempting to come inside for some of Mama's good cooking. She woke up this morning in a pleasant mood and made bunny pancakes. Jordan was so excited. Mama's stomach is growing. I placed my hand on it to feel the baby move, and it was so amazing. My little brother or sister is in there, playing all alone, and I can't wait to see what it is.

I helped Mama clean the collard greens, and it seemed like it took forever. She was seated at the kitchen table and decorated cupcakes to take over to Grandma and Grandpa's house.

Humming the song "His Eye is on the Sparrow," Mama looked up at me. "How's it going over there?"

"I'm okay. These collard greens stink, but they taste delicious when they're cooked."

She smiled and put a little bunny on each cupcake. "All my nieces and nephews are going to love these. Thank you, God, for raising Jesus from the dead."

"Mama, every year you say that. I mean, like, really? Does Jesus rise from the dead every year? How's that possible? That means that He really isn't dead. Like I said before, He's a mummy, obviously. No one dies and returns just to celebrate one day out of the year. No disrespect, Mama, but it sounds a little crazy."

She held her stomach and laughed hysterically, then waddled over to the kitchen sink to help me clean the rest of the greens.

"Girl, you almost made me pee on myself. No, obviously you weren't paying any attention in church or in Miss Dorothy's summer bible school. Jesus does not rise every year. It was a one-time event that we celebrate, just like a birthday or an anniversary. Each year, on this day, we are to remember God's power and acknowledge the sacrifice that Jesus made for us."

I didn't want to tell her that she was right, that I wasn't paying attention half the time. But, I just didn't understand how God could be everything and create everything. I wasn't buying it. If I couldn't see it with my own eyes, I didn't believe it. But I definitely wasn't telling Mama that.

*   *   *

~April 28, 1992~

Dear Diary,

Daddy called this evening, and we talked for about twenty minutes. I really want to see him. I'm afraid to ask though, because he's told me for years that he's coming or sending us something, and he never does. I love him, but I just don't want to be hopeful then disappointed if he breaks another promise. Mama told me to tell him about my eighth-grade graduation ceremony coming up next month, so I did. He said he wouldn't miss it for anything in the world. I can't wait to see his face. Does he still look the same as I remember?

He said my other older sister's birthday is today. I wish I knew what type of person she is and what she looks like. He keeps reiterating childhood memories when we lived in Milwaukee, and how she used to come over and play with me and Tori. But I don't remember that at all. He gave me her mailing address in case I want to write her a letter, but I wouldn't even know what to say.

~May 4, 1992~

Dear Diary,

Although the doctors have declared her high-risk, Mama's condition seems to have improved tremendously since the pregnancy. I keep my fingers crossed in hopes that my little brother or sister will come into this world perfect, not affected by lupus or from the dialysis.

We were released early from school due to a teacher-staff meeting. On my way out, my school counselor stopped me.

"Hey, Talisa, can I talk to you for a minute?"

Mrs. Sims was a pleasant, beautiful, black lady. Everyone ranted and raved about how smart and intelligent she was. Like Mama and Ms. Rose, Mrs. Sims didn't take no mess, so not too many students misbehaved as her direct reputation had a zero tolerance for foolishness. She stood in the doorway of her office.

"Yes, ma'am," I said as I walked through the door.

"Well, listen to you. Your mother is raising you right. Great manners, although I don't expect anything less coming from such a family." I didn't know what she meant by that.

"My mama says it shows respect, and trust me, if I respond to her with a *huh?* or a *what?* or anything other than *yes, ma'am,* I think my life would be over, Mrs. Sims."

"Well, that's how I was raised, too. I want to talk to you

about your math class. You're doing exceptionally well. I know that you'll be graduating soon and advancing to high school. But I wanted to encourage you to continue with advanced mathematics. I believe this is a strong skill of yours, so don't give up—even if it becomes difficult."

"Yes, ma'am. I won't. I promise."

"Even if it becomes difficult, give yourself the chance. Push through it and find the answers. I believe you'll do just fine as long as you stay focused. That's all I have to say. So, go now before you miss the bus."

"Yes ma'am. See you later, Mrs. Sims."

I dashed out of her office and caught the bus. Mrs. Sims recognized me—the real me. The me underneath this cinnamon skin and kinky hair. Her words made me feel unstoppable, as if I could accomplish anything, and I started to feel like she was right. I could.

*   *   *

~June 2, 1992~

Dear Diary,

I called Daddy today to see if he was still coming. He didn't answer. Maybe he's already on the road heading this way. I reminded Mama that he said he's coming, and she told me to focus on the big day tomorrow . . . nothing else.

Graduation day! The bottled enthusiasm stored inside of me was ready to erupt, and the day had finally arrived. My eighth-grade graduation. Mama bought me a cute black-and-white polka-dotted dress, and that morning she curled my hair. It was straightened, shiny and mushroom shaped. She made me feel pretty. When we arrived at the school, a lot of people were already there: Ms. Rose, Sam, Uncle Mitch, and the drill team president, Mr. Moore. Tori stayed home. I hadn't seen Daddy yet. I sat two rows from the stage. The anticipation of Daddy's appearance played double Dutch with my mind throughout the ceremony, making my thoughts bounce around like a jackrabbit.

Leslie wore a really pretty dress, too. We both received the same awards: the dean's list and honor roll certificates. My final GPA was a 3.7. Leslie and I had attended the same elementary school, the same junior high school, and now, we were on our way to high school together. This was going to be epic. Good memories were to be made and written down in the books.

After the ceremony, Mama had to go to the store, so she told me to ride in the car with Sam. He opened the door for me to get in the front seat since it was my special day. I tried to not think about Daddy. I wondered if perhaps he was just running late and would be waiting for me at the house.

"Hey, young lady. You did exceptionally well. I'm so proud of you. Excellent grades, too. You're active in sports, still a part of the drill team, and helping your mother out. You'll do good in high school. Just stay focused." Sam nodded at me in approval.

I smiled. "Yes, sir, I will."

"Things may get difficult as you get older, but just try to stay as positive as you can. Everything will work out."

Desperation drowned my thoughts; I yearned for the sight of his face as disappointment shook my core like an earthquake. I fought to hang on to his voice, his promise, and convinced myself that this time he'd show up. Sam was encouraging me to do my best, and it was great advice, but all I could think was, "Where is my Daddy? He should be the one telling me these things."

When we pulled up in front of the house, only Mama's car was there. I thought maybe, possibly, he was there in the house. Maybe it was a surprise and he was just hiding. I walked in and Tori gave me a hug. Jordan stood behind her with a bundle of balloons and Mama stood off to the side with a graduation cake. Daddy was not there, not anywhere. It was supposed to be a day of celebration—a day of love, laughter, and created memories. I didn't understand. I was a good girl; I got really good grades, and I was acknowledged for it. I did all right in basketball, but really good in track that year. Why didn't Daddy come? Why didn't he want to see me?

After everyone left, I drug myself up the stairs to my room and torpedoed into the center of my bed.

Jordan came in my room and jumped on my bed.

"What are you doing?"

"Just listening to music. What do you want?"

"Uh, I know it's music. Why are you being mean? Why are you crying?"

"I'm sorry, Jordan. I don't mean to be mean. I'm just mad that Daddy didn't come to my graduation."

"Oh. Well, maybe he had something to do or something happened to him. Let's call him now and see."

"No. I called him yesterday. He didn't call back. I don't feel like talking to him right now."

Jordan lay down next to me, put his head on my shoulder and sang "Don't Worry Be Happy." My brother is the cutest and he has a genuine heart.

"Hey, come play Nintendo with me!" He wiggled his fingers in my face, singing again. "You know you want to."

I agreed. "All right, come on. Let's do it."

I didn't call him and I didn't need an explanation. I cried and looked forward to better days. Like the day Tori was free— free at last. The halo was removed and her neck had healed. She was elated after she and Mama returned from the hospital. Her first request was for me to wash and blow dry her hair. I curled it with the curling iron since it had been impossible to do it with the halo on and straightening it took forever. She had thick, beautiful hair.

Later, on my way to bed, I passed by Mama's bedroom. Her feet were propped up on her wedged pillow to help eliminate all the water retention; her ankles were swollen to the point that her skin had begun to crack. She sat slightly up in the bed; her face was swollen, too.

"Mama, can I get anything for you?"

"No, this baby just keeps moving around and around . . . and around. It's moving so much, it's just really hurting my back." She took a couple of deep breaths.

"Should I call Sam?"

"No, don't call him—not right now. It's normal. Jordan stirred around like this, too. Of course, I was a lot bigger with him. I couldn't even see my feet when I was pregnant with Jordan. So, either this is an active boy like his brother, or a busybody girl like her sister." She playfully nudged me.

"Well, I'll be in my room. Just yell if you need something." As I walked away, I wondered if the baby could hear music. I grabbed my Discman and went back to her room.

"Can babies hear music?"

"I would assume so. They can hear the voices of their mothers. Why?"

"I was wondering . . . maybe if I put my headphones on your stomach, the baby might like it and calm down."

"You can try it. I'll try anything at this point."

I pushed play, stretched the headphones as far as they would go, and placed them around her stomach. It worked! The baby settled down after a couple minutes. This kid was already pretty cool in my book.

Since summer break started and I'm advancing to high school in the fall, Mama permitted the visitation of boys but only for a limited time. Kevin rode his bike to the house and we sat outside and talked about starting high school. Mom stood at the screen door, and after two hours, she told him it was time to go.

"Yes, ma'am," said Kevin. She nodded at him, then turned to go back in the house.

"Mama, can I walk him to the corner?"

"Go ahead. Hurry up. The streetlights are almost on, and he needs to get home before dark."

Kevin picked up his bike and as we walked to the corner, he stared at me. I blushed as he softly brushed his hand against my cheek. Then, there was an awkward silence. He grabbed my hand and slightly tugged my arm to pull me closer. We were nose to nose, and his breath softly rested on my top lip. I couldn't believe it was about to happen.

Then, he kissed me. He said he loved me. I said it back. I didn't know if I did it right or not, but he kissed me again before he straddled his bike and pedaled away.

Is this what love feels like? I wondered. I felt like I was about to explode from the inside out. Kevin melted my heart.

* * *

~June 13, 1992~

Dear Diary,

It's Tori's nineteenth birthday today. Mama baked her a cake, then after we ate, Tori announced that she was leaving. Going to get a job. To find her own place. Of course, I don't want her to leave, but she wants her freedom and to live her own life. Every inch of me wants to beg her to stay, but deep down, I know she won't. I'll miss her. No more Uno games for us. No more Nintendo battles between her and Jordan.

"Are you going to come back?" I asked as she stuffed her clothes into large, black garbage bags.

"Of course, I'll be back. I'll be around. I'm just not going to stay here."

"But could you stay here? I really don't want you to go."

"Stop whining." From across the room, she threw a pillow at my head. She flung the bag over her shoulder and proceeded to walk out the door. I followed, and she stopped standing in the grass and turned around. "Stay in school. Stay in drill team or sports. Something positive. No boys, no sex, no wild parties, and no hanging out in the streets. You hear me?"

"Yeah, I hear you. Loud and clear."

At that moment, I felt like she wasn't coming back, and if she did, it wouldn't be for a long time.

Just three days later, Mama, Sam, Jordan and I traveled an hour and a half to Peoria, Illinois for Mama's doctor's appointment. The sun's rays beamed through the back window, warming my face as I closed my eyes. I brought Uno cards in case it ended up being a long visit. We waited forty-five minutes; Jordan fell asleep in the chair and I stared at the hands on the clock as they rotated. Then, Sam entered the waiting room and shook Jordan's leg to wake him up.

"Wake up. Sit up for a second." He straightened out Jordan's t-shirt.

"Where's Mama?" Jordan rubbed his eyes.

Sam's face was blank. I wordlessly sat still. Part of me was growing petrified, and my mind was running a million miles a minute—was it bad news? What was going on? Was Mama or the baby—or both—in jeopardy?

"Your mom has to stay here in the hospital. During the check-up, she went into labor."

"It's too early for the baby to come. Mama said it takes nine months. She's only six. Sam, what's wrong with the baby? Is it the lupus?"

"We get to have the baby soon!" Jordan sang, unaware of the potential danger.

"Hold on, hold on. Not quite yet, Jordan," Sam said. "Your mom has to stay in the hospital until the baby is born. They're going to monitor her and the baby until it's time for her to deliver."

"I don't understand why she has to stay here. What else is going on? She was perfectly fine in the car all the way here." I felt like Sam wasn't telling me the truth as he looked away.

"You might be correct, Talisa. It might be the lupus, but they can't say for sure."

"Well, can we see her before we go?" Jordan stood up.

"Yeah, let's go." Sam stood up and put his arm around Jordan as they walked down the hallway. For the next three months, Mama and the baby would be in the hospital. My mind was spun. Lupus complicated everything, literally everything.

Not even a peep the entire ride home, and Jordan slept in the back seat. I had a laundry list of questions, but Sam focused on the road, not once initiating a conversation. We got home late. Sam roamed through the house and checked the windows and the side door. He avoided direct eye contact with me; had he noticed my fear, perhaps he would had stayed. I locked the door and wedged the chair up against the doorknob after he left.

"Talisa, is someone coming to get us?"

"I don't think so. It doesn't look like it."

"But, we can't stay here by ourselves, right?"

"We've done it before—just not for this long."

"Are you scared?"

Three months was a long time. "No, I'm not," I lied. Of course, I was scared. Scared as shit. But I didn't want him to worry for even one second.

Jordan went upstairs and fell asleep in a matter of minutes. After I turned off his bedroom light, I went downstairs to make some Kool-Aid and looked in the fridge. We had plenty of food, but not enough to last three months. I had taken home economics in school, so following the directions in Mama's cookbooks wouldn't be too difficult. I kneeled in the middle of the living room floor with all the lights on, squeezing a throw pillow in my arms. I hadn't noticed the tears running down my face until two drops landed on my forearm. Loneliness circled around me like a tornado, and I had no shelter to run to. No Mama, no Tori, no Daddy, and no Sam. Just Jordan and I.

* * *

~June 20, 1992~

Dear Diary,

Why is everything constantly changing? Why is everyone leaving? Jordan and I walked to Grandpa and Grandma's house today because we ran out of milk. Grandpa had packed up his car; he cussed and fussed each time he walked back into the living room. I don't know why, or what happened, but it looked like he was leaving.

PART V

Hurricane Season

CHAPTER 13

Ms. Rose and Leslie and I roamed through the high school after registering for classes. The hallways were practically empty. I'd imagined the hallways full of students, laughter echoing to the high ceilings, side conversations in between student lockers, and the energy of newness spreading from classroom to classroom. Once again, Mom's absence saddens me because I'd always imagined she'd be present for the day I entered high school. It's not her fault—it's the challenges she endures because of her battle with lupus.

As I impatiently waited for the day to arrive, my imagination drifted into foreseeable encounters of what I thought high school would be like. We continued to stroll the halls, and shockingly, there was a daycare in the high school. Leslie and I locked eyes in shock.

Ms. Rose halted in the middle of the hallway and turned with a snappy about-face. She tossed her purse over her shoulder and pointed her finger at us. Her intense facial expression stopped us in our tracks.

"Okay, listen up. Do you two see this?" She pointed at the daycare center's door.

In unison, we answered, "Yes."

"You're here to learn, to get an education." She walked closer to us, her lips tightened. "You two listen real good. You are children until you're grown and married with jobs and benefits. And until you can provide a roof over your own heads, keep your legs closed. Do you hear me? Let me find out that one or both of you are out here being nasty or come up pregnant by one of these nappy-headed boys. You'll never hear the end of it. I'm gonna say it again . . . to make it plainly clear." She moved in even closer to our faces. "Keep . . . your . . . legs . . . closed. Got it?"

Again, in unison. "Yes."

Well, we were finally ready to journey into a new experience, a new level of education, and a slew of new people. Soon-to-be students at Rock Island High School. I couldn't wait.

During the summer, the walls started to close in on me, and it felt like I was in a dungeon with no windows. No way to escape. Mom and Tori left about the same time, and for some reason, this specific time, it hurt more than usual. Jordan and I spent the summer doing whatever we chose to do. Although we were alone, we had each other. But nothing filled the void of the detachment caused by the absence of our parents. Sam visited from time to time, and he often took Jordan fishing. Jordan was excited to shadow Sam, but he always reverted back to the countless times he had craved for the experience with Daddy. I encouraged him to enjoy the moments; that's all we had. Hope converted into hopelessness, but our deepest desires to have Mom and Dad continued to cradle our hearts.

I learned to confide in my journal more than ever; it was the one place my voice could scream to the mountaintops. And no one would ever know. Although I had Leslie and other friends to talk to on the phone, deep down, I buried the emptiness behind my smile. After a while, even the atmosphere at Grandma's house was uncomforting—especially after Grandpa moved out. I had to drop Jordan off there while I attended drill team practices and performances even though he'd pleaded to stay home alone.

At home we were unchained, unrestricted, uncensored. Since I was the eldest with Tori gone, it became my domain by default. We still maintained our weekly cleaning routines. My biggest challenge was washing our clothes. Since there wasn't a washer or dryer in the house, I had to hand wash all of our clothes in the bathtub. So, to avoid potential pileups, we washed every couple of days in the sink and spread them out on the back porch to dry. Even though Jordan was there, loneliness cloaked me like a leech thirsting for blood.

The first day of high school! After walking Jordan to school, I walked to Leslie's house and Ms. Rose handed us bus fare. There were a lot of kids on the bus. The city bus's route only traveled to certain locations, and the high school sat on the top of a hill—a steep hill we had to hike in order to get to the school. The endless line for class schedules was bananas, but it was quickly condensed after the students were instructed to form lines alphabetically. I truly needed assurance that there wasn't a mix-up or change with my math class. Leslie and I linked up in the stairwell and compared our schedules, immediately disappointed that we had no classes together. However, our lockers were on the same floor, around the corner from each other.

Kevin and I spoke at lunch. He had facial hair and I liked it. We still talked on the phone. I hadn't see much of him that summer because he participated in nearly every basketball camp possible. I still blushed thinking of our first kiss. We didn't even talk about sex. He'd never pushed the issue, and I didn't want to either. Although he made my heart pitter-patter, the thought of sex scared me.

*   *   *

~September 10, 1992~

Dear Diary,

All my teachers are pretty cool. I have a couple of girls in my classes from the rival junior high school from last year. I only know them from basketball and track, but most of them seem pretty pleasant. The gym teacher told us that swimming is a physical education requirement for all freshman students. I don't know how to swim, and the thought is terrifying. And I'm damned sure it's not good for my hair! Do you know what water does to a black girl's hair? Then, to add chlorine to it, too? It's like kryptonite. I'm going to look like a runaway slave praying for a pressing comb.

Sam frantically rushed in my room one morning and once again my heartbeat echoed through my eardrums. His face was flushed as he wheezed for air.

"Sam, what is it?"

"I have to go to the hospital. They're going to induce your mom. The baby's going to be born really soon." He stated.

"Yay!" I hopped out of my bed, fueled with excitement, and anxious to see its face.

"Make sure you guys get to school on time. Lock the door. Here's twenty dollars. Make sure you get something to eat after school." He froze, took a deep breath, then smiled at me as he turned to leave.

"Wait, Sam. You said they're going to induce her. What does that mean?"

"Meaning they're going to speed up the labor process to make the baby come."

"But, why?" I was muddled. Shouldn't the baby just come on its own?

He chuckled. "I can't explain fully right now. I promise I'll call you later."

"Stop laughing. I know, too many questions, right?" I sighed.

"No, questions are your way of learning, Talisa. I'm just in a hurry. I promise I'll call you."

* * *

~*September 17, 1992*~

Dear Diary,

Well, happy fifteenth birthday to me! Oh! This would be the ultimate birthday gift if the baby was born today.

The next morning, Sam called. Mom had a boy, and I had another baby brother! Sedrick Malcolm Lewis Brooks, born at

9:32 a.m., seven pounds, fifteen ounces, and seventeen inches long. We were overjoyed.

"Yes! I have a little brother!" Jordan shouted.

We basked in the moment as we grew eager to see Sedrick. Dad called and wished me a happy birthday. I didn't even correct him. My birthday was the day before, but whatever.

We rode with Sam to the Peoria hospital to pick up Mom and Sedrick, but Sedrick had to stay in the hospital. Grandma and Aunt Denise came along, trailing behind us. When we got to Mom's hospital room, the baby wasn't there. She packed her clothes and baby gifts from the hospital staff in her suitcase. Excited to see us, she swiftly rose from the chair with open arms, and she was stunned by Jordan's appearance.

"Oh, my goodness, Jordan. You got taller. Look at you. Talisa; you didn't tell me he was that tall." She wrapped her arms around us. Group hug.

"Yeah, he grew a lot over the summer. And he eats a lot. Like *a lot*, Mom."

She shook her head. "Oh, Lord, does this mean I have to cook a lot more just for you?"

"No, ma'am." He boyishly smiled.

"Hmm, Talisa, you called me Mom? When did I get upgraded from Mama to Mom?"

I blushed. "I'm in high school now. The term 'Mama' is for little kids."

She chuckled. "OK, big girl."

I yearned to see Sedrick. "Mom, it's not that we aren't happy to see you, but where's Sedrick? Can we see him?"

"Of course. Let's go visit him."

She guided us down the hallway to the neonatal intensive care unit; a room full of tiny babies who were cradled in plastic cribs, sealed with protection. The nurse stopped us and gave us full instructions before entering: we had to wash our hands, cover ourselves with cloth robes, and put on rubber gloves. I scanned the unit through the window but didn't see him. The unit held six tiny babies, but they were all white babies.

We followed the nurse through the unit, passing four of the white babies, then she extended her arm and pointed at the baby swaddled in the light blue blanket. "Here he is. Let me know if you all need anything."

Mom leaned over and whispered, "Hi, Sedrick. This is your sister, brother, auntie, and grandmother." Her hand slid through the side of the incubator and touched his little hand. Mom slightly uncovered him. There were multiple plastic tubes, beeping machines, and little round patches stuck on his little chest.

"Mom, he's white. Is that my brother?" Jordan looked so puzzled.

"Yes, this is your brother. He's just really light-skinned, but he is black. Just like all of us." Mom stared at Sedrick, mesmerized.

I stepped to the other side of the incubator and unlocked the little circular side window. I wanted to hold him. I touched his little leg and rubbed his little feet when I noticed a red mark on his stomach.

"What's that?"

"That would be his little birthmark," Grandma said. "Some babies have them and some don't. It looks like Sedrick has a real special one. It looks like a little strawberry."

It was not easy to leave him, lying in a tiny plastic box, but when I shook his hand, he grinned and opened his eyes. He was precious with blonde, light brown hair and almond brown eyes. An overwhelming sense of attachment fluttered my heart. The doctors were wrong. Although they advocated for a pregnancy termination, Sedrick was alive and so was Mom. Because he was born prematurely, that unit would become his home for a couple of weeks until he gained more weight and the doctors cleared him for release.

Mom and Sam spoke about Sedrick all the way home. Mom being home was a relief, and the more settled she became, the more the emptiness subsided. It was a sleepless night, and I tossed and turned thinking of little Sedrick in the hospital and all of those tubes and machines attached to his little body. I got up to get something to drink and Mom was sitting at the kitchen table, sipping tea.

"Hey, Mom."

"Hey."

"Umm. . . ."

"What is it?" She set the mug down.

"Does Sedrick have lupus, too?" I braced myself.

"No, he doesn't."

"Well, why are all of those tubes and machines attached to him? Is he sick?"

She pointed for me to take a seat. "Sit down. Most premature babies are born underweight, and sometimes their organs aren't fully developed before birth, so they need special care." She sighed.

"I'm sorry, Mom. I didn't mean to ask so many questions."

"No, it's fine. One day, when you become a mother, and not any time soon though . . . ," she eyed me sternly, "but when you're older, the day will come when you'll understand the unconditional love for your child or children. The level of worry for their well-being . . . it's nonstop."

"Sam said the doctor induced you. I thought you said the baby would come on its own. Honestly, I thought he was withholding some information," I said. "Why would they do that so suddenly?"

We firmly stared at each other in silence.

She picked up her mug and sipped the tea. "You're right; he didn't give you the full story. Maybe he didn't know how to tell you."

"So, what happened?"

"They induced me because my heart and my kidneys were in distress. But they were more concerned with my heart than anything."

"Why? What's wrong with your heart?"

"I started having trouble breathing. It felt like my heart was going to jump out of my chest. It's hard to explain. The blood flowing through my heart is traveling in the wrong direction, and the valve that's supposed to keep blood from flowing backward isn't functioning right."

I was alarmed, shaken by what I could comprehend, and shifted into panic by the reality.

"So, you're saying your heart isn't working the way it should? So, what happens now?"

"Nothing. I'll continue with the dialysis treatments and go to my cardiologist's appointments in a month where they'll check my heart's status. Probably do some more testing. Who knows? Don't worry, I'll be fine."

Was she kidding me? What in the world? She clearly stated that her heart was in jeopardy. I wasn't a doctor, nor did I understand the majority of the medical terminology, but I did know from science class that the brain and heart are major components of the body—like the engine of a car. She was just sitting there acting like nothing was wrong, while I sat on the edge of my seat. She continued to sip tea. How could she just be so calm? Why wasn't she scared?

"Aren't you scared?"

She smirked. "God didn't give me the spirit of fear. I just had a beautiful baby boy. God did that. Sedrick and my heart will be just fine. He'll fix it."

"Mom, this all sounds so complicated."

"You should go to bed. It's been a long day."

"Okay. Good night, Mom."

Mom set the mug down on the table, placed her hands over

her eyes and began to pray. She was scared. I saw it in her eyes. I couldn't sleep thinking about what she'd just told me. If God was real and He could fix everything, then why wouldn't He fix her?

I wanted to give her some days to rest before bombarding her with more questions. But, this one I had to address quickly. I walked into Mom's bedroom and stood at the foot of the bed. "Mom, are you busy?"

She glanced at me over the top of the newspaper, then set it on her lap. My body temperature rose as I began to grind my teeth and searched for the right words.

"What is it?" She didn't look like she was in a good mood, but I felt like I didn't have a choice at that point. Basketball season was approaching soon, and open gym had started.

"Can I play basketball this year?" I clutched my hands together.

"When does it start?"

"Open gym started already. I believe tryouts will be at the end of the month, and the season will begin next month." I waited patiently for a response.

"That's fine. You can play, but I'm not going to be running you all around town. So, you better figure it out."

"Yes, ma'am, but if I make the team, the practices for the freshman team are pretty late."

"Figure it out." She grabbed the newspaper, unfolded it, and continued to read.

Why did I always have to figure things out for myself? I'd either walk or catch the bus to and from practice; it shouldn't be too hard. I'd just have to catch the bus right after school, get home, do my homework, eat, do my chores, and walk back or catch the late bus.

* * *

~October 17, 1992~

Dear Diary,

Mom's been pretty moody lately; some nights I sit on the edge of her bed just to talk to her, hoping our conversation will be a distraction to her own thoughts or whatever is making her sob at night. Then, other nights, she desires to be alone. I try to tell Grandma about Mom's actions, but she always says Mom will be fine.

Jordan was silent when I walked him to school—no silly joke telling or laughs.

"What's wrong with you, little brother?" I put my arm around him.

He walked with his head down and shrugged. "I don't know."

"You don't know, or you don't want to tell me?"

"I feel sad."

"Why?"

"Mama always seems to be sad. It makes me sad, too, because she's sad. It's like she doesn't want to be bothered with us."

"Oh, Jordan, I don't think it's us. I think it's something internally bothering her, something she can't fully express. But,

I know what you mean—Dr. Jekyll and Mr. Hyde. Just pray for things to get better."

I wanted to tell him about her heart, but I didn't want to scare him or have him tote blocks of worry at school.

* * *

~October 28, 1992~

Dear Diary,

Today is Mom's birthday. She was very quiet when I got home from school. I thought playing basketball would be easy, but the high school coaches are a lot harder and tougher than my junior high coaches. Today were actual tryouts. Tomorrow we'll see who made the team. Leslie didn't tryout. She said she wasn't going to participate in any sports.

~October 29, 1992~

Dear Diary,

Yes! I made the freshman girls' basketball team! I can't wait for the season to start. I received 94% on my first algebra test. After acing a couple of pop quizzes at the beginning of the semester, I confidently believe I'm going to reach my goal this semester—to maintain an A+ average in math.

Sedrick will be coming home today. Sam and Mom left this morning to go get him.

~November 1, 1992~

Dear Diary,

Since Grandpa left, I now have the responsibility of watching my great-grandmother, Mary, on the Sundays that Grandma attends church services or programs. I didn't want to do it at first, but Mom told me to. My great-grandma has to be at least eighty-plus years old, and she has the same sun-shining complexion as Mom. Depending on the time of day, I usually deliver her breakfast, lunch, or dinner along with juice and a can of Old Milwaukee beer. She has so many life stories, and they are the best. Funny and eye-opening. Over the last couple of months, I've actually been looking forward to spending quality time with her.

Between juggling school and playing sports, I had no reserved energy to even do homework. My initial plan was draining me. I walked to and from basketball practice in the rain, and as soon as I walked through the door, Mom was fitfully storming around.

"Where've you been? It's almost ten o'clock! It's a school night." My shoes and socks were soaked, and the books in my backpack felt like a bag of rocks as I attempted to maintain my balance. I glanced across the room, and Sam sat on the couch eating Chinese food while Sedrick lay flat on his little stomach.

"Practice starts at seven in the evening, and it lasts for two hours. I had to walk home afterwards while all the other girls' parents came to pick them up. I do my homework and my grades are good. I do my chores, help Jordan, and help you when you're unhappy or exhausted. So, I'm not going to apologize for having to do a billion things." Had I just gone too far? Probably, but I was too tired to care.

"Who in the hell do you think you're talking to?"

Before I could speak, Sam interrupted. "Come on, now. Give her a break. At least let the girl get out of her wet clothes."

She took a step back. "Take your narrow behind upstairs and go to bed."

I was uncertain whether my comments were disrespectful or not. I don't know what came over me. However, they made Mom defensive. If I didn't walk or catch the bus, how was I supposed to play?

* * *

~*November 21, 1992*~

Dear Diary,

I talked to Leslie. We haven't been talking a lot lately—not sure why. Because of basketball practices and the season starting, I won't be able to do both. So, I've chosen to stop going to drill team practices, but the president still insists I return after the season. The drill team is a huge part of my life and it's my oasis from home.

Stillness trailed through the house and Mom slept most of the day. Jordan and Sedrick lay in my bed until it was time to get dressed to go over to Grandma's house. Sedrick barely cried and he smiled a lot; he was a good baby. After changing his diaper and wiping him clean, I attempted to put on his clothes. Then, Mom walked in my room, picked him up, grabbed his clothes, and took him with her down the stairs. Since the beginning of the month, Mom and I had not been on speaking terms. I tried to apologize many times for being disrespectful, but her reply was always a simple head nod.

Grandma's house was crowded with family members. The aroma of Thanksgiving dinner made my stomach growl. There was enough food on the table, kitchen counters, and side tables to feed a small village. Heck, we *were* a small village. Everyone passed Sedrick around like a loaf of bread, appallingly surprised by his light complexion, but exuded love throughout the evening. The holidays had changed—or at least the dynamic had. Over the last couple of years, I'd learned that change would occur whether I liked it or not. Tori showed up, and she sat by me rocking Sedrick in her arms.

"Hey, Sis, how are you? Why are you looking like that?" Tori asked.

"I'm fine. Looking like what?"

"Like you're mad or something."

"I'm not mad; where've you been?" I asked. "You come, then you leave, and then you appear again. Then guess what happens. You disappear again. You said you'd come back in a month. It's been almost six months."

"Well, damn, Talisa. You're starting to sound like Mom. Back off. I'm here now."

"You have no idea what's going on."

"What do you mean?

"Something's wrong with Mom—something with her heart, I think."

She rolled her eyes, "Ain't nothing wrong with her. Look at her. She's fine. She just had a baby. Maybe she's just tired. Stop overthinking"

"I'm not overthinking. I talked to her right after Sedrick was born, and she said something was going on with her heart. But she played it off like everything would be fine."

"Well, until something happens, stop worrying about it."

"Yeah, easy for you to say. You don't live in the house with her anymore. One minute she's fine, the next she's crying her eyes out, yelling at us."

"She'll be fine. Stop worrying so much." She giggled.

"It's not funny, Tori. Why don't you come around more? You'll see what I'm talking about. Maybe you can help her or talk to her."

I was hoping Tori would agree, but I should've known she wouldn't.

"She'll be fine. I have other things to do." She handed Sedrick to me. "I'm going to make me a plate before I go."

"See what I mean? You never stick around." I rolled my eyes at her, and as soon as we stood up, Jordan came running around the corner yelling, "Tori! Talisa! Mama passed out! She's lying on the floor!"

I handed Sedrick to my cousin Sharae and hurried to the kitchen. Everyone surrounded her, fanning her with paper plates, shaking her hands and arms and trying to wake her up, but she was nearly unresponsive. Was this her heart malfunctioning? Aunt Joi dialed 9-1-1. The room became chaotic as people shouted and everyone attempted to assist in every way possible. Within a matter of minutes, the sirens blared through the back door, and reality once again punched me in the face. Only this time, I knew exactly what was wrong, and there was absolutely nothing I could do about it.

Sam ran past me, almost knocking me down to assist the paramedics in lifting her. The flashing lights of the ambulance continuously shined brighter and brighter as they reflected off the glass screen door. Still, I was perplexed until Jordan yanked my arm.

"Come on. Let's go. Let's go outside. We have to get in the ambulance."

Sam yelled, "You guys stay here. I'll come back to get you."

We stood still and watched the ambulance speed down the alley until the red lights faded into the distance. We sat in Grandma's living room for two hours. Sam called and told us the hospital was going to admit her again.

Tori took us home, then left. She said she was going to check on Mom. Sam didn't call or come by. I freaked out. Mom said her heart was in trouble, and I instantly thought this was a delayed complication from the pregnancy. This was real. Although she'd get in her moods and I'd lose my patience with her at times, I couldn't lose her; not then, not ever. I examined Sedrick's little face as he squirmed around in the middle of my bed and fear crept in. I had never been left alone with him. He was barely two months old.

Sleepless nights began to drain the life right out of me.

At school I was a walking, half-functioning zombie. Sedrick made noises all night long, but not whining. I was scared to fall asleep next to him, so as long as he was awake, so was I. I cleaned several of his bottles for the day's feedings. Mom had taught me how to mix the baby formula. Bathing Sedrick was nerve-racking because he was so tiny. He was too small for the baby tub, so I filled a mixing bowl with water, laid him on top of a towel on top of a pillow, and washed him. In the mornings, before school I walk to drop him off at Grandma's.

I had basketball practice that afternoon, but I couldn't go. No one was there to watch the boys. Immediately after bathing him, Sedrick fell asleep. I laid him next to Jordan on the couch while I cleaned up the kitchen and made Jordan some pancakes. Finally, Sam called and said he was coming over. My nerves were rattled as I tried not to think of the worst-case scenario. Was Mom dead? I would have literally lost my mind. Sam sat at the dining table and he didn't speak at first. He took a deep breath and leaned back in the chair.

"Sam, something's really wrong with Mom, isn't it?"

"I'm going to be straightforward with you. There is something severely wrong. I'm not sure where to even begin."

"Just tell me."

"Okay. She became nonresponsive just before we arrived at the hospital. The medics started compressions."

"Compressions?"

"Yes, chest compressions. That's when someone presses on your chest to try to get your heart to beat."

"So, her heart stopped beating is what you're saying?" My voice cracked.

"Yes, but it's back to beating on its own."

I exhaled. "So, then, she's all right now?"

"No, she's having shortness of breath, and needs assistance with breathing. She's on a ventilator every couple of hours."

"This is the lupus, isn't it? Why does this keep happening to her?"

He shook his head and mumbled, "I really wish I had an answer for you, but I don't. Even the hospitals don't know where this comes from or why these things continue to happen."

"So, you have no idea when she's coming home?"

"No, I don't. The hospital will run some tests to see what's going on. But, I can't tell you exactly when until the test results come back."

"Did Tori go to the hospital?"

"No, I didn't see her."

Sam left to get some clothes from his place. He was going to stay with us until he had to go to work.

CHAPTER 14

~December 9, 1992~

Dear Diary,

I quit the basketball team. Gosh, it hurt. I cried for about an hour. Having to take care of Sedrick is a whole new ball game. It's hard as hell. Sam stayed a couple of days, then he went home for the weekend and took Sedrick with him. I'm usually up an hour earlier now, depending on if Sam is here or not, just to prepare for the day. Getting Sedrick's bottles ready, packing his diaper bag, getting Jordan up and ready for school, double-checking our backpacks to ensure our homework assignments are turned in on time. It's hectic, but at least Jordan is self-sufficient now.

JORDAN WAS BUNDLED up from head to toe. I wrapped Sedrick with five blankets, grabbed my backpack and the diaper bag, and then speed-walked Jordan to school. Next, I took Sedrick to Grandma's and then ran a couple of blocks to catch the city bus to get to school on time. The heaviness tugged away at my eyelids as I struggled all day to stay awake. I believe I blacked out in a couple of classes, because I couldn't even recall the lessons taught. I absolutely had no focus. Although Mom had been gone for nearly two weeks, it seemed like an eternity.

* * *

~December 11, 1992~

Dear Diary,

This evening, I bathed Sedrick. It was so funny. Every time water ran over his stomach, he giggled as if it tickled him. Later, I helped Jordan with his spelling words. He does really well in English, but he still struggles with math.

Mom was home, and the battle continued.

She wobbled from one room to the next, periodically stopping to recharge before proceeding to take another step. Between the fatigue, dizziness, and lack of strength, she was restricted from lifting anything heavy—including Sedrick. While I washed the dishes, Sedrick's screeching cry reverberated from the living room. Mom was sitting at the kitchen table, then she sluggishly stood up and used the side of the table to regain her balance. She took four steps, then gripped the back of the chair, placed her hand on her chest, and took deep breaths as she attempted to take another step.

I stopped wiping the countertop. Three more steps before her body became limp and she slid against the wall down to the kitchen floor. Howling, she shoved the garage can over and screamed in anguish.

Jordan zipped down the stairs. "What's wrong?"

"It's okay. It'll be okay. Come on, Mom."

I picked her up, firmly held both of her hands as we walked to the couch. Sedrick was crying at the top of his lungs—he was just hungry, and I was sure Mom's scream startled him. She leaned back on the inclining pillows stacked behind her back and I placed one behind her head to ease her breathing. Next, I covered her with a blanket.

"Go to sleep, Mom. Sedrick can sleep with me. He'll be fine." She looked at me with such brokenness, then turned her head away to hide her face.

* * *

~December 19, 1992~

Dear Diary,

Tomorrow is the last day of school before winter break, and I had final exams this week. I'm nervous about getting the results. It's not that I can't do the work; I just haven't had the time to study or review my class notes. So, I'm almost positively sure I failed. I don't want to leave Mom here by herself tomorrow, but I don't have any choice. I'll just have to take Sedrick to Grandma's house in the morning.

~December 25, 1992~

Dear Diary,

Merry Christmas! Mom still isn't in the best condition. Short of breath, very isolated, hiding out in her room, lying in bed all day. Every time I blink, Sedrick gets bigger. Mom plays with him a lot, kisses him all over, but she still can't hold him for a long period of time or pick him up without help. Dad called today. It was good to hear his voice. I haven't talked to him in a while. It's crazy, I haven't seen him in six years, but I try to not think about it.

~January 1, 1993~

Dear Diary,

Happy New Year, my ass. When will this stop?

Sam took Mom back to the hospital because she was straining to breathe, complaining about a sharp pain in her chest. As the snow fell, Sam helped her to the car. How awful she must feel when her own body seems to be her own worst enemy!

Sam came back to pick us up this morning and we went to visit Mom.

I stood next to Mom's hospital bed and struggled to accept the fact she was going to be transferred back to the University of Iowa Medical Center in a couple days.

"Why do you have to go back?" Jordan sat on the side of the bed.

Mom touched his hand and removed her oxygen mask. "Umm, how do I put this? The blood flowing through my heart is going in the wrong direction, so they have to go in and fix it. I need a mitral valve replacement to keep the blood flowing properly." She winked at me with a slight smile of reassurance.

"Well, can we go with you to Iowa City?" I figured it could be a possibility since we were out of school for winter break.

"Maybe you guys can come after the surgery is over." She patted Jordan's hand.

The few days without Mom left us feeling empty. The snow had barricaded us in and we became prisoners in our own home for five days. After I checked the mailbox, my mouth watered and perspiration sprinkled across my t-shirt like spots of a Dalmatian dog. There it was, the envelope with my first-semester grades of high school. I shouldn't have opened it, but my curiosity consumed me as I tore the sides of the letter separating the glued tabs. I scanned the row of letters, my mouth dropped, and a fist full of disappointment pierced my pride. I had five C's and two D's, which just wasn't me. What could I do? I was trying, I really was. It wasn't that the work was too complex or problematic; I was just tired all the time. Too tired to comprehend my class notes, formulas, and summary notes from the daily lessons. If Sedrick fell asleep early, I could complete the majority of my assignments, but if he didn't, game over.

Sam came around occasionally, but not daily. No clue why not. He just didn't. He worked for the federal government; perhaps he was overloaded with work, or maybe he was out of town. I knew we were at risk being home by ourselves, but I couldn't call the police. We'd more than likely end up being separated, and there was no way I was living without my brothers. I loved them so much! So, I tried to hold on and not complain. But I was growing weary by the minute.

*   *   *

~January 12, 1993~

Dear Diary,

Sam called this morning. Mom's surgery is scheduled for tomorrow morning. They think it'll take a couple hours. He's going to take off of work tomorrow, and we're going to visit her tomorrow afternoon. Lupus is a train wreck—a pileup of multiple cars with no rescue team in sight. How can anyone get help when their own body turns against them? When Mom seems unbearable at times, I wonder if she's just tormented by her own thoughts. I often feel shameful because I get upset with her, or should I say, with the lupus. I hate the disease. It's hard to separate the disease from who Mom is. But at times, I feel like I no longer know who she is.

~January 13, 1993~

Dear Diary,

Sedrick kept rolling around all night, and I couldn't sleep because his little feet kept kicking me in the side every ten minutes. He sleeps with me because I'm too afraid for him to sleep alone. I heard that a lot of babies die in their cribs from suffocation. So I keep him near me, close, so I can keep an eye on him.

It was a slow start as I prepared for our visit with Mom—packing snacks, extra diapers, and two outfits for Sedrick. Sam arrived at 10:00 a.m. on the dot, and we were all bundled and ready to go. It took us about an hour to get there, and Grandma and Aunt Joi followed us to the hospital. By the time we arrived, they were prepping Mom for recovery in the intensive care unit. We waited about an hour. Every second of every minute was irritating, and I was losing my patience. A nurse and a surgeon entered the waiting room. Everyone hushed, then Sam stood up.

The surgeon walked over and extended his arm to greet Sam. "Hello, are you Sam?"

"Yes, I am. These are her children, Talisa, Jordan, and little Sedrick. Her mother, and her sister, Joi. How did everything go today?" Sam asked as he slid his hands into his pants pockets.

"Everything went smoothly as expected. There weren't any complications during surgery. However, the recovery will be extensive as she'll need time to heal. Her heart and body will have to adjust to the mitral valve. We're going to monitor her closely for a while to ensure the lupus does not cause any inflammation or cause any further complications. Any questions for me?" the surgeon stared as he waited for our response.

"When do we get to see her?" I asked as I bounced Sedrick in my arms.

"Let me speak with Sam for a second, then he'll let you know." He guided Sam across the room and spoke in whispers, yet loud enough that we could hear.

He told Sam the visual picture might be too overwhelming

for us and informed him that several machines were attached to Mom. That she couldn't speak and the medication had made her incoherent but stated it would only be a temporary condition. I nearly fainted when he said they had to crack Mom's ribs in order to complete the procedure. She'd received two blood transfusions and they would continue the dialysis treatments. He kept reassuring Sam that Mom would receive around-the-clock observation and care until the critical stage diminished. He leaned toward Sam and concluded, saying, "So, it's your call if you feel they'll be able to handle seeing her at this time."

Sam said he understood and shook the surgeon's hand. He stood still for a moment, then walked back over to us. "Okay, let's go. The nurse will take us to the ICU." He took Sedrick from my arms.

"Are you okay?" I asked Jordan.

"Yeah, I'm okay. I just want to see Mama."

The elevator transported us up three floors, and when we stepped out, the hallway was vacant. The sign above the door read "Intensive Care Unit." A nurse came to greet us. We couldn't physically go in because the risk of possible infection was too high. But we were able to observe through a glass window. Waiting for the nurse to draw the curtain back was torture. The anticipation was driving me insane. When the curtains opened, my heartbeat vibrated through the canals of my eardrums. I saw Mom and almost collapsed as my knees weakened.

"Oh, my God. What's happening? What are all those

machines?" I scanned the room, placing both of my hands on the glass.

She lay stiffly in bed completely covered with multiple blankets from head to toe, and only her eyes were revealed. There were four mid-size tubes hanging from her chest—two full of blood, one attached to a plastic container next to the bed, and one hooked to a machine that looked like it was pumping air. Her mouth was covered as well with a plastic guard that had a tube hanging from the right side.

It was horrible seeing her like that as I stared through the glass window, not being able to touch her or hug her. The more I observed, the more overwhelmed I became, and my armpits puddled sweat to the one hundredth degree. The whole scene was mind blowing, then Grandma touched the glass and Aunt Joi's face was full of astonishment. Sam was muted, impassive, his face frozen as if he had just seen a ghost. I stepped away, quivering all over as my body temperature rose. I became light-headed and nauseated. I threw up in the garbage can next to Sam.

"Just breathe," Sam consoled me as he patted my back.

There was an awful taste in my mouth, so I walked across the hall to the water fountain. Jordan accompanied me. We hugged and comforted each other as we sat on the bench across from the window.

"Let's go to the cafeteria to get something to eat and talk about this." Sam grabbed my hand.

I refused. "I want to stay here. I'm not hungry."

"Me, too. I'm staying with Talisa." Jordan sat next to me.

Aunt Joi cleared her throat and whispered to Sam, "I'll wait down the hall and keep an eye on them. Let's give them a minute alone."

Each time we looked at each other, the waterworks continued. At ten years old, he was now old enough to understand. And we knew each other so well we could sometimes understand each other without even speaking.

"Talisa, don't lie. Is Mama dying? Tell me the truth. Don't lie. Just tell me." He begged me for answers as his face turned to stone.

"I don't know. It looks really bad. It looks like she's in a lot of pain but the surgeon assured Sam that everything went smoothly and according to their plan." I didn't want to believe that she was dying.

"Then why do they have all of those machines connected to her body?"

"I'm not sure what every machine's function is, but I heard the surgeon tell Sam the machines are supposed to help her heart, the blood flow, and to help her breathe." I started to feel hot again. I leaned my head back and counted backward from twenty while staring up at the ceiling.

"She's not coming home soon, is she?" He laid his head on my shoulder.

I wrapped my arm around him. "No. No, she's not. Probably not for a long time."

"What are we going to do?"

"I don't know, but when we get home, I'm going to call Dad. Maybe he'll come get us this time."

* * *

~January 19, 1993~

Dear Diary,

Back to school today. Sedrick has been staying with Sam for the past five days. Even though I sleep better without him, I miss him. My classes this semester are Algebra I, Keyboarding IB, Clothing, Psychology, English I, P.E. and my favorite class, Biology. Ha! Not really.

Jordan and I had a really good morning. We both love music, so we woke ourselves up by blasting music videos we recorded on the VCR. Hip hop is the best! NWA, KRS-One, EPMD, Salt-N-Pepa, Queen Latifah. When the video "Nuthin but a 'G' Thang" came on, Jordan lost his mind. I think he thinks he's Snoop Dogg. Jordan can actually rap! His hand gestures and the way he has to run to grab his hat, acting like he's in the video are hilarious!

I called Dad and told him about Mom's condition and the surgery. He didn't say too much, and I asked him if he could come get us.

"I can't come get you guys. Your mom has a new baby."

"Sam will take care of Sedrick until we come back. Can't you just come get us?"

"As much as I would love to have you guys, I don't think I can. Legally, I mean."

Deep down, I felt like it was a lie. I didn't know why I kept trying, kept hoping for him to just be there.

Not only was home full of periodic chaos at times, at school it started to feel like it was not such a safe zone anymore. Not as exciting. Three students were in a car accident. One of them was pronounced dead at the scene and the other two were badly injured. The hallways were silent, stricken with students' tears and flowing emotions from classroom to classroom. Death was a part of life, but I'd never personally known anyone who had died.

The newspaper article about the accident circulated throughout the cafeteria and left each table mourning. The front page of the newspaper plastered a horrifying picture of the car almost completely bent around a utility pole—the metal crushed. It was heartbreaking. I knew all three boys who were in the car; one of them had been in my woodshop class the previous year. All I kept thinking was how scared they must've been. The family of the boy who passed away must've been devastated. I'd never been to a funeral and seeing someone I knew dead—someone so young—I didn't want to see that.

It was that time of year once again. Valentine's Day was a couple of days away, and Kevin and I still talked a lot on the phone—sometimes past curfew. When Mom was home, she'd caught us a couple times. She'd pick up the other phone downstairs or in her bedroom, in the middle of our conversation.

"Talisa, you know what time it is. Good night, Kevin." She waited until we both hung up. He planted such an infectious smile on my face. I guess he was my first love—my first real crush.

One night we talked for four hours; with Mom not home of course, I broke the rules. It ended up being an extremely long night. One hour of sleep. Sedrick cried and cried and cried some more—nonstop. He was feverish, so I took all his clothes off except his diaper and cracked the window so the winter breeze would cool the room quickly. Nothing seemed to soothe him.

Jordan woke up, took him out of my arms, and rocked him back and forth. "What's wrong with him?" Jordan yawned.

"I don't know. Just keep rocking him. Rub his back. Maybe he's sick. He's really hot; damn it, and I can't call Sam. He won't be back from out of town until today or tomorrow. I'm going downstairs to get a cold washcloth. Mom has to have some baby medicine in the bathroom cabinet or something. Stay here."

"Okay, hurry up. He's turning really red."

I had no idea what to look for. I turned on the cold water to wet a washcloth, and I searched the medicine cabinet. Bingo! A small red box with a lady holding a baby on the front. It read Children's Tylenol. I wasn't sure what was making him so fussy, but I did know he had a fever. I ran back upstairs, skimming through the instructions on the back of the box; the chart was easy to read. Simple.

"Well, what does it say? Hurry, he's really burning up. He's screaming like he's in pain." Jordan was panicked.

"I'm trying, Jordan; just stop yelling. You're not helping the situation right now. I have to make sure I give him the right dose." I thought maybe I should give him less than the recommended amount on the box. What if it made him worse? Mom and Sam would kill me, but his little eyes were so red. His face and body were flushed red, too.

"Come on. Hurry up."

"Just hold him still. The box says babies four to eleven months old should get two-and-a-half milliliters." I filled up the syringe. "Just a couple of seconds. Hold on."

Ever nerve in my hand pulsed and I was so scared to put it in his mouth. I placed my hand on his forehead to stop him from wiggling and squeezed just a couple of drips on his tongue.

"He spit it out. He doesn't like the taste." I started to feel defeated.

"Well, give him some more then."

"Okay, lean back just a little. Not too much or he might choke. Umm, let's just do a little at a time, okay?"

Finally, he licked his little lips. The screams and cries that tortured us decreased to whimpers and short breaths. With his pacifier in his mouth, he lay on my chest; his body was so hot. Jordan went back to bed and Sedrick started to fuss again. So, I rocked him back and forth, bouncing him from one side of the room to the other. I placed the cold washcloth on his forehead, and finally, his little body relaxed as he slowly opened and closed his little eyes. After another hour, he fell sound asleep in my arms.

I didn't want to go to school the next day, but I had two tests to take and I couldn't afford to miss them. Jordan was a bit cranky that morning, and it was slow motion all the way to school. Sedrick was sound asleep, bundled up in his little snowsuit. I dropped him off at Grandma's and told her that I'd given him Tylenol and how he cried all night. She said he was probably just teething and that she had some medicine in her cabinet for him. I ventured off to school.

The weekend had come and Sam took us to visit Mom. Speaking was hard for her, the breathing tube had been removed a couple of days after the surgery, and she stuttered while grasping for air. Unsure what to say, I sat at her bedside and held her hand while I watched the numbers on the machines fluctuate. The gauge hand on the oxygen machine remained constant as she faded in and out of sleep. I couldn't leave her side, but Sam, Jordan, and Sedrick left to get lunch. As she slept, I noticed all of the bandages on her chest. The incision started in between her collar bones to slightly above her stomach. Yet another scar. There were multiple needles in her hands, secured with strips of medical tape, and her veins were enlarged like lines drawn on a map. I kneeled down, placed her hand in between both of mine, bowed my head, and for the first time in my life, I prayed.

"Okay, God. I've never done this, so if I mess this up, I'm saying sorry right now to get it out of the way. However, if you are real, I need you to please listen to me. God, if you can hear me, please heal my Mom. Please help her. I don't always know how you do what you do, or when you will do what you do, but can you do it now? I'm begging you with all my heart to give my Mom many years of life, to allow her to see us grow up and to make her happy again. Use the doctors, God, to help her heal faster.

"Give them the medical information and research needed to better understand lupus. She believes in you. She loves you. And I'm trying to understand who you are so maybe you can show me, too. Mom says that you have the power to do all things and you created the earth. That's pretty major, by the way. Sorry . . . lost focus for a minute. So, please help her body. She's so weak. I don't want her to feel any more pain. Fix this stupid lupus. Make it go away. Mom said that we can't rush you, that things happen on your time, but I'm asking you to please hurry. Sorry if I sound pushy or demanding, but this is an emergency.

"Please forgive me if I just messed all of this up or said something wrong—I just want her to get better. Oh, and can you please find a way for her to get off of dialysis, too? It makes her sick and very tired sometimes. Okay, that's it. Amen."

* * *

~*March 3, 1993*~

Dear Diary,

Tori came by today. She didn't have much to say. She just lay down on the couch and went to sleep. When she woke up, she played with Sedrick, fed him, bathed him, and rocked him to sleep. It was nice to have her around, although I know she won't stay. She said she'd be back this weekend, but I'm not going to hold my breath.

~March 7, 1993~

Dear Diary,

It's absolutely beautiful outside! The sun is shining and people are walking the streets. We have to enjoy days like this because they never last too long. Good weather today, and cold winds with thunderstorms tomorrow. Jordan couldn't wait for a day like today so he and his best friend Eric could ride their bikes to Sunset Park to go fishing. They are two old men trapped in little boys' bodies. They fish all summer, every summer. It's their thing.

As long as Jordan isn't getting in trouble, and he comes home before it gets dark, it's okay with me. Sedrick is with Sam this weekend. I sat outside on the front porch reviewing my psychology notes, preparing for a test before spring break. I had the house all to myself.

~March 18, 1993~

Dear Diary,

I really want Mom to come home soon. I talked to her today. She sounded a lot better, and I think that just maybe God heard my prayer. I smiled when I hung up the phone. At the same time, I feel like no one cares. It seems like no one is worried about us, and it hurts. Please Mom, get better. Just come home, please.

~March 28, 1993~

Dear Diary,

Sedrick can sit up all by himself! Jordan kept poking at him, slightly pushing him over just to watch him struggle as he attempted get back up. Sedrick is just as silly because he laughs at Jordan every time.

Later, while lying across my bed, I smiled staring at the ceiling with the phone to my ear listening to Kevin's voice. After laughing about school drama, the conversation took a turn in a different direction. Even over the phone, I was embarrassed and scared, but we talked about it anyway. Sex. He'd been trying to come to the house, but I was scared things might go too far. Plus, I just wasn't ready. He said he loved me. I thought I loved him, too. I wished Tori was home. I needed to talk to her . . . like immediately. I knew having sex wasn't the answer, but I didn't want to lose Kevin either.

What a relief!

Sam never mentioned going to get Mom, so it was an unexpected surprise. Her chest was fragile as she shuffled around the house cuddling a pillow to reduce the pressure from the incision. There was a list of instructions she had to follow in order to recover properly: implement a nutritious diet, refrain from lifting objects over five pounds, and limit her walking distance until further instructed by the doctor. It seemed like a lot of restrictions. One morning, she sat on the floor in the middle of the living room with her arms stretched wide, taking slow breaths as if she were practicing a breathing technique.

Sam sat on the couch. Sedrick crawled around her attempting to grab her hospital bracelet. But when she reached to touch him, Sedrick squirmed as if he didn't recognize her. It hurt Mom's feelings; Sedrick just wasn't comfortable with her yet.

I walked to the kitchen to prepare dinner and Sam followed to get a glass of water.

I whispered, "Sam, why is she crying?"

"Because she can't pick Sedrick up. She wants to hold him and she can't right now. She's craving to bond with him. I told her he will in due time."

"Oh. So, how long does she have to wait before she can pick him up?"

"It depends on the healing process, but I'm going to stay for a while." He patted my shoulder.

* * *

~*April 19, 1993*~

Dear Diary,

Very interesting day! As I was walking out of my Algebra II class, a teacher from across the hall stopped me. He was a slightly tall, stocky, black man, with glasses propped on the bridge of his nose. He strongly resembled Bill Cosby.

"Hi! I'm Mr. Ramsey." He smiled as he extended his arm to shake my hand. I looked around to see if he was talking to me. He smiled. "I'm talking to you."

I shook his hand. "Hi. I'm Talisa. Talisa Brooks. Am I in trouble?"

"Did you do something wrong?"

"No, sir. Not that I know of."

"No, sir. Well, well, well, listen to those manners. My wife and I are supporting a state program, and we're trying to recruit minority students to see if anyone would be interested."

"What type of program?"

"It's called the Minority Teacher's Incentive Program, MTIP, and I think you might be a good candidate for it. If you're interested in knowing more about it, the first meeting will take place next Tuesday in the cafeteria. You'll have to get your parents' permission first."

"Can you tell me what the program is for so I can tell my mom? Because she's going to ask."

"Tell her it could possibly help you get into college, but you'll have to keep a good grade point average."

"Hmm, college. Yes, sir. I'll ask her."

College. I really hadn't thought about college. Sports, drill team, and maintaining good grades had been my main focus, but since I was no longer a part of either activity, maybe it was time for a new focus. Although my grades weren't the best, perhaps the program could help me.

College could mean a better future for me, but I knew being a part of this program required Mom's permission first. I paced in my room, waiting for Mom to wake up from her evening nap. No holds barred, I was just going to dive right in. *Just ask. Nothing to be nervous about. Oh, please say yes.*

"Mom, I have to ask you something."

"What is it?"

"A teacher stopped me in the hallway the other day. He thinks I'd be a good candidate for this program called the Minority Teacher's Incentive Program. The group meeting is next Tuesday after school. Can I go hear what the program is about? Leslie's going."

"What's this program for? What's its purpose?" She seemed interested, which was a good sign.

"He said—"

"Who's he?"

"Oh, sorry, Mr. Ramsey. He said the program could help me attend college."

She pondered for a couple of seconds. "Okay, go see what it's about—and pay attention."

I breathed a sigh of relief. "Yes! Thank you, Mom."

"Excuse me. Yes, what?"

"Oh, sorry. Yes, ma'am." I grinned.

She smiled and I raced down the stairs to call Leslie. I had a good feeling about the program.

At the MTIP meeting I gained an abundance of information. I was definitely interested. The program encouraged minority students to become teachers, but Mr. and Mrs. Ramsey stressed the importance of further education—meaning attending college. It seemed as if they would be mentors for the students who joined the program. They discussed Historically Black Colleges and Universities (HBCUs), just like the one on the TV show *A Different World*. It was beyond amazing because not only would they provide us with information, they were offering to take us on college visits to different HBCUs.

No one had ever talked to me about college, so I was glad I attended the meeting. I definitely aspired to be a part of the program. I'd never really thought about being a teacher either, but it was an intriguing thought.

*   *   *

~May 1, 1993~

Dear Diary,

I'm not playing basketball and missed conditioning for track this year, so I walked to drill team practice today. There were a lot of new moves, new people, and I felt out of place. Not sure what has happened, but I don't feel like drill team is something I still desire to do. There was a time when it was all I could think about . . . each step, each beat of the drums, each twirl of the flags, and each ruffle-toss set a fire within me. I don't know . . . it's just not the same. Maybe I'm growing up.

My midterm test scores had outstandingly improved, but they weren't good enough. How would I recover from the previous semester? With five C's and two D's, I didn't know what to do except devote more time to studying. And since Mom was home, there would be more allowable time for me to study, especially since the final exams were coming up at the end of the month.

When I got home from school, no one was home—peace

and quiet. I took a nap and woke up around six in the evening. The house was pitch-black. The phone rang and disturbed the silence.

"Hello?"

"Talisa, wake up. Sam had to take your mom back to the hospital."

"Grandma?"

"Yes, get up. Your brothers are here. Come get them before it gets too dark."

"Why? Where's my mom? Where's Sam?"

"I just told you—he had to take her back to the hospital. So, come on." She hung up the phone. I buried my face in my pillow, itching to scream, but I was voiceless.

So, back to the same old routine. Sedrick was adorable; he was crawling, getting into everything he set his little eyes upon, and reaching for everything within his arm's length. I sat in a daze in my English class, wondering what was going on with Mom.

"Hey, Tee, what's going on? What's wrong?" Mrs. Harper had started calling me Tee at the beginning of the semester because it was easier to remember. I didn't mind. I thought it was a cute nickname and it stuck because a lot of people started using it.

"Everything."

She grabbed my hand and listened.

"I just can't focus. My grades suck, and I barely have time to study. My mom keeps going in and out of the hospital, and taking care of my brothers is really hard, and I don't want to have sex, but he does now and he says he loves me, and I still don't know where my sister is." I was overwhelmed, and Mrs. Harper seemed stunned.

"Whoa. Okay. Take a deep breath. Slow down. Where's your mom now?" She lifted her eyebrows.

"She's back in the hospital. I don't know why just yet. She was only home for two months, and now she's gone again."

"So, who are you and your brother staying with in the meantime?"

"I have two brothers. Jordan's ten and Sedrick is almost seven months. We stay by ourselves the majority of the time. Sometimes my mom's boyfriend, Sam, stays with us during the week, and sometimes he comes to get my baby brother on the weekends."

"So, how do you get food and other things?"

"Mom usually stocks up on groceries when she comes home. It lasts for a while, but when we start running out of food, I just call my Grandma and she gets some groceries. Jordan and I walk over to her house and get a couple of things."

"Tee, you can't stay by yourself. I'm so sorry, but I have to report this. It's not safe for you and your brothers. Even if Sam does come every now and then."

Panic bubbled in my stomach like a volcano about to erupt. "Mrs. Harper, it's okay. Please. It's been this way since my mom became sick a couple of years ago. It's fine, I promise. Please, please don't tell anyone," I pleaded. "I don't want anyone to take my brothers away."

"Tee, I can't let you do this. You're just a child yourself.

You probably don't feel like one, but you are. You're sitting in my class, barely aware of the lessons being taught, with tears running down your face. To me, that's alarming."

"Please, I'm begging you, Mrs. Harper. We'll be fine. It'll get better."

She placed her hands on both of my cheeks. "That's quite optimistic." She looked at me with a hard stare. "So, tell me what's going on with this boy."

"I don't want to say pressuring or trying to force me, but he just keeps mentioning sex now. Like all the time. I'm just not ready."

"Don't do it. You are too young. If he really likes or cares for you, he'll wait." She paused. "Now, what do you and your brothers need?"

I was ashamed and I bashfully sat in silence, but she kept waiting for my answer, so I had no choice.

"Umm . . . we have food. My Mom went shopping before she left. Umm . . . ."

"What is it, Tee?" Mrs. Harper stood over me.

I muttered as my lips tensed. "I need some pads. I started my period this morning and I don't have any."

"What are you using now?"

"Don't laugh, please. I used the paper towels from the kitchen at home. I don't have any money to buy any."

She sighed and shook her head. "Oh, Tee, come with me."

I followed her to the girls' bathroom and she placed four quarters in the dispenser. Then, she handed me two maxi pads.

"Take these for now, then after school, come back to my

class. I'll take you to the store to get you some pads and take you home." She patted me on the back.

"Yes, ma'am. Please don't tell anyone. Please." She nodded curtly, not agreeing or disagreeing.

Mrs. Harper cared—she really did. It made me feel so good knowing she was concerned not just about me, but my brothers, too. I was so afraid she was going to tell someone. I prayed she wouldn't say a word.

*   *   *

~June 2, 1993~

Dear Diary,

It's official—my freshman year of high school was a bust. My grades are all horrible. I have to keep trying. It has to get better, right?

I sat on the floor next to my bed as I stared at my disappointing report card. A crashing sound forced me to jump up as I ran to Jordan's room. Sedrick fell down the stairs in his walker—talk about frightening! I was beyond dismayed, shell-shocked at the sight of his little body upside down in his walker at the bottom of the stairs. Poor Sedrick hollered at the top of his lungs. We dashed fast as lightning down the stairs. He had an enormous knot on his head from the fall. He cried and cried, and we felt so bad for him. How the hell were we going to explain a big-ass knot on his little forehead? If Mom found out, we were dead, plain and simple. Dead. I told Jordan to make sure the baby gate was up and secure. He reassured me it was.

Maybe Sedrick had tampered with the locking lever—I didn't know.

It was the middle of the night, and another daunting noise woke us. Sedrick lay sound asleep next to me. I jumped out of bed as my heart sank. I stood at the top of the stairs, waiting and listening. The noise resounded again, but louder this time, and chills massaged my spine. It sounded like someone was throwing firecrackers at the house. Jordan jumped up out of bed, too. I grabbed his wooden baseball bat, and he stood behind me. We crept down the stairs.

"Talisa, what is it?"

"Shhh . . . ."

"Is it burglars?" I stopped and looked at him. He grinned and covered his mouth.

I whispered, "Shhh! If it *is* burglars, you just told them where we are."

All of the lights were on downstairs; I always left them on at night. A few seconds later, sirens and flashing lights were in front of our house. We turned off the lights and pulled back the thick, double-rodded curtains. There was a boy lying in the middle of the street.

"Talisa, is he dead?

"I don't know. He's not moving. It looks like it. Come on, let's go back to bed."

I didn't know who the boy was, but he was small. He looked young. Very young.

PART VI

Where Do I Go?

CHAPTER 15

AFTER REGISTERING FOR sophomore year classes, Mom and I walked slowly through the halls. She reminisced and filled the moment with stories of her glory days at the same exact school. It was an amazing feeling having her there with me. It was the first time in a long time she was actually home at the beginning of a school year. She'd been home for nearly a week—and in good spirits. She was getting stronger each day and loved being home with us. We walked up the stairs to the corridor, and Mrs. Harper was standing by the windows talking to another teacher. She smiled at me and I stopped.

"Hi, Mrs. Harper."

"Tee, how are you doing?"

"I'm good. This is my mom." Mrs. Harper extended her arm to shake Mom's hand.

Mom cleared her throat and smiled. "Nice to meet you."

"Tee, stop by my class sometime. Don't be a stranger." She placed her arm around me, planting a friendly hug, and smiled at Mom. I knew then that she hadn't said anything to anyone, and it didn't appear that she was going to, especially since she'd seen Mom healthier and stronger. It was reassuring.

"Talisa, who is she?" Mom asked as we walked away.

I looked over my left shoulder back at Mrs. Harper. "She's the coolest teacher ever."

Mrs. Harper uncrossed her arms and gave me a thumbs-up as if she were proud of me.

*   *   *

~August 21, 1993~

Dear Diary,

What have I done? Actually, I know exactly what I've done. I thought I'd feel different—not sure what I expected. I wasn't even sure if I was ready. What should I have expected? But I don't feel the same. This is what you do when you're in love, right? I feel confused and so disappointed in myself. I can't tell anyone, but I feel like I really need to talk to someone. I'm so embarrassed. This was probably a big mistake.

Kevin and I had sex. Protected.

There were moments of sweetness, followed by immediate guilt. I did it because I loved him—because he said he loved me. He made me feel beautiful . . . like I was the only girl in the world. He cared for me. He was attentive. During our special moment, I felt a slight pain, but he soothed me with kisses and held me close. I smiled from the inside out. I was special to him—delicate and fragile. I closed my eyes, and I felt secure. Yet, my heart was toggling between right and wrong. Tori told me to wait. I tried. Ms. Rose commanded me to keep my legs closed. I had never talked to Mom about sex, and I didn't even know how to—not without her orchestrating my funeral arrangements in the process. These damn emotions overruled my thoughts, and before I could think clearly, it happened.

Weeks had gone by, nothing had changed and our communication was still inconsistent. I hadn't seen Kevin because he traveled a lot over the summer attending different basketball camps. Tori visited. Not for long, of course, but it was good to see her. School had begun and three weeks into the semester Kevin and I had broken up—or were no longer communicating. What we did was a mistake, and it couldn't happen again.

"We just can't."

"What's wrong with you? Why not?" He snapped at me.

"Because . . . I didn't feel right afterwards."

"What do you mean? Like in pain? Like you're hurting?"

"No, like guilt. Embarrassed. You play basketball, and you might be a great player one day. Maybe even in the NBA. I want to go to college or do something. But what happens if I get pregnant? Everything will change."

The unsettling silence over the phone made my heart ache, as if common sense was floating back into our minds.

"We'll protect ourselves. I have condoms."

"That's not one hundred percent protection. They don't always work."

"You worry too much."

"You don't worry enough. I was bleeding afterwards. It freaked me out. Kevin, I just don't want to, okay?"

"Fine. Whatever." He hung up the phone before I could even say bye.

I shed my tears and collectively gathered my feelings, but I was torn in two pieces. I loved him, but things had changed. The day before, I fretfully walked to the county health clinic. I took a free pregnancy test, just in case. It was negative, but the nurse advised me to come back in about a month to retest. I was disappointed in myself. Thinking that no contraceptive is one hundred percent effective, my thoughts sped in circles like race cars zooming around the track. What if this time it wasn't? I couldn't have a baby—I was too young. Mom would kill me, for sure.

It'd been a crazy summer without Mom. At least she could finally hold Sedrick in her arms without assistance or having any shortness of breath. The heart surgery was a success. The recovery time had been extensive, and she'd never be fully recovered, but she seemed to be functioning and progressing without any further complications.

It was time to focus. I prayed Mom didn't go back into the hospital for any reason because my GPA had to improve. After I spoke with Mr. Ramsey about my grades from freshman year, I knew I had to maintain a 3.0 or higher, especially if I aspired to attend college. I had to try. Before the last day of school back in June, he'd announced that the MTIP would be visiting several different HBCUs over the upcoming spring break. I was ecstatic.

*   *   *

~September 17, 1993~

Dear Diary,

Oh yeah! It's my sweet sixteenth birthday! Mom is letting me have a house party . . . entirely unreal. I never thought she'd go for it. There are always house parties at other student's houses, but I was never able to go. So, I'm absolutely shocked she's letting me have a party! Leslie and I have been inviting people from school all week. It's going down tonight! Details to come later!

~September 18, 1993~

Dear Diary,

Today is Sedrick's first birthday. He is the cutest ever in his little outfit. Mom placed him in the high chair and set a tiny personal cake in front of him. Sedrick dug right in. He made such a mess. He laughed, and he had no idea we were laughing at him.

The phone rang just before my party began. It was Kevin. "I just called to wish you a happy birthday."

Listening to his voice, I was full of mixed emotions. He hadn't called in two weeks, and at school, he just walked right past me in the hallway.

"Thank you." I didn't know what else to say.

Mom yelled for me to get off the phone. I told him I had to go, and I hung up.

*   *   *

~September 21, 1993~

Dear Diary,

The party was the best night, ever! Hands down. The party was insane—epic! So many people showed up. The music was loud, and the laughter was even louder. Mom and Ms. Rose stayed upstairs the whole time. It was great until the police knocked on the door and shut my party down. There were too many people inside and outside. Mom and Ms. Rose tried to persuade the cops, but they refused to see it any other way besides ending my celebration. It was fun while it lasted. The police actually shut us down!

~September 30, 1993~

Dear Diary,

Mom's dialysis treatments are worse than ever. The challenges she deals with change like someone losing at the game of Operation, pinging her heart, then her kidney. She desperately needs a kidney to become available, and she needs it like yesterday.

I was lying on the floor in Jordan's room while he played video games, and suddenly there was a weeping sound. We instantly looked at each other. What's wrong *now*? The sound of sobbing trailed up the stairs and into Jordan's room. It didn't sound like Mom or Tori. It was unrecognizable. Then, Mom's soft, comforting voice rattled as it grew unsteady.

"It's going to be all right. You're not alone. I will walk with you every step of the way," Mom said.

There was a burst of tears, and a man's voice shattered like a glass plate hitting the floor. "I don't know what to do, Sis. I'm going to die, and there's nothing anyone can do."

Our faces elongated from the words. It was Uncle Darren.

"Stop it. I'll go with you to the doctors. We'll just search for all the information possible and see what they recommend. I heard there's a lot of medication available for HIV patients now—medication to help you live with it, to manage it. You're not going to die."

Jordan scooted next to me. "Whoa, Talisa. What's HIV?"

"It's a disease. A bad disease."

"Is it worse than lupus?"

"I don't know, but I do know that a lot of people are dying from it. Just like the black tennis player, Arthur Ashe. He died earlier this year."

I realized the older I became, the more shit that was revealed. It seemed like negativity was aiming to diminish or demolish my family. Is this what we were supposed to look forward to? A future of calamity? Uncle Darren left. From my bedroom window, I watched him get in his car and drive away. What in the hell is going on? Is our family cursed or something?

*   *   *

~October 12, 1993~

Dear Diary,

I assumed the operation was supposed to improve Mom's condition, but her mood swings are escalating to new heights. I can't keep up with all the changes. Last month, she said I could play basketball this year, and once again, I made the team. Now, I'm leaving for practice, and she's giving me above-and-beyond attitude. I just want to play. I missed everything last year—everything! No basketball, no track, no drill team—everything. It's not fair!

~October 15, 1993~

Dear Diary,

I'm definitely not pregnant! I didn't think I was, but I just had to double-check. I know I should go to a real doctor, but that means I'd have to tell Mom. Not happening!

~October 28, 1993~

Dear Diary,

Today is Mom's birthday, but she's in a mood. We tried to make her laugh. It lasted for about an hour before she went back into her room to be alone. I think she has a difficult time accepting what is happening to her, or maybe she's thinking of Uncle Darren. Her moments of happiness fluctuate like the speedometer gauge on the dash of a car . . . it often leaves me baffled. Attempting to avoid her sporadic wrath, we just stay in our rooms like we used to do. Sam and Mom seem to argue more these days. Not sure over what, or for what reason. Everything keeps changing, so I try to keep Jordan and Sedrick with me as much as I can. At least they remain consistent.

Basketball practices were not easy or perhaps I was just out of shape. My legs felt like cooked spaghetti noodles, but it was just a part of improving and strengthening before the season started. Plus, that was the least of my worries. As we were setting up to run a play, Mom marched into the gym with Sedrick on her hip and Jordan by her side. I jogged over to her. Coach started to join us from the sideline, but Mom raised her hand and signaled my coach to stop.

"Mom, what's wrong?" I was so confused—scared that something was wrong with her again.

"Do you think you're grown?" The growl under her tone made me shiver.

"No, ma'am. What's going on?" I tried to whisper, but she wasn't having it.

Her voice grew intense. "You walked out the house without doing the dishes!"

I was stunned as the realization sunk in. Nothing was wrong. She was just pissed about the damn dishes. That couldn't be the only reason.

"Are you serious right now? You came all the way here and interrupted the team's practice because I didn't do the dishes?"

She stood closer to me until we were nose to nose. "Watch your mouth, go get your stuff, and get home. Now!" She was fuming. She turned and walked out of the gym.

Part of me longed to follow her. On the other hand, I internally raged, wanting to rebel and stay there or scream at the top of my lungs. Coach swiftly approached and patted me on the back and advised me to go to the locker room to take five. I was upset, irritated, and livid, and my mind was a ticking time bomb. I plopped down on the bench in the locker room and screamed, not paying attention to where I was. I threw my bag against the wall. I wanted to scream at Mom, but I didn't want to disrespect her either.

Why was she like this? Didn't I try my hardest to do everything right? Shante' and Karrin came running down the stairs. They both had attended the rival junior high school, and we'd become friends through playing sports. Since open gym and tryouts that year, we'd all become pretty close.

"What in the hell was that, Tee?" Shante' placed her hand on my shoulder.

"Nothing, I'm fine." I yanked off my practice jersey and changed my clothes to go home. I picked up my practice shoes and shoved them back into my bag.

"Tee, you don't look fine, and you damn sure didn't just sound fine. What's wrong? What the hell was that about?" Karrin grabbed my bag.

"I said nothing. I'll be fine. Y'all just go back to practice. I need to go home." I snatched my bag from Karrin and stormed out of the locker room.

"Coach, I have to go home. Sorry." I tried to walk past her, but she grabbed my arm.

"Come by my classroom tomorrow so we can talk." She looked concerned.

Oh, how I wished she could do something to help. I walked outside to get in the car, but Mom was nowhere in sight. She'd left me to walk home in the cold.

Once again, I had to quit basketball. Mom grounded me for two weeks. I was restricted from everything except attending school. No basketball for the year either. I could've tried to plea with Coach, but I thought perhaps I'd just focus on my grades. Damn, I really wanted to play. I stopped by Coach's classroom and told her about Mom's lupus. She offered an open door of possible serenity for me if I ever needed to talk. There were balls of fire bottled deep down inside of me, and my thoughts became shooting arrows attempting to penetrate a reaction. But I kept quiet, afraid that if I spoke, I might lose my mind.

School was my playground—an escape from the catastrophes on the home front. The uncaged opportunity to be free, to laugh, to be silly and carefree, or to simply be whoever I wanted to be without restriction, restraint, or responsibilities. My younger cousin, Sharae, was now in high school. She was a pure comedian and beyond the perkiest person I knew. We used to spend a lot of time together when we were younger—sleepovers, staying up all night chuckling and telling jokes. She was a freshman, and high school was definitely a bit overwhelming for her, but she was adjusting.

"Hey cousin, what's up?"

I glanced and saw that her face was outlandish, stricken somehow. "What's wrong with you? What happened?"

"Boys are so stupid," she answered.

I sighed. "Yeah, I know. Tell me about it. What happened? Are you going to lunch?"

"Yeah, in a minute. Let me tell you this first. I was in the library, right?" She asked like I should've known.

"Okay," I agreed and giggled.

"Minding my own business, right?"

I was growing impatient. "Cousin, please just tell me the story already!"

"Okay, geez, Mrs. Rush-body."

"The story, Cousin. Now." I turned my wrist to look at my invisible watch.

"Okay, okay. So, I was in the library. This boy comes up behind me and rubs his thing against me."

"His thing. What's his thing?" I knew what she was talking about. I just wanted her to say it.

She pulled on my arm to whisper in my ear. "You know . . . his thing."

"I have no idea what you're talking about." I tried to not laugh.

"Stop it. You know." She looked up at me with a blank face and whispered, "His penis. He rubbed his thing on my butt and whispered in my ear, 'I sure would like to tune up your engine.'" Her face wrinkled in utter disgust.

"Wait. First of all, how do you know it was his thing? It could have been a book, ya know."

"I know it was his thing."

"Ooh-wee, Cousin. You being nasty in the library?" I tried to joke about it, and she punched me in the arm. "So, what did you say to him?" My curiosity could've killed a cat.

She placed her hand on her hips, smacked her lips, and rolled her neck. "Boys are so nasty. I told him to get away from me."

"Well, good. If you feel like he's harassing you or something, then go to the dean's office. Report him."

"No, I'm fine. I just don't know why he'd want to tune up my engine. I don't even have a car."

I loved her. She truly had no idea. My mouth dropped as my laugh burst out uncontrollably.

"Why are you laughing so hard?"

"First of all," I pointed, "you should see your face. I'm laughing because he wasn't talking about a car, silly. He was talking about sex."

"That is just disgusting. He needs a whipping right across his butt." She stomped her right foot and turned around to walk down the hall.

As I walked to class, she yelled down the hall, "Stop laughing at me!"

God, it felt good to laugh.

*　　*　　*

~November 25, 1993~

Dear Diary,

It was a fantastic Thanksgiving. Everyone seemed to have had a good time! Mom felt pretty good today—she was actually basking in the moment.

~December 7, 1993~

Dear Diary,

Today after school, I cleaned up the kitchen and vacuumed my room and Jordan's room. One of my birthday gifts this year was a telephone, and even though it's in my room, I still have to ask permission to use it. I've been thinking about Dad a lot lately. I want to call him, but I don't know what to talk about. All of my conversations with Sam make me wonder what it would be like to have my real dad here—even if it were just for a day. Sam encourages me to excel in school, to stay focused. Although he isn't my real dad, at times, I imagine he is.

I asked Mom if I could call Dad.

"Are you okay?" She squinted her eyes.

"Yeah, I'm fine."

"What's wrong?"

Dad's absence was beginning to cleave my heart into two pieces. "I'm fine, Mom. Can I just call him?"

She patted the sofa cushion. "Come sit down. What's going on?"

I didn't know where to start, and I didn't want her to be upset either. So, I lied. "Nothing's wrong. My cramps are really hurting my stomach. That's all."

She hesitated as if she knew I wasn't telling the truth. "Okay, go on. Call him."

During the past eight years, he'd become a voice over the

phone, an image sketched in my heart, outlined with dark ink and no color to fill in the blank spaces. My fingers shook as I dialed his number, but it just rang and rang. He didn't answer, and I hung up. So many questions were unanswered. How could I love someone so much and not even know who they are? I've been craving the idea of having him there with me for so long. I started to believe in the created fictitious character in my mind of whom I wanted him to be. At times, I felt I was begging him to love me and to be part of my life. What I didn't understand was . . . why did I have to beg? Why couldn't he just love me . . . love me the way I'd always imagined?

The phone rang several times, and Mom stopped mopping the kitchen floor to answer.

Then, a lot of curse words bounced off the kitchen's walls, and Mom's face was fiery red as her bottom lip protruded. She was like a steaming teapot with a shaky lid, ready to shoot across the room and crack the glass window over the kitchen sink. That was Mom, definitely standing her ground. I loved that about her—she was no pushover, and it was encouraging. By no means was she the Wicked Witch of the North, South, East, or West, but she would fight for what was right. She was lighting a fire under my dad's ass like never before.

"I'm sick and tired of you telling them that you're coming, and you never do. Stop hurting them like this." I don't know what he replied to her, but she turned up the volume and lost all religion.

"I don't give a damn about any of that. Talisa has been calling you and calling you, and not one time did you attempt to come see them, I swear. Stop hurting them." She slammed the phone down, and it was very quiet. Jordan went into the living room with his hand covering his laughter.

"Shhh, before she hears you, silly. Be quiet."

"Did you hear that? Mama told him off. Do you think he wants to see us now?" As he danced in the middle of the room, he whispered, "Go Ma-ma! Go Ma-ma!"

"I don't know, Brother, but don't get your hopes up. We'll just have to wait and see."

Mom shouldn't have had to yell and cuss to get him to make a move. Again, why didn't he just come to see us?

* * *

~December 20, 1993~

Dear Diary,

Is this happening? I can't believe it. I don't know what to pack or what to say when I get there, but Jordan and I are going to Tennessee for Christmas. Mom must have really turned up the fire, burning Dad's ears through the phone, I guess. We're leaving Thursday morning, traveling on the Greyhound bus. Jordan and I are going to visit Dad for the holiday. So, I guess we have another brother. His name is Jason, and Dad said he would be there, too.

~December 21, 1993~

Dear Diary,

One minute I'm anxious to see Dad, the next I want to cry. The next I don't want to go. So confused. Today I wondered what it would be like to just sit next to him and hold his hand. I turned in my second poem assignment for my English class, just before winter break. I received an A+. Here it is:

"Chained Illusions"

His face appears in my dreams, creating imaginary
moments that remain imprisoned in my mind,
yet I crave his love.
Does he miss me? Does he even know who I am?
I wonder, does he know my favorite color?
They say a girl's first love is her father. How so when
he's so distant in every capacity? His picture leaves me
dreaming, thirsting to be fed by his presence.
Where are you, Daddy?
Constantly seeking for one to show me the love
I desperately urge to receive. Aching to be wrapped
in his arms as he whispers in my ear, "You're safe,
sweetheart."
Confused in this world, with no direction, fighting to
savor the prize in between my thighs and not confuse
myself of what is real love.

I can't bear the emptiness. Closed doors surround me,
frustration chisels away at every inch of my heart.
Where are you, Daddy?
When I cry for you, do you not hear me? I need you.
I need you to tell me it'll be all right. Take the worry
away. Take the pain away. Come keep me safe, for fear
is tormenting my soul.
Maybe I don't have daddy issues . . . perhaps they're
just daddy-miss-yous, drenched tears captured in balls
of tissue piled next to my pillow.
Daddy . . . where are you?

CHAPTER 16

MOM REPEATEDLY CHECKED our bags, overfilling them with snacks, and attached a long do's and don'ts list. She'd never hugged us so much—she was frantic and overflowing with anxiety. We swallowed our laughs.

She acted like a crazy woman, grabbing my shoulders and shaking me. "Talisa, you're the oldest, so pay attention. You hear me? Pay attention to everything."

I held her hand. "Mom, we're going to be fine. Stop worrying."

"Please look after your brother. Don't let him eat all of the candy in his bag before he gets there. You pay attention. Be aware of the people around you and listen closely. Put your bags in front of you so no one messes with them. And don't talk to anyone unless the bus driver asks you a question. You hear me? Every time that bus stops, you call me, no matter what time it is. Got it?" Her emotions spiraled.

Jordan hugged her. "Mama, stop crying. We're coming back. It's not like we're running away or something, geez."

"Okay, big boy. I just need you guys to be very careful."

We waved goodbye from the steps of the bus, headed down

the aisle and picked our seats halfway back. Jordan sat by the
window. He was so eager. It took a while for the bus to start
rolling, and we laughed as we looked out the window, watching
Mom talk to the bus driver. Both of her hands were placed on
her hips. There was no doubt in my mind she was providing him
with a list of instructions of what-to-do and what-not-to-do.
The bus ride was long, so Jordan and I took turns listening to
music on my Discman until he dozed off. He lay in my lap,
and I covered him with my jacket. Mom's panic made me so
paranoid, I couldn't sleep. I was beyond alert, and every hasty
movement caught my attention.

*   *   *

~December 24, 1993~

Dear Diary,

*Who in the hell voluntarily takes the bus out of town?
Never again. Ten hours on this bumpy bus. No way. After
making a hundred different stops in God-knows-where, we
finally arrived in Tennessee this morning. At every stop I
had to call Mom. With each call, it was the same repetitive
questions: "Where are you? What's the name of the gas
station or bus stop? Are you around other people? Make
sure you hold your brother's hand." The same questions
over and over again. She's too funny. She worries so much.*

We stepped off the bus and shook our tingling legs and feet
after sitting for so long. We grabbed our bags from under the
bus and scanned the lobby for Dad. For a minute, I was afraid

he hadn't come. I searched the lobby but didn't see him. Had we come all this way for nothing?

But then . . . there he was.

He stood against a pillar by the vending machines. He was tall and slender, and he had a salt-and-pepper beard, slim jeans, cowboy boots, and a baseball cap seated slightly above his eyebrows. He had a deep, southern accent.

"Hey, hey. Look at you two. Oh, my goodness, would you look at this?" He hugged me, and his baritone voice vibrated throughout the lobby. His cologne reeked, his narrow eyes looked nearly closed, and his slender, muscular physique was just as I had remembered. He bent down to hug Jordan.

"Boy, you're going to be a tall one, just like your daddy. Look at these hands . . . those long arms and legs. Shoot, boy, you just might be taller than your daddy when you get older."

Jordan couldn't resist, and he dove into Dad's arms. Dad kissed him on the cheek.

"Well, come on. Let's go. Your brothers are waiting at the house. They can't wait to meet you." He smiled at us and I stopped.

"Wait, what? You said brothers, as in plural not singular. You said we had a brother." Yeah, I had an attitude. Jordan's face was blank and I immediately grew defensive.

"Yes, you knew that, Talisa." He was attempting to convince me of something I knew nothing about.

"No, you told me about our older sister, Chelise. Then, about another brother before we came. Now, there's another one, too?"

"Well, yes. Another brother and a younger sister."

I knew he was my dad, but I wanted to punch this dude in the face. I was astounded. "Wait, a minute. Stop. We barely know who you are, and now you're telling us we have a little sister, too? Where is she? Is she here somewhere?" My bag dropped to the floor.

Dad was speechless and had a smirk on his face. "Girl, you look just like your mama." He stroked his beard and chuckled. "I see you got a bit of your mama's fire in you, too. We can talk more when we get to the house. Stop the fussin' and come on."

Jordan pulled on my arm and whispered, "Yeah, come on. Don't be mean. Let's just go. It's Daddy. Don't mess things up."

I couldn't deny my brother's face all full of excitement. He didn't get it. Our dad had another child or children who were living with him. If he could do that, why in the hell didn't he ever come to get us? Lord knows we needed him. Jordan was just happy to see him, but I needed to know where Dad had been for the last eight years and why he never came to visit us. Seeing him face-to-face puzzled and intrigued me at the same time. It felt like we were in the presence of a complete stranger.

*   *   *

~December 25, 1993~

Dear Diary,

Merry Christmas! Dad cooked breakfast this morning. All of the boys were in the living room laughing, chatting, and watching TV. Yesterday afternoon, I met my other two younger brothers for the first time. They're both from

Wisconsin. Jason, the oldest of the brothers, is thirteen, and Seth is eleven, the same age as Jordan. The numbers are very close, no mystery there. It means it wasn't just Mom and Dad when we lived in Milwaukee. Dad's a rolling stone, obviously. I wonder how old my younger sister is. Where does she live? Why isn't she here, too?

Jordan was overjoyed being surrounded by brothers his age. He was truly backstroking in a pool of bliss with no flotation devices. Our family in the south was very loving, affectionate, and naturally hospitable. Each house we visited welcomed us with open arms, and they accepted us immediately without question. We met aunts, uncles, and cousins for the first time. They all hugged and kissed us repeatedly, and the loving feeling was overwhelming.

Back at Dad's house, the boys immediately fell asleep, but it wasn't as easy for me. I went to the kitchen and found Dad sitting at the table, reading.

"What's wrong? Why are you still up?" He removed his glasses.

"I can't sleep. I just wanted to get some water."

He tapped his hand on the table. "Come sit down for a minute. Let's talk."

There were seconds of awkward silence. "Oh boy, your aunties are surely fond of you guys. Everyone was just raving about you all."

"Yeah, everyone was so nice."

"Why do you sound so surprised? You guys have a lot of family up north."

"Family, sure, but it's just different. I can't describe it, but it's not like the family here."

"How's your mom?"

"Good days, bad days. She shuts herself off from the rest of the world, and us sometimes. The dialysis treatments drain her energy sometimes."

"I can't imagine anything knocking your mama down. She's a feisty one. When she used to get up on that stage, modeling at those fashion shows, strutting her stuff, people were wowed."

"Wait, what? Mom modeled? Like lights, camera, action-type model? Are you serious? I know she went to college, but when did she model?" My mouth opened wide.

"Yes, she would model for fashion shows in college. It's what she went to college for—fashion design. Such a creative mind. She was gorgeous." He gazed into the air.

"Oh, my goodness. She never said anything about this."

"Hearing about this disease, I can only imagine how she feels. And this new other baby—" He paused. "How's he doing?"

"Sedrick is fine. He is so cute and funny. He's walking and talking now. He can say my name, too."

He lowered his head and fidgeted with the corner of the newspaper. His demeanor gave me pause, but I ignored it.

"Dad?" I hesitated.

"Yes, what is it?"

I cleared my throat, "Why didn't you come? Why didn't you come to help us?"

He leaned back in his chair, as though he knew I was going to ask. He placed his hands on the top of his shaved, bald head, while taking a deep breath. "I just had a lot to take care of here. My mother was ill, and my work schedule just didn't always permit."

Deep down, I guess I expected countless excuses which would never fulfill the blank space in my heart. I desperately desired so much more from him. But reality crudely shook my core, and I realized my questions would remain unanswered. How would I come to terms with this? I pushed myself away from the table and asked, "Do you love me? Do you love us?"

"Why, yes. What in the world would make you ask me that? I love you all to death."

"Then, why didn't you come? All those times I called you, all the times I cried, begging for you to help me. I needed you, and you did nothing. Where were you?"

His lips didn't move, and he studied my face. He reached for my hand, but I pulled it back. It hurt seeing him, and I'd assumed he'd be the tranquility I longed for. I walked away, and he followed me down the hallway. Then I stopped before closing the bedroom door.

"Talisa, wait. Talisa . . . ." He cleared his throat and leaned in to hug me.

I stood like a statue, and my tears drenched my face.

"I don't need a hug *now*. I needed it *then*. I needed you to be there." I slammed the bedroom door behind me.

The road trip back home was shorter than the bus ride. Dad drove and he sang gospel songs the whole way. Not the gospels songs Mom listened to on Sundays like BeBe and CeCe Winans songs, I'm talking about the old Negro, spiritual, in-the-field-picking-cotton-type hymns. It was way too much for my ears to bear. He said he was studying to be a minister and advised me to start reading the Bible for guidance through life. The overall visit shed some light on some things, but it also open doors to some unpleasant realities. Dad dropped us off and showered us with affection.

"Talisa, I know that you are, or were, upset with me. But I just want you to know that I do love you with all my heart." He kissed me on the cheek.

"Dad, I just don't understand. I just don't. I'll talk to you later." I grabbed Jordan's hand and walked into the house.

*   *   *

~January 1, 1994~

Dear Diary,

Happy New Year! Me and my cousin Sharae and Leslie went to the new teen club for the New Year's celebration party. We danced all night long.

~January 10, 1994~

Dear Diary,

My first semester grades came in the mail today. I'm so proud of myself! I have four A's, two B's, and a C-, damn Biology II class.

I often fell asleep with my headphones on because music relaxed me. While I slept peacefully, Tori practically kicked down my bedroom door. She held her purse in one hand and a baby car seat in the other.

"Hey, little sis." She was glowing.

"Umm, what's that?"

"I thought you were supposed to be all smart and stuff. It's a car seat."

"I know *what* it is. I'm talking about what's *in* the car seat." I rolled my eyes and walked over to see the baby.

She removed the cream-colored blanket. "It's your nephew. His name is Quentin. Say hi to your auntie."

"First of all, you're not going to strut in here acting like you didn't say what you just said. What in the world? You had a baby?" I grabbed her hand. "And you're married? Wait a minute. I thought that guy was just your boyfriend. I need to sit down."

"Yes, to both questions. I had a baby boy." She slowly lifted the baby and kissed him on the forehead.

"Well, I can see that. He's a cutie. Look at those pretty, big, round eyes. Can I hold him?" I was an auntie, and it felt pretty cool. I just wanted to love all over him.

"Yes, girl, please. You can hold him, feed him, raise him if you want to. I need to take a nap." She flopped down on my bed and fell back.

"How old is he?"

"One month old." She closed her eyes.

I kicked the side of the bed. "Oh no, get up. You don't get to sleep right now. You've been gone forever and you come back with a baby. Did it hurt?"

"Did what hurt?"

"Pregnancy? Having a baby?"

"Hell, yeah. That shit is the worst. The contractions are horrible. Worse than cramps, girl. But, I had a C-section, so no coochie pain for me. But these damn staples in my stomach. Hold on!"

"What?"

"Why are you asking me about pregnancy?" She jumped up from the bed and walked up to me. "You better still be a virgin. Are you having sex? You pregnant?" Her face resembled Mom's.

"Calm down. I'm not pregnant."

She put her hands on her hips. "You said not pregnant. But I asked you two damn questions, and you didn't answer the second one. Now, again . . . are you still a virgin?"

"Tori, please, leave it alone."

"You're not, are you? Why'd you do this? Set the baby down."

I gently laid the baby on the bed and shrugged. "I don't know, Tori. He said he loved me."

"Aw, hell naw, Talisa." She grabbed both of my arms and shook me. "That's what they do. That's what they say to get what they want, and you fell for that shit. Men are takers. They just take what they want."

"Okay, Tori. Okay. Afterwards, I knew it was a mistake. I should've waited. I thought I loved him and he loved me. But now I see that wasn't the case. I guess."

"Well, don't be sad about it. What's done is done. Nothing you can do about it now. Just don't do it again. Wait for a guy who really cares about you. Wait until you get older and he appreciates you. Don't just give it away. I didn't want this for you, Talisa. I wanted you to wait. Does Mom know?"

"Hell no. I'm still alive, ain't I?"

"Did you protect yourself?"

"What do you mean?"

"Oh, my goodness. Birth control, contraceptives, a condom?"

"Oh, yes."

"Anyway, you need to go to the doctor."

"For what?"

"To get checked out."

"But I'm fine. I don't need to go to the doctor. Why are you panicking? My periods have been regular for the past few months. I'm not pregnant. I went to the free clinic and took a pregnancy test. It was negative."

"It's not just about the possibility of pregnancy, Talisa. No contraceptive is one hundred percent, and there is so much more out there, like diseases . . . like HIV. What in the hell are they teaching you guys at school?"

HIV. Like Uncle Darren? I was instantly nauseated.

"I have health class this semester. I don't know what we're going to review just yet."

"Well, good. When your teacher gets to the sex lesson about babies and sexually transmitted diseases, pay damn attention. You hear me?"

"Yeah, *I* hear you. Quiet, before *Mom* hears you."

She looked so disappointed in me, but there wasn't anything I could do. What was done was done.

*　*　*

~February 10, 1994~

Dear Diary,

I am in love with my black literature class. I had no idea some many African American people were famous for their creativity. Poems of passion, conflict, confidence, and pride as a people. This class is truly inspirational.

Early morning complications disturbed my peaceful sleep. Mom woke up in agonizing pain, her legs cramped and muscles throbbed. Our usual routine was to wrap her legs with extremely hot towels and eventually her muscles would relax, her cries would stop, and her heavy breathing would subside.

"Just try to relax, Mom." I rubbed her left leg.

"Thank you for helping me. I pray for a kidney all the time. I just wish one would become available for me." She wiped the sweat from her forehead.

"How will you know when one's available for you?"

"The hospital will call once they have a match for me."

"Well, I'll try to pray, too."

"You know how to pray. Just talk like you're talking to me right now."

*　*　*

~February 25, 1994~

Dear Diary,

God, please! Please let a kidney become available for my mom soon. Amen.

The spring dance, "Swirl '94," was arriving soon. I had no intention of going, but I was asked by a classmate. All the girls at school nearly fainted when Malcolm Penn strutted the hallways. Don't get me wrong; he was pretty handsome. The girls at school had given him a secret nickname: "Sexy Chocolate." His cologne lingered in the air. He appeared shy to me, so I was surprised when he asked. After speaking with Mom, she gave me permission to go, but she asked to speak to his parents first. I was finally going to a school dance. I didn't want to place judgment, but I had to make Malcolm aware of just how the intended evening would go. This date would not include sex.

Within a couple of days, Malcolm's mom came over, and she and Mom had a lengthy conversation. Malcolm and I sat at the dining room table where we chitchatted and laughed. He was a respectable guy. When Malcolm's mom spoke of their family's regular church attendance and her children's participation in the church, Mom was sold. She agreed to let Malcolm escort me to the dance.

In preparation for the spring dance, Mom and I had our first mother-daughter shopping escapade. Sam watched Jordan and Sedrick while Mom and I shopped for a really cute, black dress for the Swirl dance. We picked out some low heels with rhinestones along the sides, earrings, two bracelets, and a tiny black-and-white clutch purse. When I pulled the curtain to the side and stepped out of the dressing room, Mom's tears immediately flowed.

I speed-walked over to her. "Mom, what's wrong? Are you hurting? We can leave. I don't have to go to the dance."

"No, Talisa. You just grew up so fast, that's all."

"Well, don't be sad about it, Mom. I'm still going to be your daughter."

"I know. When you came out of the dressing room just now, I had a flashback—good memories though."

"Speaking of memories, Dad said you used to model in college. Is that true?"

She blushed. "Yeah, that's true."

"Wow, that's pretty awesome, Mom. So, you designed clothes and stuff, too?

"Yes. Dresses, women's suits—you name it, girl. I used to love creating the most beautiful pieces, and people were in awe."

"That's what Dad said, too. Why'd you stop?"

"That's a story for another time. Let me see you again. Turn around."

* * *

~March 13, 1994~

Dear Diary,

Wow! Malcolm is an amazing guy. We had so much fun. A group of us went out to eat after the dance. We laughed nonstop, and the jokes were endless from one end of the table to the other. Malcolm is different. He brought me a flower; he opened my car door, and every door I walked through, he opened. He paid for my dinner. He didn't touch me inappropriately. We were like the best of friends. It was an amazing night. When he dropped me off, he opened the car door for me to get out and walked me to the front door. He thanked me for coming with him. I kissed him on the cheek, and he smiled. Thank you, Malcolm, for being a gentleman.

~March 14, 1994~

Dear Diary,

Spring break is in one week. I'm so excited. The Minority Teacher's Incentive Program is taking our first trip to visit different HBCUs. I wasn't sure if I would be able to go, but Mom said she'd pay the fee for me to go. I hope she has enough money. I've been dancing in my room for days. I got my first stereo this past Christmas. When no one's home, I turn the speakers all the way up. I have such a love for music, and dancing makes me feel so free. When I return from the trip, Mom is going to take me to finally get my license. I've completed all of the required driving hours. Mom said that now she won't have to keep running to the grocery store. Uh-oh.

~March 25, 1994~

Dear Diary,

So, yes, I have to figure out how to get into college. The visitations to the HBCUs were fantastic. We learned a lot about black history and the legacies of each institution. I got a lot of information, and the atmosphere was captivating.

I will never forget this—never. HBCUs are definitely the top institutions on my list . . . well, the list I just created. I'm so glad Mom agreed to let me be a part of this program.

An invisible, thick haze dangled over my head as I struggled to stay awake in every class today. The night before, Mom was at war again, nearly defeated, defenseless, and hanging on the edge of a cliff with one hand. I lay in bed thinking I was dreaming about someone repeatedly calling my name. I opened my eyes. It was two o'clock in the morning, I wasn't dreaming. It was Mom's distressed voice calling me in the night.

"Talisa! Talisa! Talisa!"

I raced down the stairs and Jordan stuck his head over the banister.

"Hey, what's going on?" He rubbed his eyes.

"It's Mom. I don't know. I'll go see. Just go back to bed."

I walked into the living room and dining room, but there was no sign of her. Where was she?

She called out for me again. "Talisa!"

I turned toward the kitchen and saw her feet sideways on the floor, her legs in the doorway of the bathroom. She struggled to get up, and each time she slipped back into her own vomit and blood that covered the bathroom floor.

"Sit still, Mom. I'm going to call the ambulance."

"No, just help me up." Her voice rang in excruciating pain.

I lifted her and sat her up against the cabinet below the bathroom sink. I ran back upstairs to get her some washcloths, towels, and new pajamas. I used a whole roll of paper towels to clean up some of the mess, then I finished by mopping up the rest. I walked out of the bathroom so she could change her clothes while she continued to lie on the floor next to the toilet.

"Mom, do you want some water?"

"No, I'm cold." I ran to grab a blanket and a pillow.

I slid behind her, covered her with a blanket, placed the pillow on my legs, and as I lifted and rested her head on my lap, she sighed. One minute she was perfectly fine and in good spirits, laughing, cooking, and having fun with us, the next was turmoil caused by lupus.

"Mom, is it dialysis?" I wrapped a cold, damp washcloth around her neck. She was so cold but sweating profusely. "Do you feel like you're going to throw up again?"

"A little, but I think most of it has come up already."

"Do you want me to get you something?"

"No, you've done enough, Talisa."

I rocked my legs and rubbed her back. "It's going to be all right, Mom. We have to keep praying for a kidney."

"I hate this, I hate this, I hate this!" she repeated as she slapped the floor.

"Calm down, Mom. If you get upset you might make things worse. Just try to go to sleep." She calmed down, stopped crying, and closed her eyes.

As she slept, I stared at her, dreaming, picturing her up on a stage in a long brown and gold dress with gold heels, her makeup flawless as she walked to the end of a stage, turning to show off her stuff as she strutted back up the stage. I imagined she turned and winked at me.

This must've hurt her—not just physically, but her heart, her mind. I figured that's why her moods fluctuated so much. I'm sure she'd dreamt of those days of designing clothes and being at fashion shows with the spotlight shining on her slender body, long legs, and gorgeous face. I bet she was absolutely stunning.

I fell asleep sitting up against the shower doors—my fragile mom in my lap. "Lupus, please go away," I begged.

CHAPTER 17

I**T WAS BEAUTIFUL** outside. I sat on the front steps listening to my Discman, and a blue car kept rolling by the house. The first time was noticeable, the second time I was aware, and the third time I grew suspicious. The car finally pulled up in front of the house. It stopped. I jumped up to run in the house, and just when I was about to call for Mom—

"Hey, Tee, wait," a boy laughed.

I turned back around. It was Derrick. He was a senior when I was a freshman the previous year, and his sister was a sophomore. I knew her quite well.

"Derrick, what in the world? You scared the crap out of me, creeping up all slow and jumping out the car like you were about to do something to me." I exhaled.

"I wasn't going to hurt you. You've been out here all day."

"You stalking me? You drove past here several times. What's that about?"

He grinned. "I just wanted to stop and talk to you for a minute."

I turned around to see if Mom was standing on the porch. "Well, you better talk fast."

"Why? Are you on punishment or something? What did you do? I thought you were a good girl."

"Whatever. I'm not in trouble. My Mom just doesn't like people in her yard, or on her steps, or in her house that she doesn't know."

"Oh, you mean boys?"

"Especially boys. So, if you have something to say, you better talk fast." I barely finished my sentence.

Through the screen door, Mom stood there looking down at us sitting on the steps. "Excuse me; do I know you, young man?"

Derrick jumped up fast, and I tried to hold back my laugh, "No, ma'am. I'm Derrick." He extended his hand and Mom cracked the door to shake it.

"Uh-huh. How do you know my daughter, Derrick?"

"From school last year, ma'am."

"Last year?" She looked puzzled. "You don't go to school now?"

"Yes, ma'am. I'm in college. I graduated from high school last year."

"Hmm, uh-huh, and Derrick, just how old are you?"

Derrick was sweating bullets. "Nineteen, ma'am."

"Hmm, someone was raised with some manners. Talisa, twenty minutes, you hear me?"

"Yes, ma'am." She walked back in the house and the screen door slammed shut.

We giggled, and Derrick stared at me. "Man, your mom is no joke. She ain't playing around, huh?"

"Nope. So, what did you want to talk about?"

He cleared his throat. "I wanted to see if you might want to hang out some time, maybe go to the movies or something."

"Or something? I'm going to need you to be specific."

"Dang, okay. Do you think I could take you to the movies?"

Leaning back on the steps, I blushed. "You know I have to ask my mom, right?"

"Damn, you won't be going anywhere. Never mind."

I chuckled. "Probably not, but it can't hurt to ask."

"Well, can I call you sometime? Or boys can't call the house either?"

"Yes, I can talk on the phone. Just don't call at night after nine during the week and ten on the weekend."

He busted out laughing, picked up my foot, and looked at my ankle.

"What are you doing? Put my foot down."

"I'm looking for your ankle monitor. Sounds like you on lockdown."

"Whatever."

"So, can I call you sometime?"

"Hmm, I guess so. It's 786-0101."

"Okay, let me get out of here before your mom comes back. I'll call you."

"Just don't call tonight." I shook my head at him.

He waved as he got back in the car. Oh, my goodness, he was

so handsome. Tall, caramel complexion with soft eyes. And his personality was charming.

~May 10, 1994~

Dear Diary,

Preparing for final exams at the end of the month. Most of the lessons this semester were easy, except for Biology II. The studies of biological behavior of living things, energy flow patterns, and physiology of plants made me yawn. What am I really going to do with all of this? It seems pointless since I don't want to be a scientist. I'm going to have to spend a lot of time studying for this final exam. This is still my lowest grade with a C+ at midterms.

I talked to Mom about possibly going to the movies with Derrick, and she said yes. She gave me permission. What? I felt her forehead, thinking she must be sick or something. She just said it has to be a movie during the day and on the weekend. Derrick and I have been talking on the phone nonstop. We actually have a lot to talk about, no inappropriate conversations. I'm crushing on him, like a lot. We made plans to go to the bargain movie theater on Saturday afternoon to go see Above the Rim. I really wanted to see this movie when it first came out, only because Tupac Shakur was in it.

The thought of walking into the building made me nauseated. My first time in the dialysis center wasn't as bad as what I'd imagined it to be. I drove Mom to receive treatment, but normally she'd come alone. The scenery of machines pumping blood and solution in and out of patients made me woozy and faint. For some reason I couldn't leave Mom alone, so I sat for a few minutes waiting to see how the treatment process went.

"You don't have to stay here."

"Are you sure, Mom? I can just wait outside or something. It's eerie in here."

"Tell me about it. But I have to until a kidney becomes available."

"What's that machine?"

"It's a hemodialysis treatment machine."

"What does it do?"

"Well, in a few minutes the clinic technician will come, insert the needle into my graft in my leg, and the machine will start the cleaning process."

"What cleaning process?"

"It gets rid of all the wastes, salt, toxins, and fluid from my blood. One needle will pull blood from my body and go into the machine where it will go through a filter called a dialyzer. Once it goes through the filter, the blood will return through the second needle and go back into my body. That's it." She leaned back to relax.

"You make it sound so simple. Does it hurt?"

"No, it doesn't hurt. Well, at least not during the process, but you've seen the aftermath first hand. I usually get really light-headed immediately afterwards, so I have to sit for a while before I can drive home."

"Well, I'm going to stay with you this time."

"You don't have to, but if you're going to stay . . . let's talk."

Uh-oh. Usually when she said that I was about to get an earful.

"Okay. Talk about what?"

"How's Derrick?"

I was taken aback because we didn't normally talk about boys.

"He's a cool guy, really funny. A true comedian. We have good conversations on the phone."

"Well, look at you blushing over there. Has he asked you out on another date yet?" She smiled at me.

"Yes, but I'm not sure what we should do."

"Why don't you guys go bowling? You like to bowl."

"That's a good idea. Thanks, Mom." I couldn't believe I was talking to her about a guy. It was so surreal.

"I think he's scared of you," I said.

"Good. He should be."

*   *   *

~*June 4, 1994*~

Dear Diary,

After a couple of letters and many phone conversations, I'm starting to feel like I'm getting to know my other older sister. She graduated from high school today. Mom was in an excellent mood, so she drove us all the way to Milwaukee to the ceremony. It was a four-hour drive. I helped drive because driving on the highway is easy. When I first saw Chelise, she was tall like me, but taller. I could see Dad's features in her face—his smile and eyes . . . there's just something about our eyes. Their depth is mysterious. Her smile is as bright as mine. She thanked us for coming, then left with her family. It was a little awkward because I don't know her, but I want to.

The second date with Derrick resulted in a few waves due to a touchy conversation. Derrick picked me up, and we went to his house. He introduced me to his family, but I already knew his sister. I met his grandma. She is the sweetest lady. Unfortunately, his mother had passed away some years before, but I didn't know how. So, he and his sister live with their grandparents. After dinner, we watched a movie in the basement. It was his personal space, and it definitely had man cave written all over it. We sat on the couch, talking.

"So, I have a question for you." He leaned back and swung his arm around my shoulders.

"Okay, what's your question?"

"Did you used to date Kevin Miles?" I wanted to pass out. Kevin had been a pain in my ass since the mistake. Even with Malcolm, Kevin started some stupid-ass rumor about me still being in love with him. It was funny to me, but annoying. Malcolm spoke to me, but after the dance I could tell he shied away and my intuition told me it was because of Kevin.

I dreaded answering. "Yeah, I guess so."

"You guess so? Did you, or didn't you?"

"What does it matter?"

"It really doesn't. He makes it seems like he has you signed, sealed, and up on the shelf for keepsake."

"No, he doesn't. In fact, I haven't talked to him in months. Why do you think that?"

"Dudes talk just like females."

"Fine, he was my first crush. First love, I guess. Things happened. It went too far. It was a mistake."

"Let me guess. By too far, you mean sex?" Gosh, this dude asked a lot of questions.

"Look." I stood up. "I didn't agree to come over here to be interrogated."

"Whoa, wait a minute." He stood up and grabbed my hand. "Tee, I didn't mean anything by it."

"We're not having sex if that's what's on your mind. You can forget it. Can you just take me home, please? Now?" I snapped and pulled my hand away and walked up two steps.

"Hey, wait a minute. I don't want sex, Tee. I like you. A lot. I asked my sister about you, so I thought maybe you were still with Kevin. That's all." He raised his hands up in the air. "Can you please sit back down?"

I was unsure of Derrick's intentions and if his overall goal was sex, even if he denied it. Kevin had denied it. We sat on the sofa and watched TV. I think my actions scared him a bit.

After the movie, he dropped me off at my house and walked me to the door. "Hey Tee, listen. I would never ask you or force you to do anything you didn't want to do, okay?" He lifted my hand and kissed it.

I relaxed my shoulders. "Sorry for assuming the worst back at the house."

"It's all right. No apologies necessary. Just know I would never disrespect you, and I wouldn't hurt you in any way." He hugged me, walked down the front steps, then waited until I locked the screen door.

Oh, my goodness, help me! Damn it, there went those butterflies again.

On our third date, we went to the park and played H-O-R-S-E on the basketball court. We were playing a little one-on-one when a group of guys stepped on the cement court. They greeted each other as if they were friends, then I noticed a stocky, dark-skinned guy with bad acne lingering in the back, smoking a blunt, just observing. He never spoke to Derrick, but he stared at him with piercing eyes. After they left, Derrick took me home.

Mom actually invited him in, and I was shocked as hell. What was going on? She talked to him for some time while I changed out of my sweat-drenched clothes and took a shower. I went back into the living room to sit next to Derrick. They were still chatting. She excused herself, told Derrick good night, and told me that it was getting late.

"Your mom's actually pretty cool."

I was still stuck in shock at her openness.

He and I hugged tightly on the porch. He kissed me. Every nerve in my body went numb. He smiled at me afterwards. Then he kissed the dimples on my cheeks.

He grabbed both of my hands. "So, I was thinking . . . how do you feel about being my girl?"

My alter ego was moonwalking across my shoulder, screaming in my ear, "Go ahead, girl. You got 'em!" I didn't know what to say. "Umm, it's a nice thought. Can I think about it?"

"Yeah, I'm not trying to rush you. Before you go cutting me to pieces, this isn't about sex, either."

We laughed.

My bed felt like I was floating amongst the clouds thinking how good it felt to not feel the pressure of sex. Derrick seemed like he was into me. Like, for real. I liked him. Not just as a potential boyfriend, but he was cool to be around. A friend—a comical friend.

*   *   *

~June 23, 1994~

Dear Diary,

Happy 12th Birthday, Jordan! We went to Grandma's house to celebrate. He seemed to have enjoyed his special day. Our number of cousins has almost doubled from a couple of years ago. There's so many kids running around, I can't keep count.

Derrick stopped yesterday and accidently left his pager at the house. I called his house phone after we came back from Grandma's.

"Hello?"

"Derrick. It's me, Tee."

"Hey girl."

"You left your pager at my house." There were voices in the background and laughter ringing through the phone. "Geez, that's loud," I said.

"Sorry, a couple of the fellas are over just hanging out. I've been looking for that damn thing all day."

"Well, I got it. I'll just hold onto it. Come and get it when you can but call first."

"All right, cutie," he said. "I'll see you tomorrow."

~June 29, 1994~

Dear Diary,

Still no word from Derrick, and I still have his pager. It seems like he's disappeared. No phone calls, and he hasn't been by or anything. This is odd and making me uneasy. Maybe he doesn't want to see me anymore, but he could've just told me. His pager stopped buzzing a couple of days ago. The battery died. I called his house phone again. No answer. No call back.

PART VII
Silent Cry

CHAPTER 18

DERRICK DIED OVER the summer.

According to the coroner, his body was found several days after he took his last breath. The police said he was shot once in the head. He lay dead on his back, in his bed, for days. His body was badly decomposed and left a lingering stench throughout his grandparent's house. Based on his position, and that he was home alone in the basement, they labeled it a suicide.

I was alone, in silence. Alone again. I'd never attended a funeral until then, and as I sat in the church observing his family and friends forced to accept a loss of life, it was beyond devastating. An abundance of heart-throbbing flashbacks pressed against my chest and made it hard to breathe, to think. How could someone be there one day and gone the next? Suicide? No way. What in the hell happened? He was a friend—a close friend. I knew death was a part of life; I just didn't expect for it to be a part of mine at that particular time. Not then, not yet. His face intermittently appeared in my dreams, and like a mirage it disappeared into thin air the moment I'd open my eyes. The presence of him felt so real until the light from my lamp revealed an empty room.

I didn't get to say goodbye, have one last hug, one last kiss, or the chance to hear him tell one more joke. He was gone, vanished. My mind cycled through rigorous levels of acceptance. As the days continued, the more perplexed I became. Although I constantly felt his presence, tragedy had crushed my heart. It was hard—way too hard. I never wanted to experience that. I wouldn't have wished it upon my worst enemy.

Everyone kept reiterating the importance of time—that only time would heal the wounds, the heartache. Occasionally, my days felt full of purpose. Nights were spent battling restlessly between my pillows. Reality shook me, woke me up. Once again, change had altered my life; whether I agreed or disagreed, I had no control over it.

I wanted to rewind to a time before Mom was sick, before Tori kept leaving, before Uncle Darren was diagnosed with HIV, before Grandpa moved out, before Mom and Dad split, before I lost my virginity, before Derrick died. I just wanted it back. Back where simplicity was double Dutch, tic-tac-toe, and Barbie tea parties. I just wanted it all back.

Derrick's passing made me ever-afraid of Mom dying. She needed a kidney. What would happen if she didn't get one? Death had never seemed more real than it did at that moment. I never thought it could touch my heart so deeply, but it did.

Rumors about Derrick floated through the town—gossip

at its worst and best, negative and positive. No one would ever know why. Many would speculate, judge, and criticize. It didn't matter. I would always hold his smile, his laugh, and his friendship close to my heart. A week after the funeral, two bullets were fired into my bedroom wall. The police came. I couldn't stop shaking. Perhaps a part of Derrick's life was a mystery—a tantalizing mystery that I was unaware of, but apparently someone thought I knew otherwise.

They wanted to rule his death a suicide, but after bullets flew through my bedroom wall, there was no way. Deep in my heart, it wasn't true. Someone killed him. He didn't kill himself. Mom couldn't fathom the menacing possibility of me potentially being in danger, so within two days, I flew on a plane for the first time to Houston, Texas, to Aunt Bernice's house for the rest of the summer. I didn't know Aunt Bernice. She had always been quite distant from the family, although back in the day she and Mom were two peas in a pod.

So, I spent the rest of the summer getting to know my aunt. She was unique, humorous, and unafraid to articulately express her points of view. I loved that about her. She wrote poetry, and we spent days talking about writing and the importance of an extensive vocabulary. I expressed my interest in writing poetry. She awakened my creativity and ignited the small flame of passion hidden behind my belly button waiting to be freed. She further emphasized how writing could be therapeutic, cathartic. It was like she'd sensed how much Derrick's death had shaken me. We talked about everything. She was a beautiful person, a lone wolf, and a pillar of knowledge. She truly cared, and she hugged me a lot. I needed that.

*   *   *

~September 17, 1994~

Dear Diary,

Happy birthday to me. I don't feel like celebrating at the moment. I'm just glad to be back home. I missed Mom, Jordan, and Sedrick terribly. Tori came by. I was happy to see her and have the opportunity to spend time with my nephew, Quentin. He's crawling now. So cute! Mom made a cake, and we went over to Grandma's house to blow out the candles.

When I returned from Houston, Mom had moved us into a different house. Given the potential danger, Grandpa insisted Mom move into a house he'd bought years before. So, we no longer lived in the same neighborhood. We had new neighbors and new surroundings. The atmosphere was different; this neighborhood was quite diverse. While our old neighborhood was predominantly black people, this one was not. It had big, beautiful Victorian homes with manicured yards. Something about it provided a sense of relief, of comfort. Maybe of safety.

Grandpa lived just a block away by himself. He'd occasionally bring us groceries, and although Mom insisted he didn't, he brought them anyway.

Mom cooked, and Jordan and I walked to take Grandpa a

plate of food. He was up in age and his semi-arthritic knees often made it difficult for him to stand for long periods of time. He shouldn't have been up attempting to cook, but Mom said Grandpa was as stubborn as a mule. He would do it anyway. He dared against all odds. Mom had the same strong-willed nature.

Although we had moved, I still attended the same high school. For some unforeseen reason, I assumed I could just get back into playing basketball without any physical conditioning. It was hideous. I gasped for air as my heart beat against my ribs like a stick to a drum. I even began to laugh at myself after a while, but I was persistent. I walked off the court like Scarecrow from *The Wizard of Oz* when he took his first steps. My lethargic body howled for water. I was worn out, empty, as if I'd urinated every ounce of liquid previously stored in my body. But I didn't quit, and nothing would prevent me from actually playing on the team.

*　*　*

~October 28, 1994~

Dear Diary,

Tori came over with the baby and they spent the night. She's pregnant again. I hope it's a girl. Too many boys running around here. Today is Mom's birthday. Her sparkling smile lighted the living room as we circled around her, dancing, while the music played loudly. Our boisterous laughter rang to the hilltops and tumbled back down.

~November 10, 1994~

Dear Diary,

Well, I believe I have underestimated myself, quite honestly. I thought I looked like a Harlem Globetrotter reject on the court during the open-gym session today. I guess the coaches saw something different because I made the basketball team. Mom gave me permission, as well. Coach pulled me to the side today. He thought my efforts during open gym and tryouts were impressive, and those were his words exactly. This gave me reassurance and the fortitude necessary to keep up throughout the season. I just have to focus on maintaining good grades.

~November 24, 1994~

Dear Diary,

Happy Thanksgiving! I believe I've grown beyond the big hoopla attached to holiday celebrations. I just wasn't in the mood. Everyone seemed to have enjoyed themselves. There were a multitude of babies running around everywhere.

After I ate, I sat next to Uncle Darren because he sat alone, in the corner, just staring at everyone. He has lost a tremendous amount of weight. His hair has become extremely fine and thinning on both sides. He rocked back and forth with a green blanket draped over his shoulders. Quivering uncontrollably, he tapped my hand and smiled. I grabbed his hand and smiled back. He doesn't talk much anymore, and his poised, dapper, fashion-suited strut is now a thing of the past. His slow shuffle often causes an imbalance as he leans on the sides of his house slippers.

I thank Mr. Nelson, my health class teacher from last year, for thoroughly explaining HIV and AIDS to me after I asked him a series of questions. How idiotic is it for people to treat Uncle Darren the way they do? If people would educate themselves about the disease, their ignorance wouldn't get the best of them. They aren't going to get HIV from touching him or by him breathing on them. The disease isn't airborne.

Usually, Mom and I had comprehensive discussions about the unexpected effects of lupus, but this conversation drew the curtain back and threw a spotlight on me. It almost felt like we were friends instead of mother and daughter. As I was on my way downstairs to get my pickle out of the fridge, Mom called me into her room. She scrambled to stack the newspapers from her bed into a pile and placed them onto the floor to make room for me to sit.

Oh damn, this isn't good. I haven't done anything. Calm down. Just be cool.

"I'd like to talk about you and Derrick for a minute." She leaned back on the bed, crossing her legs.

"Yes, ma'am." I inhaled a deep breath.

Why this? Why now?

"Were you sexually active with Derrick?"

Oh, my goodness. What in the world was this? She'd never

asked me about sex. Tori was usually the one who always gave me lectures and chastised me for even having thoughts about sex.

"No, ma'am." My armpits became sticky.

"Don't lie to me. Are you telling me the truth?"

"Yes, ma'am. That's the honest truth. I didn't want to, and he said he understood. So, we didn't."

"Well, are you a virgin? Be very careful how you respond. Don't lie."

Damn it, I didn't know what to do or how to respond. Part of me wanted to be honest, but my gut was shaking and shivering like a prisoner's if he was developing an escape plan. Out of all the questions in the world, she had to ask me that one. I didn't want to discuss this with her. I started to sweat through my pajamas.

"No, ma'am." I leaned back slightly just in case she decided to knock my ass out.

She didn't respond. She sat there quietly, staring deeply into my eyes. "So, you're telling me that you aren't a virgin?" Oh, my goodness, she was repeating herself. This was torture to an unknown degree. I was trying to be honest.

"No, ma'am. I'm not a virgin."

"Do you know what birth control is?"

"Yes, ma'am."

"How do you know about these things?"

My voice deepened into a sparing whisper. "I learned some from school, a bit from Tori, and some from the summer health classes with the drill team."

"So, you know what can happen, right? You recognize the possible consequences of your actions?"

"Yes, ma'am. Pregnancy and STDs."

"Do you need to be on birth control?"

"No, ma'am. I'm not having sex. It was stupid. I shouldn't have done it, and I don't want to do it again until I'm older."

"Well, okay. That's all I wanted to discuss with you. You can go to bed now."

Hell no. That went entirely too smoothly. She wasn't distraught, or shouting, and her head didn't rotate like the girl from *The Exorcist*. Nothing. As I eased out of her room safely, I scanned her face for clues. Something was brewing behind her serene eyes and unpersuasive smirk. She plotted, but for what?

I was in third-period chemistry when an office runner interrupted the class. He handed the teacher a note, then shouted my name. An excused slip from class was rare for me since I never had to report to the principal's office. I hesitated, and when I opened the office door and saw Mom's sly face . . . shit.

"Hey, Mom. What are you doing here?" I tried to hide my panic.

"Hey," she smiled. "I need you to come to the doctor with me, so I'm signing you out of school early today."

Oh, wow. I turned off the panic button and shifted into cruise control. "Did they find a kidney for you? Is there a match?"

"No, not yet." She flung her arm around my shoulders. Weird.

"Okay, so what's wrong?"

"Nothing's wrong, I hope, but stop with all the questions.

There will be plenty of questions to ask once we get there." She grinned.

It was just me and Mom, and the drive was short. Once we arrived, I sat skimming through various magazines assorted on a pine coffee table. There were pretty flowers and a small glass bowl filled with peppermint candy at the front desk.

I continued to thumb through a magazine, and eventually, I realized they were all magazines for pregnant women. My heart slammed. Say it ain't so. Was Mom pregnant again? I hadn't even seen Sam around lately, at least not staying the night. I investigated the room and speculated Mom's actions. The gold sign by the front desk said "Women's Health Gynecology." Mom sat next to me, waiting and waiting. It took forever, then a nurse opened the door.

"Talisa Brooks."

Wait. What? I sat very still.

The nurse called again. "Talisa Brooks? Is there a Talisa Brooks here?"

I looked at Mom. "Why's she calling my name?"

"Get up, grab your book bag, and come on." She grabbed me by the arm.

"What's going on? Why does she want to see me? I'm not sick!"

"Hush, girl, they will explain once we get in the exam room."

"Exam room? To examine what, Mom?" I was nervous, annoyed, and scared.

"Lower your voice, Talisa. Stop it. Calm down."

On the exam room's wall was a diagram of a woman's

reproductive system and shelved pamphlets about women's health, menstrual cycles, and breast examinations. Damn it. I knew the discussion last week was a setup, and now she wanted me to sit and talk to a complete stranger about my vagina. This was not cool.

"Okay, Talisa, do you know why you're here?" The nurse smiled.

"No, I don't." I looked over at Mom pointedly.

She hummed.

"Well, this is a routine procedure for women. Every woman has to have it done, especially sexually active women."

"But I'm not sexually active." The nursed looked at Mom.

"She's no longer a virgin. So, in my eyes she's active, whether it's now or in the past." Mom nodded at me. "Sit still, Talisa. Stop fidgeting."

"Okay, Talisa. Today, you'll have your first pap smear. I just need you to undress from the waist down," the nurse instructed.

"Umm, no, not okay. My first what? What's a pap smear? Mom, really?" I was becoming angry as the nurse continued to explain the procedure.

"Nope, I'm not doing that." I stood up to leave.

"Ms. Brooks, perhaps you two should take a minute or two to talk this over. I'll step out to see how long the doctor will be." The nurse left the room.

It was quiet for a couple seconds. "Talisa, listen. I need to know that everything is all right."

"But Mom, I told you everything is all right. I was protected. And now you want a complete stranger looking and touching my cooch. You're giving a complete stranger permission to see everything." I reached for the door, but Mom's face froze me in my tracks.

"Girl, you better sit back down. You decided to play grown-ass woman by opening your legs. So, this is what grown-ass women do. I just need to make sure that that so-called protection did what it was supposed to do—protect. Now, get undressed, wrap this sheet around you, and sit your ass on that table. Once the doctor comes to examine you, put your feet here and here." She pointed at the stirrups. "Now, take off your pants and panties, and don't even think about complaining."

"No, Mom. I'm not doing this. If you make me do this, I'm going to pee all over the table on purpose."

"First of all, that's nasty as hell and very un-ladylike. Second, you don't get to tell me what you are or aren't going to do. Get undressed, now!"

"Mom, please don't make me do this. I promise I won't do it again. If you're trying to teach me a lesson, I got it. Like for real, I got it."

"Yes, you will. Talisa, this is a good thing. You'll have to do this for the rest of your life. It's just part of being a woman. Usually, you wouldn't have to get a pap smear until you're older, but you've been active. It's not that I don't trust you, but these boys are the ones I don't trust. Everyone isn't as safe and clean as you may think." She took the bag off my shoulder. "Now, please. Get undressed."

It was an embarrassing experience.

Although Mom definitely bamboozled me, her intentions

were good. There were five babies in the daycare center at the high school, so I understood Mom's concern. Tori told me not to have sex and wait until I was married to have a baby. After watching Jordan and Sedrick and Quentin from time to time, I knew I could wait. Sedrick was two, and although he wasn't a crying, screaming baby, there was still a lot of work involved. Fixing bottles in the middle of the night, changing his diaper eighty times a day, teething tantrums, and toting him back and forth to Grandma's. Exhaustion at its highest peak. So, yes, I could wait.

CHAPTER 19

~December 24, 1994~

Dear Diary,

Dad and I talk a lot more these days. We even had the sex talk. He wasn't mad when I told him I wasn't a virgin, but he advised me on how to conduct myself in a different manner going forward. I'm trying to not harbor the past, although it's never going to fade away. I've learned to accept and settle for what's given, even if it's just a five-minute conversation. Sometimes, it's hard to not think about the what-ifs when I starve for him to be here more often.

I hold tightly to his every word because that's all he gives me. I yearn for him to love me the way I've always imagined, to hear him say that I'm special, that I'm beautiful. I've fallen in love with the idea of who I want him to be and devastated by what he actually is. I'm tired of hoping, I'm tired of wishing, and I'm tired of allowing my heart to beat so fast for a love I only occasionally receive. I want to love *him, and deep down, I do. I want to believe he loves me, too. I just don't know how to love someone who never truly shows their love for me. Words are just words. What's the true meaning of them without any action?*

THE OLDER I become, the more disinterested I am in the holidays. Grandpa and Grandma set the tone for these particular days. They called it family time. I had no gift requests. But Mom did buy me three new CDs by Brandy, Soul for Real, and Aaliyah. Jordan helped Sedrick open his gifts, and it was definitely a Kodak moment.

Mom seemed slightly pale to me, but because everyone seemed to be enjoying the day, I refrained from interrogating her. But I kept a close eye on her as she maneuvered through the house with the pace of a turtle. Maybe dialysis was really starting to take a toll on her again. She'd never looked so pale though. Sam came over and played with Sedrick. He noticed Mom's pale complexion and advised her to take it easy. I didn't think Mom and Sam were together anymore. I didn't know what happened, but he didn't spend the night at all. He just occasionally showed up.

Sedrick slept in my room a lot. He grabbed his blanket, his bear, and binky, and stumbled in my room like an old man with no balance. We played the tickle game where he pointed to a spot on his body and I tickled it until he was flushed. His sweet, infectious smile could brighten anyone's day. His laugh was the electrifying sound you wanted on instant replay. We started calling him Sedi, a funny little nickname.

I picked him up and went to see if Jordan was awake, which he was. I glanced across the hall. Mom was still in bed. She was usually up before the birds chirped in the morning, except for the days she wasn't feeling up to par. A pit formed in my stomach, and I turned on Mom's light. She appeared lifeless. She mumbled in between shortened breaths, and I couldn't understand a word she said.

"Mom, can you hear me? Mom?" I shook her.

Her eyes rolled backward, then Jordan ran in the room.

"What's wrong?"

I'd never seen her like that before. "I don't know."

"I'm going to call the ambulance." Jordan dashed across the room to the phone.

"No, wait."

"What do you mean wait? Look at her. Something's wrong." He climbed onto the bed. She was still mumbling.

"Call Sam, then take Sedi downstairs."

"I want to stay here. Come on."

"No, I don't want Sedi to see her like this. Now, call Sam and get downstairs. Make sure you unlock the front door."

Her delusional state made me frantically panic. I pulled the covers off of her, fanned her with newspapers, and struggled to open the window, hoping for a cool winter breeze. I lifted her up, sat behind her, and struggled to remove the robe she usually slept in. Her skin was boiling hot, and her body was limp. I used every muscle in my body to lift her and remove the robe. Her deadweight fell upon me, and my legs were stuck underneath her as her head fell on my shoulder. The mumbling continued.

I fanned her with an old newspaper from her nightstand. "Mom, it's okay. It'll be okay. Shhh."

I heard the door open and Sedrick screamed, "Daddy!"

I heard heavy footsteps rapidly run up the stairs.

"Talisa, what happened?" Sam was winded.

"I don't know. We woke up and she was like this. She's burning up, sweating all over, and she keeps mumbling, but I can't understand what she's saying."

Sam touched her arm and bent over to pick her up. "Grab her purse, her medication bag, and the blue folder next to the bed. Bring everything downstairs." With Mom in his arms, he speeded down the stairs repeating, "You'll be all right. Hang in there. You'll be okay." He put her in the car, came back to grab her things, and told me he would call. I shut the front door, and we stared out the window as he drove off. Jordan covered his face with his hands as he wept. Sedrick wrapped his little arms around my right leg.

He tapped my knee. "Can I go with Mama?"

I patted his little head. "Not this time, Sedi. Not this time."

Jordan lay down on the couch. I camped out on the bathroom floor waiting for Sedrick to use the training potty. I washed him up, put on a new Pull-Up, and put some animal crackers in a bowl and a little juice in his sippy cup. I turned the channel to the *Power Rangers*, and I laid him down on the other sofa and covered him with his blanket. Slowly, I walked back upstairs to my room, and I shut my door. I grabbed my pillow from my bed, went into my closet, shut the door, put the pillow to my face, and screamed. I couldn't stop crying. It hurt. Pieces of me were fading. How long would she be gone this time?

* * *

~*January 3, 1995*~

Dear Diary,

Mom's back home. An infection of some sort affected her entire body, nearly causing her to go into septic shock. After taking the prescribed antibiotics, her fever subsided, and her vitals are back to normal, or close to steady. Her sun-kissed complexion is starting to glow again.

~*January 10, 1995*~

Dear Diary,

Yay! Tori called today. She had a baby girl. About time we had a baby girl. This is a great feeling. I have a niece, and I can't wait to love all over her. Her name is Shanice. That's pretty. I'm so excited; I can't wait to see her. My report card came today. It's not disappointing, but it's not Harvard acceptable either. Let's see . . . an A in Current Events and Athletic Gym; B's in Algebra II, Accounting II, Spanish II, and C's in American History and Chemistry.

It was 5:07 a.m. when the phone started ringing a million times. I wondered who was calling so early in the morning. My alarm was set to go off in two hours, so I put my head under my pillow and prayed that Mom would answer it already. When it stopped, I curled back up into my blankets. There was a scream, and then another scream. I jumped up to open my door.

"Thank you, God. Thank you, God. Thank you, God." Mom was dancing in the hallway.

My first thought was yep, she has finally lost it. I knew it was only a matter of time. Of course, I didn't say that to her.

Instead, I asked, "Mom, what in the world are you doing?"

"There's a match for me. A kidney is finally available." She wrapped her arms around my neck.

We celebrated in the hallway, overjoyed by the news. We jumped up and down.

Jordan opened his door. "Why are y'all so happy so early in the morning? What's going on?"

"The hospital called and they have a kidney for Mom!"

Jordan joined us in a group hug.

"Sam's on his way to pick me up. I have to be there within four hours. You two go to school. Talisa, take the car, take Jordan to school, and be careful." She handed me the keys.

"What about Sedi?" I couldn't stop smiling at her.

"We're going to drop him off at your grandma's." She pranced back into her bedroom, and Jordan and I continued celebrating in amazement. Sedi peeked his little head around the corner and smiled at us. Jordan picked him up, placed him on his shoulders, and we sang "Oh Happy Day."

Jordan thought he was Tupac, and right in the middle of the song, he just started rapping. I guess he was just so excited, he lost control—and he was serious, too. Sam arrived, then he and

Mom left and took Sedrick with them. We blasted "Funkdafied" by Da Brat on repeat all the way to school. While I was driving, I did a double-take. Jordan's noticeably changing features had begun to show his entry into manhood. A thin layer of hair set upon his top lip. He was getting so tall and handsome, too. What a beautiful morning!

The next morning, we prepared to visit Mom. A kidney was what she needed. Now, things should turnaround for the better.

On the way to Iowa City, Sam and I talked about taking the ACT test, as if I didn't have enough to study for. The prep testing announcement was listed in the counselor's office. The counselor advised me go to the bookstore to buy an ACT guide and practice test book in order to see which areas I needed to study, practice, or prepare for. There was no waiting until the last minute.

Sam and I were so engaged in the ACT discussion, that time flew right on by and we arrived at the hospital quickly. The room was chilly, and Mom was wrapped in blankets like a cocoon. Her faint smile reset the mood as her eyelids occasionally closed, but she found her way through the blankets and held our hands. Her muttered speech made her sound disjointed. The sedation from the medication had her in a twilight zone, floating among the clouds. I picked Sedrick up so he could give her a kiss on the cheek for strength.

"Hey, Mom, how are you feeling?"

She answered, "Tired."

"Yeah, you look like you've had enough. You'll be back up and dancing soon." I patted her hand.

Jordan leaned over the bed and hugged and kissed her. She smiled. "What's on your lip?"

"What? There isn't anything on my lip."

I tittered. "She's talking about your peach fuzz, silly."

"The soon-to-be mustache, Jordan," Sam said. "Tell her it's your manhood coming in." Sam high-fived Jordan.

"Oh, Lord." Mom shook her head, smiling.

"Yeah, Mom, he's been looking in the mirror a lot. Isn't he too young to be getting a mustache?"

"No, he probably won't get a full mustache right now," Sam said, "but it's definitely on its way."

Jordan rubbed his chin and repeatedly touched his top lip and licked his lips. He leaned back and crossed his arms. "I'm smooth."

I looked at Mom. "He's going to be too much. You know that, right? Like, too much."

Mom smiled. "Yeah, he is. Leave my handsome son alone."

I was extremely grateful for this kidney, and Mom's overtiredness was only temporary. But at least she didn't have to have dialysis treatments anymore. We didn't stay long because she needed to rest.

I knew Mom had to get strong, healthier. But, I needed her home. I was so tired. I couldn't keep my eyes open long enough to properly function. Sedrick had a stomachache the previous night, so we spent the majority of the night lying on the bathroom floor. Although Sam was there, Sedrick still whined for me. I gave him some water with a pinch of baking soda. At first, he fought me, yelling "Nasty." He finally took a couple of sips, and after two hours, he finally went poop.

He immediately passed out on my chest afterwards, but I still couldn't sleep. I dozed off but immediately sprung up to make sure he was all right. He bounced up in the morning with tons of energy and in such a playful mood. I wasn't in the mood at all, but his silliness made me smile. Trying to dress him gave me a headache as he ran around like the Roadrunner from Looney Tunes cartoons. Sam was getting ready for work. Finally, Jordan caught Sedi, and he sat on Jordan's lap so still and quiet as Jordan put on his clothes. That kid.

Tori called. I told her about Mom.

"That's good," she said.

There was something about the tone of Tori's voice—it was reserved. She was usually very talkative and inquired with a hundred questions. But she was lax, silent, and detached, as if she wanted to say something but either couldn't or wouldn't. Still, I noticed. She called to ask if I would babysit the kids while she went out for a couple of hours over the weekend. My plate was already full, but since I hadn't seen my new niece, I told her yes.

* * *

~February 10, 1995~

Dear Diary,

Shanice is adorable. She's so tiny, with the cutest dimples when she smiles. It makes me want to kiss her all over her face. When Tori walked in the door, something about

her was different. We barely talked. She just dropped off
Quentin and Shanice and said she'd be back in a couple of
hours. I glanced at all of the babies. Sedrick is two, Quentin
is one, and Shanice is just a month old. Our house was full,
but Jordan helped out a lot. He really enjoyed both of the
boys, and they rolled plastic balls all over the floor. There
wasn't much packed in the diaper bag Tori dropped off—
only five diapers for Quentin and six newborn diapers for
Shanice, with three bottles and a can of formula.

Tori never showed up, nor did she call.

At first, I wasn't concerned. But as the day progressed, I
became nervous. I had no way of contacting her, and all I could
do was pray nothing had happened. I swear, she better not still
be out partying, either, I thought. There were only three diapers
and a half can of formula left in the bag. I paced in the kitchen
and trying to think of various possibilities. One thing was for
sure—I couldn't just leave them there with Jordan so I could go
look for her.

I scrambled through my school notes from the last semester,
and I found Erica's phone number. Erica was my older cousin—
absolutely beautiful, but many in the family called her the black
sheep, a lost soul.

I saw her about a month ago when I was walking home from
basketball practice. She was hanging out with some guys. She
was drunk or high or something, screaming, "Hey! My little
cousin, growing up so fast." She'd thrown her arms around me
and squeezed me firmly. She wrote her number down in my

notebook and told me to keep in touch and call her anytime. She might've known where Tori was. It was late afternoon and Tori still wasn't back.

I waited a couple more hours. The sun was setting; there were only two diapers left, and no more formula for Shanice. So, I called Erica, but she didn't answer. I waited thirty more minutes. Called again.

"Hello?" She sounded like she was asleep.

"Erica, this is Talisa."

"Hey, Cousin. How are you?"

"I'm all right. Have you seen Tori?"

"No. No, I haven't. Why? What's wrong?"

"She asked me to babysit last night for a couple of hours. She never came back to pick them up. I'm running out of diapers, and there's no more formula for the new baby."

"Wait, she had another baby?" She sounded completely clueless.

"Yeah, a baby girl. Her name is Shanice."

"Oh, that's a cute name. She's foul for leaving you with them like that. I'll go get you some diapers and formula."

"Okay, thank you so much."

"Do you know what size diapers?"

"No, Quentin is one, and Shanice is a month old. Does that help?"

"I'll figure it out. I'll be there in a little while, okay?"

"Okay, thank you again, Cousin. See you in a bit." I was relieved because I didn't know what else I was going to do.

When Erica came, she brought the formula, diapers, and a

pizza for us—a total savior. She stayed for a little while and then said she was going to look for Tori.

*   *   *

~February 13, 1995~

Dear Diary,

I couldn't go to school today because Tori still isn't back. After bathing Sedrick and Quentin, they instantly fell asleep, which gave me a short break from the madness. Shanice only cries when she's wet or hungry, but oh boy, was she blessed with a set of lungs. It's a big difference from when Sedrick and Quentin were first born. Jordan is pretty self-sufficient now, so I don't have to do much for him anymore. He's twelve, about to turn thirteen, so that's helpful.

CHAPTER 20

EVERYONE WAS ASLEEP before 10:00 p.m. All of the babies lay in my bed as I stretched out on the floor. As soon as I closed my eyes, I heard banging on the front door. It startled me. Everyone was sound asleep. I tiptoed down the stairs and grabbed the wooden stick next to the back door. The banging started again. As I walked through the house, I felt my body wanting to scatter into frantic pieces. I trembled from head to toe.

"Talisa. Talisa. Open the damn door." Yelling and laughter projected from the other side of the door.

"Tori, is that you?"

The voice was muffled. "Yes, it's me. Open the door."

When I opened the door, she stood unbalanced and some guy stood behind her, grinning at me.

"Where in the hell have you been?"

"Uh-oh. Don't whip me, Mama. You should see your face right now."

"Are you drunk? I'm glad you think this is so funny, Tori.

You left me here without enough formula or diapers. I couldn't go to school today!"

"Move, let us in. Come on now. Move out the way. We need to lie down for little while." She waved her hands for me to move out of the way.

I was burning like a blowtorch. "Umm, what do you mean 'we'? He isn't coming in here."

"Talisa, cut it out. Move out of the way!" She yelled louder and louder.

"Get in here." I grabbed her by the arm and pulled her in the house. "Excuse us. I need to talk to her alone." I slammed the door in his face.

"What's your problem? Where have you been?" There was my heart again, beating faster than ever as my level of annoyance increased.

"He is so fine, ain't he?" She smiled and giggled without a care in the world.

"Are you serious right now? You think I'm joking with you right now? Are you listening to me, Tori? What the hell?"

She yanked her arm away from me. "Damn, Talisa. Just let him in." She reached for the doorknob.

"Hell no. I don't know him, and he isn't coming in here, Tori." I blocked the door so she couldn't open it, and I heard him walk away. Tori glared at me.

"Damn, you get on my fuckin' nerves. Always got to be the good girl, damn. Mama's girl." She stormed into the kitchen.

I walked upstairs to check on Jordan and the babies, and surprisingly, after all the yelling, everyone remained asleep. But then, I heard Tori talking to someone. I ran back downstairs to see if she let the guy in the house, but instead she was talking on the phone.

"She's your favorite. Stop lying. You never wanted me, did you?" She paced back and forth with her hand on her hips as she screamed through the phone. "I just wanted it to stop, Mom."

What was she talking about? I hurried to the kitchen and snatched the phone out of her hand.

"Mom, it's okay. Everything's all right. You can go back to sleep." I hung up and Tori pushed me into the wall. My head hit the clock next to the microwave. I fell to the floor and the phone cord came completely out of the wall jack. The phone rang. As I tried to stand up I became dizzy, and heaviness arrested my legs. I staggered into the living room to answer the other phone.

"Mom?" I was breathless.

"No, this is Dr. Kirkland at the University of Iowa Medical Center. Is everything all right? Your mom is pretty upset here in the ICU, crying and demanding that someone call you. Are you in danger?" He paused.

"No, sir, I'm fine. My sister was just upset about something, but it's all right now. Please tell my mom that everything is fine."

I hung up the phone, and when I turned around, Tori was standing in front of me, her face full of fire, damn near infuriated. We stood face-to-face. Her eyes were bloodshot, glazed with a yellowish tint. She shoved me again, but this time she drew a butcher knife with her right hand and pressed the blade against my neck. The cold stainless steel sent spurts of frigid chills through my veins. With my back against the wall, I couldn't move. The harder she pressed, the more my speech was impaired as I grew frightened by the blade puncturing my skin. I inched up the wall, hoping to decrease the pressure, but I couldn't move up any further.

"You're not perfect, schoolgirl." She gritted her teeth.

"Tori . . . please . . . stop it. What's wrong with you?"

Tears floated in my eyes, blurring my vision. Tori laughed hysterically. She was a fighter. I'd heard rumors of Tori fighting in the streets. She was notorious for standing her ground at all costs. We'd argued before, as sisters do, and Tori used to tease and taunt me when we were younger, but never anything of this magnitude.

"Tori, let me go. Please."

"Shut up, you damn cry baby." She took a step back and giggled again.

I kicked her in the stomach and yelled, "You're crazy! Fuckin' crazy!"

She bent over and gasped for air as she continued to wheeze, "I'm going to beat your ass!" She raised her arm with the knife in her hand and charged at me.

Fight or flight kicked in, and without any hesitation, I unlocked the front door and ran in the snow all the way to Grandma's house. I kept looking over my shoulder to see if she was behind me, but she wasn't.

I banged on the door until Aunt Nita finally opened it. "Talisa, what are you doing? Where are your shoes? Your coat?"

I was distraught, crying my eyes out. "Can you come to the house? Tori's trying to kill me or something . . . she came at me with a knife . . . the kids are still there."

"Oh, shit, come on. Get in here. Put on these shoes, this coat." Aunt Nita grabbed her keys, and she and I and Grandma went back to the house. My hands shook as we all rushed inside.

"Talisa, where are all the kids?" Aunt Nita looked at me.

"They're upstairs sleeping."

I didn't mean to leave them; I had just reacted, captured by fear. Aunt Nita kept trying to get the knife out of Tori's hand. Tori swung each time, and actually cut the sleeve of Aunt Nita's coat. Tori kept her eyes on me and attempted to reach around Aunt Nita. Grandma's abrasive approach did not faze her, and Tori was uncontrollable and wouldn't stop.

Jordan ran down the stairs, yelling, "Tori, stop it!"

She ran toward me with the knife again.

It happened so fast. She flung the knife, and a flash of the blade shined in my left eye. I ducked, and it went whizzing into the wall with a thud. Shaken, I stood up and realized that it hadn't hit me, but she seriously had just tried to kill me. Inflamed, I pushed her to the floor, got on top of her, and I hit her, and hit her, and hit her. I don't know what came over me.

"You always mess everything up. Always making Mom cry!" I screamed. Aunt Nita started yelling at Tori like never before, and shortly after, the police arrived.

The police pulled me off of her and pushed me into a corner of the room. They picked Tori up and handcuffed her. We locked eyes. Things were out of control. Something was terribly wrong with her. We'd never fought like that before. Never. Not like that. What had happened? Did Tori secretly hate me?

My mind spun like a looping rollercoaster, thinking of what I could have possibly done to upset her, but there was nothing. I didn't do anything. What was she talking about on the phone with Mom? Deep down, I didn't want to fight her. I just sat in the corner crying. Aunt Nita kneeled down and patted me on the head.

"I didn't want to hit her. I promise I didn't. But she just wouldn't stop." My heart was aching.

"You had to defend yourself. I'm sorry it had to be from your own sister. But it is what it is. Now, she just got a dose of her own medicine. Stand up and quit crying." So, I did.

Tori was released the next day, and she picked up the kids from Grandma's house. With no communication between us at all, I sat in my room starving for answers only she could provide.

The whole incident continually replayed in my mind. I wanted to apologize for hitting her. I wanted to just sit and talk about it. Everything was chaotically infused by what? For what reason? I racked my brain searching for answers, but with no indication as to why. The repression of everything increased my vulnerability, leaving me a castaway deserted on an island with no survival kit. I briefly talked to Mom, and she said she would be home in a week or two. I omitted the fight from our conversation because I didn't want to break her heart. It definitely would've torn her to pieces.

*   *   *

~February 26, 1995~

Dear Diary,

This is a horrendous feeling. I didn't want to fight with Tori, and I damn sure didn't want to hit her. She just was so persistent. What was going on? Why did this have to happen? I love my sister; I swear do. But right now, I don't understand her, and maybe I never truly did. Based on her actions, I'm lost. I know she and Mom have their differences, and at times I just want Tori to calm down. She's hurt, but I don't know by what or who or how.

The day began peacefully. I was home alone, and Jordan spent the day fishing with Eric. Sam took Sedrick for the weekend, so I studied for the majority of the day and reviewed some class notes. After a while, my head drooped as sleepiness defeated me.

The phone rang. It was Nelson, a classmate from my chemistry class, and he was a part of my study group. He had been absent all week and wanted to copy my notes. He asked if he could come over. Nelson was a loner and wasn't talkative, but I would always talk to him. He seemed so shy. He came by, and it didn't take long for him to copy the notes.

"Where are your parents?"

"My mom's in the hospital."

"Oh no. What happened?"

"She was diagnosed with lupus years ago, and it's been one challenge after another ever since."

"Lupus. What's lupus?"

"It's a disease that causes your body to fight against itself. As for my mom, it affects her internal organs badly. But she said there are other types, too. It affects people in different ways."

"Oh, I'm sorry. That sounds like it sucks."

"You have no idea."

He touched my hand. It was weird. "So, you stay here by yourself?"

"Yeah, pretty much. But I have two little brothers. They just aren't here now. They'll be back."

We sat in the living room watching rerun episodes of *The Fresh Prince*. My eyes were heavy. Drowsiness held me up against the ropes, and with a one-two punch . . . I dozed off.

The next moment I recalled, a coldness touched my stomach, and I opened my eyes. Nelson's hand was under my shirt. He abruptly kissed me, and I pulled back, pushing him away. When I resisted, he climbed on top of me, and I squirmed.

"Get off of me. What's wrong with you?" I shrieked and tried to push him off.

But he was stronger. He grabbed both of my wrists and pinned them over my head. I kicked and kicked and kicked.

I pleaded and begged him to stop. "Please, get off of me."

He forcefully continued to touch me and kiss my neck. My hands were bound by his strength as he held them above my head with one of his hands. He slid the other hand into my shorts, into my panties, into my vagina. He didn't speak—not one word. He took his hand out of my shorts and licked his fingers. I started to cry as he yanked down my shorts. I wiggled to break free, and I tried to pull my shorts up, but he pushed me back down. He pulled a condom out of his pocket and held it in his mouth, attempting to tear it open. I slid off the couch, and I placed my hands on the floor, trying to crawl away, to run. He unbuttoned his pants, grabbed my ankle, and yanked me back closer to him. He forced me onto my back and pinned me down again.

I cried and cried. "Please, Nelson. Stop, please. I won't tell anyone if you just stop, please."

No matter how many times I begged, he ignored my cries, my screams and pleas. His hypnotic glare paralyzed me as he forced himself in between my legs and pinned my hands above my head again. His thighs were muscular, and his penis was fully erect. Blatantly, he pushed himself into my body. The latex of the condom tore at my vagina, and I dissolved into my own tears—panting. It hurt—it hurt so badly. I yelled at the top of my lungs, praying someone would hear me, but no one did. And no one came.

His breath got hotter and hotter on the side of my neck until he collapsed on top of me. After he finished, he didn't speak.

I curled into a fetal position as he ran to grab his books from the dining room table. He darted out the door. I managed to run to the door to lock it and then fell to the floor in tears. Why did he do that? He seemed so nice. I cried until I vomited on the kitchen floor. I fell to my knees and cried even more. I wanted to call Tori, but I had no way to contact her. I wanted to call Mom, but I couldn't. I shouldn't have let him in. I shouldn't have told him he could come over. I felt so stupid and embarrassed.

After I took a shower, I sat in the corner of my room and squeezed my pillow, screaming, crying. A knock on the door imprisoned me, holding me hostage in my own bedroom. I was unable to move and captured by the mental picture of his cold, devilish eyes staring into mine. I froze as the banging on the door became louder and louder.

"Talisa. Talisa. Unlock the door. It's me, Jordan." I jumped up, ran to the door, and tried to wipe away my tears. There was a throbbing ache between my legs that silently screamed for help.

"What's wrong, Sis?" Jordan set his fishing pole against the wall.

I struggled to hold back my tears, and I threw myself in his arms.

"Sis, you're scaring me. What's wrong? Why's the living room so messed up?" He hugged me tightly and patted my back. He was my little brother. I couldn't tell him. I couldn't say the words. He just held me in his arms.

"Tee, whatever it is, it'll be okay. Just tell me," he repeated.

I just couldn't find the words. I felt nasty and disgusting. I was ashamed and afraid Jordan would look at me differently. Maybe everyone would. Why did it happen? Why did Nelson do it?

* * *

~*March 5, 1995*~

Dear Diary,

I lay in bed all day, listening to music, staring at the ceiling. I was numb. Jordan kept coming into my room periodically, asking me what was wrong. I couldn't tell him. I was ashamed, so ashamed. How could Nelson just take what he wanted? Why did he think it was okay? I kept screaming over and over again for him to stop. I said no, and he didn't stop. I couldn't go back to school because what if he'd told? What if everyone knew? Who would believe me if I told? As it replayed over and over again in my mind, I felt more and more defeated. I just couldn't break loose. He was just too strong. Did he think I was easy? Did he think I was a whore? Why? Why? Why?

~*March 7, 1995*~

Dear Diary,

I didn't go to school yesterday or today. I feel so defenseless. Nelson stole something from inside of me. Pieces of me that I can't get back, damn it. I want to know why. The look in his eyes flashed self-satisfaction as his penis thrashed in between my thighs while I screamed. While I drowned in my own tears, he smirked as if it were pleasurable to him. I know I can't hide forever. I can't run away. I went in

Mom's room and grabbed her Bible off of the nightstand.
I wrapped it in my arms like a shield. I slept all day.

~March 9, 1995~

Dear Diary,

I skipped chemistry class all week. I feel like such a coward hiding like this, but I can't face him. I was intimidated. Why didn't I fight harder? This is my fault, but I don't know what to do about it. I shouldn't have given him permission to come over. That's why I can't tell anyone. Who would believe me? I didn't handle it right. I should never have let him in. I thought he was a nice person. I wish I didn't feel so sick to my stomach. I'm so stupid. I just didn't think he was like that. Perhaps Tori was right—men just take what they want.

It had been over a week. Mom seemed to be slightly back to being herself. She'd been playing music all day, singing and cleaning up, rearranging the furniture, and dancing around the living room with Sedrick. I wanted to be happy, but I was still trying to hold back my tears.

When I walked through the school hallways, I tried avoid Nelson at all costs. If I could dissipate into thin air and be whisked away by the wind, I would've flown high beyond the clouds. Where no one could find me. Later, I sat in my room just listening to music.

Mom opened my door. "Talisa, didn't you hear me calling you?" Her hands were on her hips.

"No, ma'am. I didn't. I had my headphones on."

"What's going on with you? You've been cooped up in this room since I've been home. You need to get up. Come downstairs with us." She started dancing around, and I tried to smile. I couldn't tell her. I wanted to, but she was so happy for once. I didn't want to ruin that for her.

"Okay, I'll come."

"Well, stop looking so down. Get up." She tickled my feet, and reluctantly, I giggled. "Are you ready for the spring break trip?"

"Do I still have go?"

"Umm, yes you do. I paid money for you to go. So yes, you're going. What's going on with you? Why don't you want to go all of a sudden?" She narrowed her eyes at me.

"I don't know. I just think I need to study more and get ready for the track season."

She sat on the edge of my bed. "You like this program. You were excited about being a part of the program. Now you don't want to go? Talisa, what's going on?"

"Mom." I almost told her. Almost. But then . . . I couldn't. I couldn't tell her about my stupidity.

"Yes, what?" she urged. I sighed and devoured my words.

"Nothing. I'm just tired."

Mom stared at me for a long time, then grabbed my foot and wiggled it side to side. "Well, whatever it is, this too shall pass. Nothing lasts forever."

"Yes, ma'am."

"Just make sure you come downstairs to get something to

eat. Now that you're finally picking up some weight, you might want to keep it." She stood in the doorway, staring, and then winked.

I knew her intuition was tugging away behind her smile and that she knew I wasn't telling the truth. But for some reason she didn't press the issue. I lay back in my bed, trying to convince myself that the spring trip just might be what I needed.

*   *   *

~March 28, 1995~

Dear Diary,

Oh, my goodness. The spring break trip was the best ever. We visited several HBCUs. Hands down the best time ever. It was completely inspirational and walking through the Dudley Beauty Corporation building made me feel like I could have my own business one day, too. It's a corporation that manufactures, produces, and distributes hair care and personal care cosmetics. There were black people throughout the business, from administrative assistants to the president of the company.

I have never seen anything like this—especially not back home. This was real, and it was black people just like all of us. History has recorded the limitations and restrictions placed upon black people due to racism and prejudice, but I have just witnessed accomplished, professional, and educated black people. An entire business. It's made me realize that anything is possible. This was truly amazing.

So thankful for Mr. & Mrs. Ramsey for giving us this positive experience.

I had a panic attack, or anxiety, or something, along with shivering chills and a boiling, heat-coiled fever. I gushed sweat everywhere. After leaving my second-period class, I went to my locker to grab my notebooks for the next class. A lot of people knew my locker combination. We shared lockers sometimes— just the girls from the basketball and track teams. It made it easier to get to classes without carrying a ton of books to different floors. I stood on my tippy-toes to look in the back of the locker when I felt someone standing behind me.

He whispered in my ear, "I will never forget how you smell, how you taste." Nelson licked my ear lobe, then walked away.

I jetted to the bathroom. The hall monitor followed me, called my name, and knocked on the bathroom stall.

"Talisa, are you all right?"

I cleared my throat and took a deep breath. "I'm fine. I just don't feel good. I feel like I'm going to throw up."

"Well, let's go to the nurse's office. Come on out."

They called Mom, and when she came, the nurse and hall monitor asked to speak with her privately. I don't know what was said, but Mom kneeled down in front of me. "Talisa, what's wrong?"

My eyes watered. I wanted to tell her, I swear, but I just didn't know how or if she would even believe me, so I lied again. "Nothing, Mom. I'm just cramping, and my stomach hurts like never before. Can I just go home?"

Mom's astonished look made my stomachache filled with guilt. I shouldn't have lied to her. She examined my whole demeanor and her eyes squinted doubtfully. "All right; come on. Let's go."

*   *   *

~April 10, 1995~

Dear Diary,

God, if you are there, please help me! Please take this pain away, please! Why did you let Nelson do this to me? Why? Please help me to understand. Just help me.

~April 20, 1995~

Dear Diary,

Mom and I had a deep discussion about her transplant experience. It was very informative and shocking. It's amazing how people's organs can function in another person's body. I guess science isn't so bad after all. No more leg cramping in the middle of the night, no more fevers, leg swelling, dialysis, absolutely nothing anymore.

"Where did the hospital get the kidney from?"

"It came from a little girl. She was just twelve years old. Unfortunately, she died in a car accident."

"Oh, that's really sad. I don't know how to feel. On one hand, I'm happy you finally have a kidney. On the other, a little girl had to die in order for you to get it."

Holding her hands in a prayer position, Mama replied, "I'm just so thankful, but I have been praying for the little girl's family. I'm sure it has to be very hard. I wouldn't know what to do if I ever lost any of you."

"I'm sure."

"I pray for all of you. Tori, too." She placed her hand on her heart.

"Yeah." I was definitely not going to bring up the fight between Tori and me, and of course, I hadn't heard from Tori since. "So, how do you feel now? Does it feel weird knowing that someone else's kidney is in your body?"

"No, it doesn't feel weird or anything. I started crying when I was finally able to go to the bathroom by myself. No medicine, no dialysis treatment. I'm just so grateful."

*   *   *

~May 1, 1995~

Dear Diary,

Okay, breathe. You can do this. Today, I actually attended my chemistry class, and it was terrifying. Deep down, I wanted to show Nelson I wasn't afraid of him, but once he walked in the classroom, my hands became clammy. I was glued to my seat, my breathing was irregular, and my mouth felt like I was chewing a cotton ball. He sat one row over to my right, three seats ahead of me. Before the bell rang to dismiss class, he turned and winked at me. Powerless. I peed on myself. Mr. Shepherd came over to me, wondering why I was still sitting after the bell had rung. My eyes flooded over because of the humiliation. "I used the bathroom on myself," I told him.

Mr. Shepherd gave me one of the lab coats and an excuse slip for the next period. I went to the nurse's office then walked home to change my clothes.

~May 16, 1995~

Dear Diary,

The end of the track season. The last meet was held today, but many, including me, are off to super-sectionals this coming weekend. Although everything seems to have turned around for the better, deep down I'm still disappointed in myself. I try to block the scene of Nelson on top of me, but it seems like a never-ending battle. I just want to extract the image from my brain. I've been practicing on praying more, seeking to understand my own actions, as well as the actions of others. I haven't been reading the Bible, but over the summer I would like to read more, to grasp a better understanding of how and what to apply to my life to make it better overall.

~May 20, 1995~

Dear Diary,

Well, I think I did the best I could. I placed fourth in the sectional track meet in shot put, finishing at 33'9 ¾ feet.

The girls were like giants, body types like football players. But I tried. My season best is 34 ½ feet in shot put and 80'11 feet in the discus. Overall, it was a good season.

~May 27, 1995~

Dear Diary,

Memorial Day! I'm going to be a senior in the fall. Am I going to college? Which college? How do I apply? Did I take the right classes for college? I know I have to study, do more ACT practice tests, and take the test again. I scored a seventeen on the school's prep practice test, I heard the higher the score, the better chances of getting into college. I would love to go to a HBCU. I'll try to see if I can talk to Mr. Ramsey this week before the school year is over.

~June 2, 1995~

Dear Diary,

I received my grades today, and damn, I'm so disappointed in myself. Skipping so many chemistry classes hurt my GPA. Taking the final exam was a waste of time. I wasn't prepared, either. The teacher never even called Mom, nor did my counselor. I received a D in Chemistry this semester, an A in Athlete Gym, which I believe is just given to all athletes participating in a sport at the school. As for the remaining five classes, all C's. Now my GPA has dropped to a 2.6 from last semester. I needed to maintain at least a 3.0, but I couldn't concentrate this semester.

The past has become a mental thunderstorm full of nonstop flickering images in my mind. I am subconsciously conquered by my own thoughts. Ugh.

PART VIII

Picking Up The Pieces

CHAPTER 21

NO HOSPITALIZATION, NO aches, no pains, no complications, and no lupus flare-ups at all over the summer. It seemed like the perceived notions projected by the doctors and researchers were a bit inaccurate. Mom and Sedrick were both currently in good health. The kidney transplant was a success, her mood swings had decreased, and her energy levels increased.

Tori visited from time to time, and she was expecting her third child in December. We talked. Not like before, but at least we were able to laugh during our conversations. We never spoke of the fight—not even to Mom. The summer went by entirely too fast. I found myself sitting on the front porch trying to accept the fact that in exactly four days, I was going to be a senior. What was I going to do?

As cluttered thoughts played tug-of-war with the left and right sides of my brain, an overwhelming feeling of pressure made me queasy. I had no plans, no path, and no direction to journey into. In less than a month, I was going to be eighteen years old. Legal. It felt like I was broken into tiny pieces and stirred in a pot of complexity with a pinch of purposelessness. Vastly nervous.

I had the opportunity to speak with Mr. Ramsey regarding future plans, my class schedule for the year, and how to build a work ethic. My summer goal was to get a job. I was hired in June as a cashier for Hardee's fast food restaurant making minimum wage at $5.45 an hour. What was my life's plan? With graduation skating around the corner at an accelerating pace and the hourglass running out of sand, I needed a plan, immediately. What that plan was—no idea.

When I looked around, I saw exactly what I *didn't* want, and I *didn't* want to be trapped in a small town. My mind drew images that were beyond my wildest dreams, my heart craved for substances of success, and my feet pitter-pattered to their own beat. I was determined to obtain more and strive to be the best me. The best me ever. The rerun episodes of *A Different World* kept me inspired. I had to be so much more than what society believed I should be; a fallen statistic, society viewed young black females as lazy women collecting welfare and having baby after baby.

I didn't want that.

Why couldn't we be smart, educated, and talented? Why was there such a negative connotation attached to our skin color? Over the summer, I indulged in various books of the Bible, and it was a difficult read, certainly not like reading an actual novel. The previous years had taught me a great deal; learning to cope with situations and circumstances beyond my control was strenuous, especially when the unexpected rose to the occasion. Learning how to deal with adversity was challenging. Prayer seemed to help, although memories echoed in my chest from time to time, and my soul still starved for real happiness.

Derrick's smile would always be engraved in my mind and heart; the memories were invaluable. Over the past four years, five classmates had died. Each time my heart would break; they were so young. No one tells you during childhood about the things life will toss your way, turning fantasy into folly. Damn adults should speak the truth already—at least that way we would be prepared.

A month before, I sat in the park up the street, persuading the voice in my head that I wasn't a victim.

IT WAS NOT MY FAULT.

I shouldn't have been embarrassed over his actions. Nelson was wrong. Not me. I bottled his hostile behavior and placed shame upon myself. I didn't want to be a victim, nor did I want anyone to pity me.

Senior year! Everyone was ecstatic and wandering sketchily through the halls. The charismatic, contagious energy drifted through the air. Senior classmen cheered and chanted, "The class of 1996 is here!"

My entire class was a multitude of individual brilliantness. We were close, like a family in a way. I had two reasons for attending school: one, to receive an education, and two, to escape my own thoughts. I surrounded myself with friends to fill the void of being alone because, in the past, home had felt lonely. I was thankful for the friends I did have and for those who loved to just laugh with me. Our school pride was infinite; we were diverse, we were captivating, and we were ready to perpetuate our gifts into the world.

*   *   *

~September 17, 1995~

Dear Diary,

I don't want to grow up, but I'm too old to be a Toy-R-Us kid. Sigh. Happy eighteenth birthday to me! No party this year. I had to work, but Mom still made me a cake, and some family members came over to celebrate. This semester I only have four classes: Literature and Composition, Federal Government, Consumer Economics, and Trigonometry. I was eligible for the work-study program at the beginning of the school year, so I attend school the first half of the day and work the rest. The program restricts the number of hours students can work per week. Twenty hours is the max. I don't plan on playing basketball this year. I'm over it. Tired of trying. Besides, it's just too late for me. However, I will definitely be participating in track and field in the spring.

Everyone was ranting and raving about homecoming. Because it was senior year, I told myself I would attend every dance, event, and school function. But I was tired. While sitting in second period, the principal's voice blared through the intercom.

"Good morning, students and staff. The results for the

homecoming court have been calculated. The candidates for this year's homecoming court are...."

My head fell down on the desk as I hoped to sneak in a quick nap. Every year it was the same types of people nominated: the top athletes, the perkiest cheerleader, Mr. or Mrs. Popularity. When he finished reading the nominations for the boys, he continued on to the girls, reading two female names and then ... mine.

Wait.

What the hell?

I popped my head up. The entire class was jumping and surrounded me with glee. Everyone was so excited—even my teacher. This was crazy, and I was struck with amazement.

After the bell rang, the hallways were swamped with cheerfulness and praise. *What? Me?* Sharae and Leslie were elated and jumped up and down at my locker. How did this happen? There must've been a calculation error. Homecoming court? It couldn't be. As I walked the hallways, I was still perplexed by the announcement, but internally jubilant. The senior class elects who would become king and queen would be announced at the homecoming ceremony on Friday, the same day as the homecoming football game and parade. This was just way too much!

I walked home from school in shock, and Mom was gone. I rushed to change into my work uniform and sat on the front porch. She usually dropped me off at work, and within five minutes, she pulled up and honked the horn. She jumped out.

"Is it true?"

"Is what true? Why are you smiling like Ronald McDonald?" I tried to be nonchalant.

"Shut up. Stop cracking jokes. I heard the little girl at the grocery store tell the cashier you were selected as one of the nominees for homecoming queen." She crossed her arms, tapping her fingers on her right bicep.

I shook my head. "So, what you're saying is, you were ear hustling, Mom?"

She giggled. "Hush, girl. So, it's true?"

"Umm, I don't know what you're talking about."

She walked around the car and pinched my arm. "Talisa Lynn Brooks, if you don't confirm the gossip I just heard right now—"

I burst into laughter. "Whoa, did you just call me by my government name? It's just gossip, Mom." I reached for the car door handle.

Her peering eyes were fastened to my face as she walked to get back in the car. She had intense suspicion written all over her, so I had to tell her.

"Okay, okay, okay. It was me."

She yelled, "All right now. That's my girl! Yay!" She hugged me, bouncing up and down, rocking me back and forth.

"Mom, really?"

"Why aren't you excited? Is something wrong? Did someone say something to you?" She put her hands back on her hips.

"No ma'am. I'm just shocked, that's all. I'm not one of the popular kids. No big-time athlete or anything."

We got in the car and started to drive off.

"What makes you think you have to be labeled to be noticed?" Her nostrils flared.

"I know a lot of people. Of course, I'm cool with everyone. Hearing my name announced over the intercom . . . it was surprising. Students in the hallways yelling my name, hugging me, giving me praise. I don't know what I did to get nominated. Teachers were high-fiving me, Mom. It was bananas."

She drove two blocks and pulled the car over. "Listen. You're a good person with a good heart. You have a great personality, character, charisma, and a beautiful smile."

"No, I don't."

"You don't what?"

"Have a beautiful smile."

"Why would you say that? Yes, you do."

"I have a gap in my teeth. It's ugly."

"Talisa, no it's not. It's part of you. It makes you different. Special. Kevin liked it. Derrick liked it. Beauty is in the eye of the beholder."

"Well, if you say so."

She stared out the window. "Well, you are. Inside and out. And don't you let anyone tell you any different. You hear me?"

"Yes, ma'am." I flashed a smile at her as she began to drive.

"You're funny. Girl, you have more jokes than I care to hear sometimes. But, that's what makes you, you . . . and people see that. People know. They just may not always tell you."

"So, you don't like my jokes?"

"Out of everything I just said, you ask me about some jokes. Hush, get out, get to work. Don't forget my box of chicken when you get off."

"See, I knew you were warming me up for something. You created this whole *Lifetime* movie scene in the car for some chicken. You're not slick, Mom."

She chuckled and gave me a thumb's up as I walked away. Hardee's did make some tasty, lip-licking fried chicken.

*   *   *

~September 22, 1995~

Dear Diary,

I just can't believe it? I can't believe this has happened! I won homecoming queen for the class of 1996. Can you believe it? From the crowd of students in the bleachers, to my classmates standing beside me, everything was incredible. I will never forget this day! I brought Jordan with me to the football game. He's getting older, taller, and I like hanging out with him. All the girls are eyeing him already. He's only in eighth grade, and this facial hair is drawing a lot of attention. The high school girls are constantly complimenting and overfilling his cup with flirtatious comments. This is not sitting well with me at all. AT ALL. Even still, winning was amazing. I put my tiara on my dresser, and sometimes, I catch myself looking at it. It stands for something more than simply winning. It stands for possibilities.

~October 28, 1995~

Dear Diary,

Happy birthday, Mom! We danced and the music filled every room throughout the house. The cake from the grocery store bakery was decoratively beautiful. She enjoyed every minute. I bought Mom flowers and Turtles chocolate candy. Minimum wage doesn't mean I'm rolling in dough. I barely had enough money to buy her a gift—I just wanted to see her smile. And she did.

Tori came by with the babies. She's so funny and back to being her witty self, but she drifts away at times. Our laughter continued through the evening and I guess the past has become just that—the past. But there's something skeptical hidden behind her smile, and although she tucks it away, it surfaces periodically. I still don't know what happened or what even caused us to fight in the first place. I just want us to be sisters, best friends. I'm willing to let bygones be bygones, but we should address the underlying incident face to face. When she comes around . . . well, she avoids me sometimes. We continue to laugh. I don't know what drove us to such a crossroads, but we're sisters. Love conquers all, right?

~November 11, 1995~

Dear Diary,

Study, study, study. The pressure is building as I apply myself to prepare for the ACT. The process is beyond time consuming, demanding, and mentally draining. During the week, I had a brief conversation with my counselor. For the first time in four years, she advised me to stay in the local area to attend the community college. Worthless. Just worthless. She won't even attempt to provide me with any other options.

But rumor has it the majority of these counselors are just trying to collect their checks and push us out the door. For the last couple of years, I've dreamed of attending an HBCU, or some university, so before I left the office, I skimmed over the pamphlets stacked on the shelf for college and university application information.

The Western Illinois University pamphlet stood out, mainly because it was outlined with my favorite color, purple. I tucked it away in my notebook. I'm going to take the next couple of months to study for the ACT, and hopefully in February I'll be ready to retest. I'm praying to increase my score. I've been thinking about the next step—graduation is literally around the corner. I can't stay here. I want to succeed, be adventurous. If I go to Western Illinois, I can come back on holiday breaks and during the summer, and also, I wouldn't be too far away from home.

~December 13, 1995~

Dear Diary,

Tori had a baby girl yesterday—another niece—and her name is Shanea. She is a chunky, healthy baby, and we all went to visit her in the hospital.

~December 25, 1995~

Dear Diary,

Merry Christmas! For the past couple of years, I've dreamt of having enough money to buy Jordan another WWF wrestling ring. Although he's older now, he still doesn't let me forget. He probably never will. If I could rewind time, I would've been more careful around Jordan's things. I swear, every year since he was five, he's reminded me of the moment I stepped right in the middle of his wrestling ring. It cracked in four different directions, and from the way he screamed, you would've thought someone was torturing the kid. He passed out on the floor, pretending to be unconscious, and when he finally got up, it was World War III. He was so hurt.

~January 1, 1996~

Dear Diary,

Happy New Year! The countdown begins. Six months to figure out which path to take and how to get to college. Last night was epic though. New Year's Eve and everyone in the house was hyped. Sam, Mom, Jordan, Sedrick, and even Tori stopped by for a while, then she left the kids with us for the night. We danced and danced, and for once, the house felt like home. I smiled a real smile today.

For two weeks, Mom's mood swings had been like a ticking time bomb. Lupus had become the judge and she was the prisoner sentenced for life. Without parole. In between the constant yelling and angry tantrums, it had become unbearable, and my patience was running thin. I thought this part was past us. It snuck back in the house like a thief in the night, once again creating the atmosphere of a danger zone. One day, the road of sanity was clear, the next we found ourselves standing on a field of land mines. At times, I just wanted to run away.

I dreamt I had wings—beautiful, white fluffy wings with purple tips and lightly dusted gold glitter gracing each feather. I dreamt I flew away to a vacant island where I was free. Free to be whoever I wanted to be. But sadly, I didn't even know who I was.

After a couple of hours of her yelling, I grabbed my coat and walked out the door. It was freezing outside, but I didn't care. I trailed through the snow, stepping in already placed footsteps to Grandma's house, hoping to clear my head. But it only added more confusion to my flaming brain as I sat at the table trying to explain Mom's inconsistent behavior to Grandma.

"Grandma, you're not hearing me. Something's wrong with Mom, and it's not lupus. Not this time."

"Oh, she'll be fine. She's just probably having a bad day, that's all."

"A bad day? There are a whole lot of bad days. She yells at us for literally no reason. She sits in the house all day doing absolutely nothing. She stays in her room watching television or going through old mail again and again and again."

"Yeah, I know."

"You know." I lifted an eyebrow. "Well, if you know, stop saying she'll be fine. Because she's not fine at all." I was probably going too far, but at that point, I didn't give a shit.

"You calm down. Go home."

"Sure, go home. That's all you've been telling me since I was damn near eleven years old. Just go home. I don't know why I even came down here in the first place." I scuffled to put my coat back on.

"Watch your mouth."

"Grandma, you're no different. Not once did you ask me if I needed help or if I was okay. Not once. We were by ourselves, alone. I was all alone, and I had to deal with everything. All. Alone."

"You were fine. There's nothing wrong with you." Her expression was blank.

I pushed back from the table to stand up. "Fine? Grandma, no, I'm not fine. Far from being fine. Neither is my mom, but who cares enough to give a damn, right?" I yanked the doorknob and slammed the door behind me.

I climbed the hill to get to the park and sat for an hour until my toes became numb. I was irate. I felt out of control. I walked and cried, walked some more, and cried some more, because it just felt like no one cared. At times, I felt like I was losing my mind. I was trapped in a repetitive cycle driven by what everyone else needed. But what about what *I* wanted? What *I* needed? I'd done everything I thought I was supposed to do. I didn't want the rest of my life to be like that. I wanted to be free.

No more crying, no more heartache, no more misperceptions and foiled plans.

*   *   *

~January 17, 1996~

Dear Diary,

New semester. The last semester of high school, back to an all-day schedule. I've taken a couple of electives to fulfill the requirement to participate in the school's sports program. Track season will begin in a couple of months. This is it. The final stretch. Today I completed the admission application to Western Illinois University, and I stopped by the gas station for a stamp and mailed it out. When I told Mom, she was quiet. She didn't have much to say besides, "That's good." I know my freshman year grades truly hurt my overall GPA, and my second semester junior year grades—especially chemistry—were . . . well, not good. But, I'm just hoping for a miracle. I pray I get accepted.

After talking to a couple of classmates, they told me to make sure to get the package for financial aid from the counselor's office. Since Mom's been on public assistance and receiving disability because of the lupus, I think I'll qualify. But financial aid may not cover all the expenses like tuition, room and board, and the meal plan coverage. I definitely don't want any student loans, or I'll be trying to pay it off until I'm ninety years old.

~January 26, 1996~

Dear Diary,

Let's go! All registered and scheduled to take the ACT on February 17th. I don't know if I'm ready or not. At this point, time is not on my side with graduation approaching in a couple of months. I have to go to college. Reading the newspaper, watching the daily news, and observing people, I figure it's the only way to succeed and gain as much knowledge and education as possible. Working minimum wage is getting me absolutely nowhere. If I aspire for greater, then I will be greater. I have to figure this out, like now. Right now. The pamphlets from the college and universities list a lot of important information, but the number one issue is tuition.

Oh, my goodness, college is really expensive. I can't pay for this working at Hardee's. Mom doesn't have money to send me to college. Dad, well, I'm not going to even play with that idea. I didn't know college was so expensive. Who has that type of money? Scholarships. Scholarships have to be the focal point right now. How do I find additional funding to go to college? It's so much money. I'm starting to feel like maybe I won't be able to go.

~February 1, 1996~

Dear Diary,

Spoke with Dad today. Guess what? He's getting married to some lady who has a young daughter. I'm not sure if he was requesting or insinuating that we go to the wedding. I've thought about whether we should or shouldn't go. Jordan and I are still deciding. Maybe this'll help our connection. The wedding isn't until March. This may be an open door of opportunity to meet more family members we've never met before.

The ACT test wasn't too complex. The limited time to complete each section was nerve-racking, and I tried to not let the jitters interrupt my attention span. I looked over the student financial aid application, and a lot of the questions required some information only Mom could fill in. I wasn't sure if it was because Mom didn't want me to go to college, or if something else was going on, but lately she seemed highly agitated with me. I hadn't done anything that I knew of.

"Mom, do you have a minute?"

"What is it?" Her eyes were focused on the newspaper.

"I'm trying to fill out this FAFSA form. It's a financial aid application, and it's asking for some of your personal information." I set the paper down on the table, and she didn't touch it. She didn't even look up.

"Just leave it there. I'll get to it."

"Yes ma'am." I walked back upstairs.

The thought of going away to college made me miss Jordan and Sedrick already. I skipped my last class to leave school early, just to make it in time for Jordan's basketball game. He played exceptionally well, and it was amazing to see him out there playing with his own style. I couldn't believe he was so big. I sat in the stands and waved at him. He smiled at me with that killer smile. He had charming dimples that were striking the hearts of young girls already. After the game, we went to McDonald's and chatted for a while.

"Did you see how I shook him? He was dizzy," he said.

"Yeah, I saw you out there. Doing your thing. Gosh, you grew so fast. We're the same height. I'm five feet ten inches. You're only thirteen. This is crazy. So, what do you think about going to Dad's wedding?"

"I mean, I don't know. I'll go if you go."

"Part of me wants to go to see more of our family that we don't know. But . . . part of me doesn't because he doesn't come to any of our events or celebrations. I don't know."

"Man, are we going to have to take the bus again?" He scrunched his face.

I laughed out loud. "What's wrong with the bus? I thought you liked taking the bus."

"You got jokes, Tee. Hell no, I don't like taking the bus."

"I don't know if he's going to come get us or what. Guess we'll have to ask."

So, we rode the damn bus again. We were on our way to Dad's wedding, except this time we each had our own music, and Jordan's legs were a lot longer. He sat in the aisle seat, sitting sideways the entire trip. We talked the majority of the trip about sports, school, and "oh-no girls." Well, he was going into high school soon, so it was about that time. When I was his age, I was already talking to Kevin on the phone, *and* Kevin had ridden his bike to my house, so I couldn't fret about it too much.

Once we arrived in Tennessee, we stood in the lobby of the station. It was déjà vu, a flashback from the trip two years before. I had attempted numerous times to push the past aside, but over the last almost ten years, I'd only seen Dad twice.

The wedding was nice, and random people approached us with a million stories about our grandparents, aunts, uncles, and countless other family members. So, we had a stepmom and a stepsister. Interesting . . . . Actually, not so much since we didn't visit often, and once I got to college, I figured I would more than likely just go back to Mom's house on my breaks to hang out with my brothers.

My southern aunties were complete sweethearts, so loving and caring. I'd connected with them all and hoped to build a relationship with them. My Aunt Gloria was funny and appeared to be a free spirit dipped with southern sweetness.

"You've grown since the last time I saw you," she said.

"Yes, ma'am. Not taller, that is, but I've gained a couple of pounds."

"I see. You're not completely skin and bones anymore."

"Oh, no ma'am. I'm up to a size eight in women's jeans now."

"All right. Watch out there now."

"It's about time. I thought I was never going to get any boobs or a booty."

She smiled at me. "Well, Niece, that's not the case anymore. Looks like those Hunt genes have kicked in. Girl, I used to have it. A sure 'nuff fire starter. You just make sure you carry it like a lady."

"Used to have it? What happened to it?"

"What do you mean?" She stood up and placed her hands on her hips, then swayed her slim frame back and forth while shaking her booty. "Girl, I still got it. It ain't gone nowhere."

Overall, the trip to Memphis was a good time with laughs and love, which was always a decent combination in my book. And oh boy, the food. Southern cooking is the best, with savory flavors that linger on your tongue for days. Once the celebration was over, I had the opportunity to speak with Dad about my graduation. He sat in front of me holding my hand. We were eye to eye.

"I will be there, no matter what," he promised.

"Well, like the invitation says, it's on June first. On a Sunday. Don't forget. Jordan's graduation is May thirty-first, and I'm sure he'd be excited if you came to his, too."

"Two for one special. All right. I'll find the time and be there." He kissed me on the cheek.

The anticipation led me to believe him as his words provided comforting confirmation. This time, I hoped, he would keep his promise.

* * *

~March 28, 1996~

Dear Diary,

Spring break! I sat today thinking about the previous spring break trips to different HBCUs with the Minority

Teacher's Incentive Program. It's been truly inspirational. During the previous trips, we attended these HBCUs: Clark, Spelman, Morehouse, Jackson State University, and University of North Carolina at Chapel Hill. Oh! We also went to Louisiana State University where we had the opportunity to stand on the same basketball court that Shaquille O'Neal plays on.

No trip this year due to low funding. Of course, I would love to fulfill my dream of attending a historical black institution, but I'm not sure how I'd even get there. Last week, I received my ACT score. My overall score was nineteen. Not too bad. I'm pretty sure it'll get me into college. I just have to finish this semester with good grades. No slacking.

~April 6, 1996~

Dear Diary,

Earlier this week, I quit my job. I figured I had two months left of school, and I was going to make the best of the remaining time. Since Mom seems to be physically healthy, perhaps I don't have to be at home all the time. I'm so over doing dishes, cooking, doing laundry, and watching my brothers. I'm just over it. I love being with my family, but I want to hang out now. I need to see what I like. See what I want.

I was asked to prom by a classmate named Gary Tobbs. He was also on the track team. After Derrick passed away, I lost the interest to date, and after the incident with Nelson, the dent in my heart still ached. The terror still haunted me. The thought of being alone with a boy still terrified me, but I knew I couldn't remain internally secluded forever. I told myself that I would attend everything possible to celebrate the upcoming new journey to life. But I had nothing to wear, and I hadn't even asked for permission to go yet.

"Mom, do you have a minute?"

"Sure, what is it?"

"Someone's asked me to prom. Can I go?"

She stopped writing on her tablet. "Yeah, of course. You should go, have fun."

"There's just one thing."

"What's that?"

"Since I'm not working, I only have sixty-eight dollars left, and I'm not sure if it's enough to buy a dress."

"Don't worry about it. We'll figure it out." After standing still for a couple of minutes, I thought maybe this would be a perfect opportunity for Mom to get back to what's she was passionate about—sewing. "Why are you just standing there? Is there something else?"

"Well, would you sew me a dress?"

She set her pen down, stood up, and stared at me with a huge smile across her face. "That's a perfect idea. We can go to the fabric store this weekend and look at some patterns. Let me guess . . . you want to wear your favorite color, purple, right?"

"Actually, I was thinking more like red."

"Oh, really? Hot mama."

CHAPTER 22

* * *

~April 30, 1996~

Dear Diary,

This is nerve-racking, I have to admit that I'm scared out of my mind. All of a sudden, I feel so unsure. What if I don't get into college? What will I do? Where will I go? I know I don't want to stay here in Rock Island. I want to succeed. But succeed at what? I just need Western to accept my application. I need financial aid to approve me for enough money so I don't have to apply for student loans. Playing sports would've been a great opportunity to receive funding for college, but, well, you see how that went. I'm nervous. I truly am.

M om's distraught behavior when I walked through the door made my head throb. *What was going on now?* Sam sat next to her in attempt to calm her. Sedrick ran and hid behind me. I picked him up and went upstairs to Jordan's room.

"Hey, what's going on?" He was lying across his bed watching *Yo! MTV Raps.*

"Close the door. Grandma called right after I got home from school. Ever since then, Mama's been a bit emotional."

"About what, though?"

"Something that has to do with Uncle Darren. I don't know the full story."

I slowly opened the door. "That's because you don't know how to listen." I set Sedrick down on Jordan's bed, gave him the bag of potato chips from my book bag, and proceeded to the hallway. Yeah, I was being nosy—nosy as hell.

"I know this has to be hard. Unfortunately, there is just nothing anyone can do to slow down the progression of his condition," Sam whispered.

"He's getting weaker by the minute. I know he's not getting any better. I'll be there for him, but it's just difficult to watch him fade away."

"I know."

"I take him to his doctor's appointment. Wash his frail body from time to time. And all the while, I try to hold on to his smile as I picture him as just a boy." She burst into tears. "I want to continue to help him, but it's too dangerous for me to come into contact with him now. I just barely received this kidney. What if my immune system weakens? I feel selfish for even saying that. I'm scared. But, I want him to know I'm there for him."

"Well, continue to take the same precautions you've been using," Sam suggested. "He'd probably be more comfortable if you continue to take him to his doctor's appointments, though."

Mom's voice calmed, and as I glanced over the banister, I saw Sam hug her.

"He's my baby brother," she cried. "I told him he wasn't going to die, but he just keeps getting worse. It's just so hard."

It felt like a marble was lodged in my throat. I knew exactly what she meant. Watching a disease diminish someone you loved when you couldn't do a thing about it was disheartening.

Uncle Darren's condition began to weigh on Mom's shoulders. On top of her own remaining battles with lupus, things continuously added to her plate. She'd often get lost in her own thoughts.

With prom a week and a half away, Mom called me downstairs for a final fitting. It was perfect—a sleeveless, long, satin red dress with small straps connected from the bust cups to the choker around my neck. She pinned the waistline in just a few more inches. She'd taken all my measurements a week ago: dress size eight, thirty-four D bust, twenty-seven-and-a-half-inch waist, and hips rounding at thirty-eight and three quarters. Mom had impeccable sewing skills, and the design and creativity she carved into my dress was remarkable. After I slipped back out of the dress, she immediately returned to the sewing machine. I could tell her mind was racing and her heart was aching. Her presence was distant although she stood directly in front of me.

After a couple of days passed, track season was officially over. Many of us went off to super-sectional competitions. I didn't place as I high as I'd imagined, coming in at fifth place. Therefore, I didn't qualify for State competitions. But it was fun.

The day of prom arrived hectic and hot. We all prepared for the monumental moment to come, the class of 1996 promenade dance. All of my classmates were pumped, hyped to the hundredth degree; the phone rang like a million times with excitement projected through the receiver. This was our moment, our time to make memories we would all talk about twenty years later. I was relieved that Mom was in a good mood, and when I ran through the door, she had everything already laid out for me.

"Awesome." I kissed her on the cheek. "Thank you, thank you, thank you." I undressed and ran to the bathroom to take a shower.

Mom yelled through the bathroom door, "Gary called! He said he'll be here around six thirty to pick you up. So, you have exactly an hour to get ready."

I yelled back, "Okay."

It still felt like a hundred degrees outside, and I didn't even know how to do my hair. After getting into the dress, I tried my best to style it, but it was a mess. Because I couldn't wear an actual bra under my dress, Mom bought some breast cups that were supposed to just stick to your skin. You know, to hold the girls together for support. Mom applied them for me.

"Umm, Mom."

"Stop squirming around. Hold still."

"Mom, you're making me really uncomfortable. Geez, your hands are cold. Do you have to like actually touch my boobs?"

"Stop it. Unless you're more comfortable doing it yourself. I'm just trying to help you."

Sedrick hopped on my bed, jumping up and down. "I can help. Let me try, Talisa."

Mom and I looked at each other and burst into laughter. He had no idea what we were talking about. "Umm, Sedi, you can't help me. Not this time, buddy."

He sat in the middle of my bed with his lip hanging down, pouting. "But I never get to help. I can try to fix it." He melted my heart with that little face.

Everything came together perfectly. Gary was on time with the prettiest white and gold corsage, and when I stepped outside on the porch, I took multiple deep breaths, convincing myself that this moment should be cherished. I kept telling myself, *He's not going to hurt me.*

As I sat in his car, I was entirely inwardly defensive. All I could think was that if he attempted to touch me, I was going to use every muscle in my body to whip his ass. Even if I had to pretend like I was crazy. When we arrived at the recreational center, the ambiance was spectacular. Everyone dressed to impress, and bright glittery red and gold balloons floated throughout the room, casting an array of sparkles to the ceiling. Small bits of confetti brightened each table. The dance floor was overly crowded as the music filtered the soles of tapping shoes. We danced a couple of times.

Gary was a nice guy, although I didn't like him like that. A group of girls from the track team came together to take a picture. Memories to hold on to forever. The group joked around, and then we made our way to the dance floor. I pulled Leslie by the arm and drug her to the floor. We all danced until we had to take off our heels. In that moment, I was free. In that moment, everything was simply amazing.

At school, prom night conversations filled the hallways with laughter as we all recapped the majestic night. After walking home from school, I was exhausted. Not that I was out of shape, but I was cramping bad. It felt like someone was tugging away at my belly button and twisting it in a million circles. I couldn't wait to dive into my bed.

Mom was having one of her days, but I ignored it and headed straight to my room. When I flopped down on my bed, an envelope popped up into the air and landed on the floor. I reached for it and sat in silence, holding the envelope. I read the purple letters in the top left corner: *Western Illinois University, Office of Admissions.* I kicked my shoes off, leaned back on top of my teddy bears and pillows, and curled up. This was it—the moment I'd been waiting for.

And I couldn't open it.

I placed the envelope on my chest, smothered it with a pillow, and closed my eyes.

Okay, God. You know I'm not very good at this whole praying thing. But can we talk for a minute? As I hold this letter close to my heart, I'm hoping that the words inside are a gateway to a new future for me so that I can succeed, become more knowledgeable, and venture away from home. Although I really want this letter to say that I've been accepted, if it doesn't, please show me another way to succeed. Amen.

I woke up when a three-year-old kid with hot Dorito breath jumped on my bed and put his nose to my nose.

"Talisa, are you sleeping?"

I giggled.

"Not anymore, Sedi." I tickled him until he was red-faced. He sat on my lap holding three of his Power Ranger figurines as I procrastinated about opening the letter.

"What's that?"

"It's a letter from a university."

"What's a university?

"It's a big girl school."

"Like the big girl school, you go to now?"

"No, Sedi. It's an even bigger girl school than that."

His eyes widened and his jaw dropped. "Whoa, that's a big school. Do you have to catch the bus there?"

Oh, my goodness, this kid with all the questions in the world.

"Let's just open the envelope, okay?"

"Okay, can I help?" he asked.

I made a small tear in the corner and let him open the rest. I unfolded the letter and set Sedrick on the floor.

"What does it say?"

I was so nervous. The letters were blurry at first, but there it was in black and white.

"Oh shit! It says, 'Congratulations, we are pleased to announce your admission for the fall of 1996.'" I hopped around. "Yes, yes, yes."

"Yay, shit."

I stopped jumping. My eyes bucked like a deer's eyes shined

by headlights. "No, no, no. Sedi, you can't say that word. It's a bad word."

He smiled. "But you said it."

"I know. But, I didn't mean to say it so don't say it anymore, ok?" I held both of his arms to his sides.

"So, I can't say shit."

"Stop it. No, you can't. Don't say it again. I mean it or I'll have to give you a whooping."

"I have to whoop you, too. You said shit, too." I wished I could take the battery out of his little brain and press reset.

"Sedi, STOP! Please don't say it anymore. If Mom hears you, she's going to be really mad." He covered his mouth and mumbled between his tiny fingers. "Ok, I won't."

I ran down the stairs, and Sedrick followed me. I stood off to the side of the couch and smiled at Mom.

"What is it?'

"I was accepted to college at Western."

She continued pushing the buttons on the remote without looking up at me. "Okay, that's good."

What? "Okay, that's good?" That's all she had to say?

"Well, can I go?"

Sedrick hopped on the couch next to her.

"Talisa, have a seat." She set the remote down on the arm of the sofa and sat up straight. "I really wish I had the money to give to you for college, but I don't. I'm sure you'll qualify for financial aid. But there are other expenses that have to be covered. I suggest you call your dad."

I soaked into the loveseat, feeling defeated once again. What was I supposed to do? Staying home was not an option, not the answer. I knew being home would not allow me to live out my dream to succeed in life. The acceptance letter was my first-class ticket to soar amongst the clouds.

Disoriented and irritated, I walked back upstairs and showed Jordan the letter.

"Talisa, does this mean you get to go to college?"

"Yeah, that's exactly what it means."

"I want to be happy for you, but I really don't want you to go away."

"Yeah, I don't want to leave you guys. But I can't stay here. I have to better myself, get a better education, so I can get a better job than Hardee's making $5.45 an hour. That's not what I want."

"Go. Do what you want to do then."

"I have to get there. I don't have a car or any money."

"Did you ask Mom?"

I looked at him, "Yeah, she told me to call Dad."

"Was she serious?" He scrunched his face.

"Yeah, I think she was."

"What are you going to do?"

"I don't know."

"I'll be sad if you go."

"I'll come back for holidays, spring break and summers. It won't be forever. I will still be able to hang out with you guys. And go to your basketball games."

"Yeah, but it won't be the same." His shoulders slouched.

"A better education could mean a better future. An actual

job." I knew he would miss me; I would miss him, too. But, I didn't see a better future for me if I stayed home.

As I sat in the bleacher staring at Jordan, a sense of proudness overwhelmed me. It was humid, hot, and an unpleasant smell in the small gym at the junior high was unsettling. I sat next to Mom and Sedrick, waiting for Jordan to walk up to the stage to receive his eighth-grade graduation certificate. I was praying Dad would show up. Once Jordan sat down, he looked over at us. He smiled at me, I waved, and then he continued to look back at the door multiple times. Damn, I wanted to tell Jordan not to worry about it, but I recalled sitting in almost the same exact seat waiting for Dad to walk through the door at *my* eighth-grade graduation. I too, hoped, anticipated, that Dad would appear at my graduation. But each unrecognizable face that walked through the door was a punch in my gut. Sadly, I couldn't stop Jordan from feeling those exact feelings, and I would've done anything for him not to feel them.

But I couldn't do anything, and neither could Mom. Jordan smiled and told jokes afterwards, pretending Dad's absence didn't affect him. He was deflecting, and for a moment, I saw myself in his eyes as his laugh grew boisterous, a bit too loud, a bit too unconvincing. I felt like he was teaching himself to mask the pain—the hope of having a present father. I knew the feeling all too well.

I walked past his door later that evening. I heard him crying. I stretched my arm out to reach for his doorknob when Mom's voice startled me from behind.

"Don't."

I jumped, "But he's crying."

"I know. Every bit of me wants to call your dad. You both are going to have to make up your own minds."

"What do you mean?"

"It means, pay attention to how people treat you. Even family. Then, you decide how you choose to deal with them. Got it?"

"Yes, ma'am. But he's in there by himself, and he's hurt."

"Talisa, go finish getting ready for bed. Leave your brother to figure it out." She walked back into her room. I turned to look at Jordan's door one more time before closing my door. My heart broke for him, but I did as Mom said.

*　*　*

~June 1, 1996~

Dear Diary,

Today is the day! Graduation Day! This is it! Mom woke up in a cheerful mood, thank goodness. She was up cooking before the sun lit the sky. Music was playing and she decorated the house with red, gold, and white streamers and hung posters on the walls. Jordan helped her set up folding chairs on the back patio while I walked through the house smiling. Today is going to be epic.

Mom hung a huge "Class of 1996" sign on the front door, and Ms. Rose brought over some balloons. Leslie and I were going to celebrate this final moment together.

All of the students met in the auditorium around 11:00 a.m., many in disbelief, others already in tears, some basking in the moment. We helped others with their caps and gowns, and just as I was about to pin the gold tab on another student's gown, a newspaper reporter approached us. She asked if she could take a picture of us, and we both agreed. The ceremony was held on the football field, which was roughly a block from the school. It was hot marching over to the stadium, but well worth it. As we lined up alphabetically, we heard the music play through the stadium speakers. There were hundreds of people in the stands. I couldn't have found Mom, Jordan, Sedrick, Sam, and the rest of the family even if I had had binoculars.

They called my name to receive my diploma. It was an amazing feeling knowing I had done it. Even though my overall GPA was 2.87, I'd still done it. My ACT practice test score was seventeen, but I'd studied before taking the actual test where I scored a twenty, so I'd done it. I applied for college, and I was accepted. I'd done it. I applied for financial aid, and I hoped I had done it right.

After the ceremony, everyone took a hundred and one pictures, and then they went their separate ways. I was surrounded by the entire family, and I was showered in kisses and hugs. With so many family members present, I was still looking for *him*. But he never came. False hope. Why did I keep looking for something different, still seeking for the moment when he would be there for me? We'd traveled by bus for long hours to get to him—not once, but twice. He had looked me in the eye and affirmed that he would come, but he lied. He was a no-show. As the crowd diminished, I sat on the steps of the auditorium, and Mom finally walked over.

She stood in front of me, muted at first; our eyes connected and her soft expression consoled me. Then she grinned. "I'm proud of you."

She meant it, and her face gleamed with joy. I'd never heard her say that before, and the words resonated in my heart.

"Thank you, Mom."

"Well, come on. We have to get to the house. A lot of people are going to be there, so let's go."

"Mom, I need to walk. Okay? It won't take me long to get home, I promise."

She stared at me for a second, and in that moment my hurt was her hurt. She placed her hand over her heart to show that if she could, she'd take what I was feeling . . . away. She knew I needed a moment—a moment to collect my thoughts and feelings.

"Okay, Talisa. Okay." She walked to the car, and I walked back across the grassy field.

Still wearing my gown, I tossed my cap in the air. People were driving by and honking their horns as I approached the park. I sat on the swing and kicked my feet, letting the sand run in between my toes as my tears fell. I didn't even know why I was crying, because I was also smiling, swinging on the swing with my eyes closed as the breeze cooled my face. I took a walk by the colorful flower beds before I walked down the hill to go home. The array of colors encouraged a smile. I stood at the top of the hill, looked up, and giggled. "Everything is going to be all right. Everything. I just know it." I had set my mind to what I needed to do, and I had done it.

The front, side, and back yards were full of family and friends, and as I walked up, everyone started clapping. Part of me felt delighted that so many recognized my accomplishment, however, the little voice in my ear was appalled by their presence. Everyone surrounded me with praise, love and acceptance—for me. Where were they when I needed help? But I maintained my focus, which was to enjoy my day without negativity attached to it. With each handshake and hug, I repeated to myself: *Stay positive. Push through it.* Part of me was tired of pushing through and not vocalizing my opinions. I sat outside on the front porch to get some air, and Jordan joined me.

"Hey, big time." He smiled and kissed me on the cheek.

I smirked. "I'm not big time. This is just one step to the future."

"Yeah, but you get to go away to college."

"You will too once you graduate from high school, so try to stay focused. Jordan, you're a basketball player. Be smart. A lot of people think the majority of black boys are in sports because that's all they have going for themselves. So, study hard. You can be both . . . smart *and* an athlete. You hear me?"

He smiled. "Yes, I hear you."

"You hear me, but are you listening? I'll call you all the

time. Every break I'll come home. But in the meantime, be a leader, Jordan, not a follower. No gangs, no drugs, and don't get anyone pregnant. You hear me?"

"Huh? What you say? I blacked out for a second."

I rolled my eyes. "I'm not playing with you. Stay focused."

"I hear you, Sis. I mean, I'm listening. But, what was the last part? The last thing you said?"

I pinched his arm.

Mom yelled through the screen door, "Talisa, your dad is on the phone. He wants to talk to you." I looked at Jordan. He looked away.

"Jordan, do you want to talk to him?"

His face was blank, no smile. "Nope."

I grabbed his hand. "Jordan, I will always be here for you. You know that, right?"

"Yeah, I know, Sis. I'll be here for you, too."

"It means I got you, always. Okay?" He looked at me with curiosity in his eyes, and I squeezed his hand.

"I got you, too, Sis. Always."

I pulled him in the house, and we walked through the crowd. Mom stood in the doorway of the kitchen holding the phone. She handed it to me, and I stared at it for a second. I thought of all Dad's words, his promises, and his absence. My pain. Jordan's pain. I looked at Jordan and smiled. I nodded at Mom and hung up the phone. Mom didn't say a word, and Jordan and I high-fived each other.

I threw my arm around his shoulders. "Come on, Brother. Let's go eat."

*   *   *

~June 3, 1996~

Dear Diary,

My head feels like a ton of bricks. Every sound, every movement is bouncing around in my brain like someone turned the volume up to the max. Leslie and I partied, and I mean partied like never before. We visited graduation party after graduation party until we ended up at a hotel party. We were eventually kicked out, and I'm not sure which drink did the most damage, but right now, it's obvious alcohol is not my forte. The punch was spiked at one of the locations, and it was either the Mad Dog 20/20 or the Night Train that was being passed around. We were definitely drunk. Mom wasn't even mad when I got home. She just giggled and watched me crawl up the stairs, swearing to never drink again.

PART IX

Big Girl Panties

CHAPTER 23

I T WAS TORI's birthday, and after contemplating whether or not to walk the six blocks to her house, I decided to take the journey. As I walked, I giggled to myself thinking about the first time Mom had given me permission to hang out with Tori. She had taken me to my very first concert, and it was a night I'd never forget. Despite our differences, I loved her—more than she would probably ever know.

The scene was a bit sketchy as the bass boomed from car trunks and beer bottles littered the front steps of Tori's house. People had gathered on the porch and in the yard, and as I walked through the crowd of people, they stared at me as if I didn't belong. I didn't care. The front door was wide open, so I walked into the house. Quentin ran up to me with his little arms open wide. My nephew was so big; I hadn't seen him for some time. I hugged him tight and carried him into the living room. My nieces were in their playpen—Shanice alert, smiling, trying to climb out, and Shanea sound asleep through all the noise.

"Well, well, well. Look who decided to show up. What are you doing down here?" Tori stood in the doorway.

"Yeah, I wanted to say happy birthday. It's not like I have your phone number or anything."

She rolled her eyes. "Come on outside." I picked up Quentin and Shanice and walked out to the front porch.

"So, are you going to tell me the real reason you walked down here?"

"I told you—"

"I heard what you said. I'm asking you about what you're not saying." She sipped from her red plastic cup.

"I was accepted to Western Illinois University. I don't have a way to get there. I don't have any money, so—"

"So, what? I don't have any money, Talisa. Not like that. So, what are you asking?"

"Damn, Tori. I'm not asking for money. I'm asking you to help me get some money." Quentin and Shanice climbed down the stairs to play in the grass.

She looked at me, leaned her head to the side, and squinted. "You can't be asking me what the fuck I think you're asking me. Are you shitting me right now?" She grabbed me by the arm and pulled me in the house, yelling for some girl to watch the kids. "What in the hell is wrong with you?" She was pissed, pacing back and forth. "That is the dumbest shit you could ever do, I swear."

A crushing force had pushed me into a corner of defeat, increasing the pressure on my shoulders as my mind spun in frustration. Where do I go? What do I do?

"I just don't know what to do. I want to go. I have to get out of here, Tori. I can't just sit here. I just thought you could point me in the right direction or give me a name. Help me out. I'll work for it."

"Do you hear yourself? You sound stupid as shit. Drugs? You want to sell drugs?"

"What else am I going to do?"

"You go figure that shit out, but I'm not going to tell you where to go for this mess. I don't sell drugs, Talisa." She paused and mumbled. "Now, I might buy a little weed every now and then," she snickered.

"I'm not laughing. I'm serious, Tori."

"Ask Mom."

"I did. She told me to ask Dad. We haven't talked about it since, but all week she's been on my ass about getting a job."

"Ask Sam."

"Ask Sam what? I don't even see Sam a lot anymore. Even when he's around, it's not for long."

"What about the family?"

"Are you shittin' me, Tori? Like who? Everyone is in their own world; they're not concerned about what's going on . . . isn't that obvious?" I flopped down in the chair and placed my hands on my head.

"Well, damn, little sis. You sound like you need some weed to relax, girl."

I sighed. "I don't need weed. I need you to help me. Will you . . . please?"

"Talisa, listen. You don't want any part of these streets, trust me. This ain't for you." She pulled out the chair next to me and patted my back. "Look, it may seem like you have no options. But you'll figure it out. But this bullshit you're asking me is not the answer." Deep down, I knew she was right. I was only feeling desperate.

"You just need to trust God."

I burst into laughter. "What?"

"What are you laughing at? I believe in God."

"I'm not saying that you don't, Tori, but do you have to bring *Him* into this particular conversation while you're holding a drink in your hand?"

"Girl, Jesus turned water into wine. I'm just trying to enjoy my cup. Now, quit all that crying and come out here and get some of this barbecue."

She was right . . . I had to just figure it out. No one sat down with me to talk about attending college. I became determined after the spring break trips. Hell, I wouldn't have ever met my school counselor if I hadn't scheduled an appointment with her.

I had to just figure it out. On my own.

The day before Jordan's birthday we went to the mall. I didn't have a lot of money to get him a gift. He picked out a new CD. We walked past the armed forces office. A huge poster of a white woman dressed in a uniform caught my attention.

At the beginning of the school year, ten armed forces recruiters had posted up in the cafeteria. The Air Force recruiter stopped me and recited a scripted speech. I thought about it and mentioned it to Mom, but she didn't have much to say at the time. I toyed with the idea because I wasn't sure if I would get into college, and it sounded like an exciting adventure. Still, since I'd received my acceptance letter, I couldn't think of anything else but going to college. When I felt stuck in between a rock and a hard place, the thought of joining the military resurfaced as an open opportunity.

Jordan was sitting on a mall bench eating a slice of pizza. I pulled open the door to the armed forces office.

"Sis, what are you doing?"

"Jordan, it's just an option. Wait here."

I talked to each recruiter and watched a couple minutes of the Marine Corps boot camp training on video. I decided the Air Force seemed like a good fit for me. Maybe.

"What did they say?"

"Don't tell Mom, promise?"

"Promise."

"Well, the Marines and Army are definitely not for me. And I'm terrified of water, so that crosses out the Navy. So, I think the Air Force might be best."

"If you do this, you can't come back for a long time, right? It's not like college where you can come home for holiday breaks."

"Actually, he said that I can. I just have to complete basic training first, then there might be a slight break before I have to go to something called tech school to learn everything about the MOS that I choose."

"What's MOS?"

I flipped over the brochure. "It's military occupation specialty. In other words, a job in the Air Force."

"Don't you have to ask Mom first?"

"Nope. I'm eighteen."

"Whoa. Are you really going to do this?"

"I don't know, but don't say anything to Mom. I'll tell her if I decide to join."

For days I contemplated the idea of joining the military, or should I try to go to college. Now, at eighteen I was ready to spread my wings in hopes of venturing into the world. As I begin to tread the waters of what the world had to offer, big trouble aroused. Mom gave me permission to go with some of the girls from the track team to Chicago. I told Mom we were going on a college campus visit over the weekend, and that the older sister of one of the girls was taking us. Lies. We actually went to Chicago to see some guy one of the girls met over the track season.

During the trip, while we were hanging out with random people in a parking lot, the police pulled up. They ran all the parked cars' license plates and asked for our driver's licenses. One of the officers approached us and told us that our vehicle was going to be towed. Because it was a rental car, and neither of us were twenty-five or older, the car wasn't supposed to travel beyond a certain number of miles. I thought we were in trouble. I couldn't even think straight because I couldn't afford to mess up, not then, especially since I was thinking about joining the military. We were three hours away from home with no transportation and no way to get back.

I had some of my graduation money on me, but not enough to get all us back. I couldn't believe it. The cops just left us stranded there in the parking lot. Luckily, the guy we drove there to visit told us he would take us home. The police called the rental company, and the rental company called my friend's sister who had rented the car. The sister told their dad, and the dominos fell as all of our parents were notified. The total cost of the tow back home was eight hundred dollars. When I got home, Mom and I argued, then I barricaded myself in my closet.

Mom and I hadn't been seeing eye-to-eye since the incident from the trip. The guilt of lying to her weighed me down and seeing the disappointment in her eyes dressed me with embarrassment. Something deep down in my heart was telling me that it was time be open and honest with her. I pulled the kitchen chair from the table and sat with my fingers intertwined.

She set the newspaper down on the table. "What is it, Talisa?"

"I'm going to join the military. The Air Force, actually."

Surprisingly, her expression went from stern to gentle. "Okay, if that's what you want to do."

"It is."

She leaned forward. "Sounds like you have your mind made up."

"I know I mentioned it at the beginning of the year, but now I'm sure."

"When?"

"When, what?"

"When are you going to join?"

"I've already talked to the Air Force recruiter at the mall. He said anytime I want to come to take the practice test, I can.

Since I'm eighteen and have a high school diploma, I've already met two requirements."

She crossed her arms and leaned back. "Okay. When you go, I'm going with you."

I grinned at her, "Yes, ma'am. I'm going to call the recruiter and schedule the practice test. But, Mom. . . . Will you be all right?"

"What do you mean? This is your decision."

"I know. But, what if you get sick again and I'm not here?"

"Talisa, you have to do what is best for you. Your dreams and aspirations are yours and you can't push those to the side for anyone. You will regret it later in life. Don't worry about me, I'll be fine."

"I just want to succeed and try new things. Explore new opportunities. But I don't want to leave you guys."

"Listen, there is nothing here. All these young people getting into mischief, all these young girls running around pregnant. There is nothing wrong with wanting to strive for more."

I didn't need Mom's permission, but I wanted her approval . . . and perhaps, her blessing.

*　*　*

~July 16, 1996~

Dear Diary,

This is happening really fast. I took the practice test today. I scored a thirty-two, which is below the required score for the Air Force. This is the ACT all over again. I'll have to study harder. One more thing—I have to lose ten pounds.

I'm not meeting the height and weight requirements either. I'm five-ten and one hundred fifty-seven pounds, but the Air Force requirement is either a max of one hundred forty-seven pounds, or below twenty-eight percent body fat. I need to shred some pounds or inches. I never thought I was fat, but all right, let's do it. No more snacks or junk food. The recruiter suggested more vegetables, better nutrients for my body, and more exercise, whether it's walking or running. So now I have to study, and study hard. If I can't attend college, this is my only other option.

After we left the office, Mom took me to the bookstore and I jumped out of the car fueled with determination. I ran in the store, purchased an Armed Services Vocational Aptitude Battery (ASVAB) practice test book. The sales clerk smiled at me and said good luck when she placed the book in the bag. I told her, "Thanks. I got this." We smiled.

~June 21, 1996~

Dear Diary,

I observed from the window seal as the small particles of freshly, cut grass began to irritate my eyes. This time of the year my sinuses flare up causing non-stop sneezing and continuous tear drops. Her face glowed even brighter when the sun rays spotlighted her as if she were standing center stage. Mom sat in the wicker, brown chair on the back porch with her feet propped up on an old, dull green plastic storage bin. She stared up at the sky, I assumed daydreaming until I saw the tiny bubble of water seated along the creased lines of the side of her right eye.

Now that I'm older, I get it. I understand her sadness, her fluctuating angry and maybe even her deep depression. I wondered if she'd dreamt of a different life, perhaps a different outcome. Lupus changed everything for her, she had no control, but if she could only see that she made it through. Maybe her smiles would be more genuine. Today, she drifted into a mental hiatus attempting to escape reality. Her moments of happiness are the best, but they seem to only be temporary before she drifts away. Once, again. Part of me doesn't want to leave her or my brothers, what if they need me? What if she gets sick again and I'm not here? I have to believe everything will be all right, and I must believe that there is a plan out there for me. A future, for me.

~July 31, 1996~

Dear Diary,

I've spent the last two weeks studying like crazy, walking to the school's track to run laps, and eating more carrots and lettuce than Roger Rabbit. Everyone's preparing for college, and I visited house after house after house as I checked off my list of early goodbyes and good lucks. Friendships, classmates, and acquaintances—I'm *learning the difference. We're all growing in different directions, and some of us are already falling apart. I'm just trying to focus on my goals since I committed to joining the Air Force. It's been my main focus. My only focus.*

After a month of studying, I was prepared to take the actual ASVAB test. After speaking with my recruiter, he scheduled my test at a testing site in Davenport, Iowa, just across the bridge. It wasn't far. I was scheduled to take the test at the end of August, and I was two pounds away from meeting the weight requirement. I was aiming to be below that before I took the test. Mom told me that Dad had called. I hadn't talked to him since before graduation, and I wasn't in the right frame of mind to talk. Not yet.

"Do you think I should call him? Should I tell him I'm joining the military?"

"Talisa, you have to decide whether you want to or not. I can't tell you what to do."

"I just don't know what to say. Am I supposed to keep pretending everything's all right when it's not?"

"Listen, if it's bothering you, then speak up. Are you scared you're going to hurt his feelings?"

I hung my head, mumbling, "Sometimes."

"Not everyone is going to treat you how you think they should, so pay attention. Listen to your gut. Stand up for yourself. Understand?"

"Yes, ma'am. I understand."

After eating Sunday dinner, the phone rang several times before Mom answered. It was Dad. I was lying on the couch flipping through pages of the ASVAB practice book, when she stood over me and handed me the phone.

"Hello?"

"Talisa, it's me. Dad."

"I know."

"Well, are you done being mad?"

"Are you calling to argue?"

He paused. "No, I just wanted to talk to you. How are you doing?"

"I'm fine. Studying to take the ASVAB test for the military."

"What? Oh Lord. Why the military? Why not go to college? You're smart; I know you are."

I itched to provide him with every detail, but I was too exhausted to repeat everything.

"Are you doing this because I didn't come to graduation? I sent you some money and a card."

"You're kidding, right? Money? A card?" My body temperature rose. "Dad, I'm tired. So tired of hoping and wishing for you to just be here for me. I'm not asking you for anything other than that. That's it."

"I couldn't get out of work. I just didn't have the time or extra money for multiple trips."

He had to be shittin' me. My head spun. "So, when you said you wouldn't miss it for anything in the world? To me, that means you get here regardless and make time. What do you mean multiple trips?"

"Yes, me and my wife and stepdaughter had plans for a trip." He paused, and I knew he was waiting for me to hang up in his face again, but I didn't. I kept my cool.

"Dad, you know what?"

"Talisa, I'm sorry. Don't be mad."

"I'm bound and determined to succeed. I will pass this test. I will be joining the Air Force. There is nothing that I need from you. I've always been fine on my own, and I think I'll *continue* to be fine on my own. So, enjoy your new family. I have to go. Take care."

His voice turned to a whisper. "Talisa, please . . . wait. I'm sorry. I love you."

"Later, Dad."

I hung up the phone.

* * *

~September 1, 1996~

Dear Diary,

An exuberant run this morning. I can't describe this feeling. Out of breath. I'm confidently assuring myself that my current decision is the right one. I passed the test. The military job position isn't available until the beginning of next month, which places me on the Delayed Enlistment Program. I've passed each requirement so far, and in thirty-five days, I'm headed to basic training in San Antonio, Texas. I have to go back to the Military Entrance Processing Station (MEPS), and I'm ready. Aunt Bernice is back from Texas. It's good to see her, especially with

Mom. They're truly enjoying each other's company. Their sisterhood and laughter make me smile.

~September 17, 1996~

Dear Diary,

It's hard to believe I'm nineteen years old today, but here I am in the flesh. No big celebration. Quite the chill, relaxing day. Mom gave me a really cute card with some money. Aunt Bernice wrote me a poem and gave me a figurine of two mice in a tea cup. She said it's me and her, brainstorming over tea.

That night, I lay on my bedroom floor, thinking about my future. What do I really want? Who do I want to be? Who am I? As the wheels turned slowly in my head and I bounced from idea to idea, I was entangled in a puzzle with missing pieces that I had to go find. I opened my new journal, and my ink pen sang a soft, slow melody to the textured pages as the two danced in harmony. Paper to ink, ink to paper, a current committing them to a forever-embedded song. My song. I wrote the words as if they were speaking directly to my soul. And maybe they were.

"*I AM*"

I AM who I choose to be, simply me,
Unapologetically me, no restraints, no restrictions,
just me.

Uncensored, unstoppable, unchained to the domain of a societal trap attempting to imprison the knowledge and wisdom I possess.

A pre-statistic they say, as if lying on my back to bear a government check—I mean, a child—is all my existence is good for.

I AM me, bold and bodacious, sweetened by the nectar slowly dripping from the birch tree, broken from the weight of my ancestors, hung like Christmas ornaments.

I AM almond eyes, thick thighs, cinnamon-complexioned radiant skin,

I AM poised with a purpose,

I AM decorated with determination,

I AM witted with willpower,

I AM not a victim, but a victor,

Me, simply me, I AM.

One week away from a new journey. A new adventure. My next step would be my first actual step into adulthood. My heart was wrenching, the throbbing of my chest felt like someone was tapping the center of it like a hammer to a nail. The day was full of farewells and good lucks. First, I stopped by Grandma's house. We talked just for a few minutes before I climbed the stairs to visit my great-grandmother and Uncle Darren.

Great Grandma Mary was so funny and cute. Our Sundays spent together would forever be etched into my heart. As I sat beside her holding her soft, but wrinkled hand, she smiled at me, and I captured a mental picture of her soulful glow. My heart crushed as I leaned in to kiss her goodbye. I began to perspire, shaken to the core by the thought of this being the last time I might see her. I would never want to see her pass away, but I knew then that death was inevitable. As I stood up to leave, I kneeled down to hug her one more time, and she grabbed my hands.

"You go show those boys that girls can do it, too." She winked at me.

"Yes, ma'am."

I opened the door to walk down the hall to Uncle Darren's room. The room was stuffy, and sunlight barely peeked through the drapes. On a wooden chair tinted gold by the shaft of light next to his bed, a fan was positioned, blowing light air. He was wrapped in multiple blankets with only his face revealed. I stooped down and hunted for his hand through the blankets. His entire body shook, and sweat beads were cradled over his eyelids. His eyes were closed, and I squeezed his hand.

"Uncle Darren? Can you hear me?" I whispered. His eyes opened slightly as his right-sided grin made me smile in return. "I joined the military. I'm leaving in almost a week." He grinned, closed his eyes mumbling, but I couldn't understand a word.

I prayed. He was so weak, so tired, barely coherent. I walked out, cried my eyes out for a couple of minutes, splashed water on my face, and left. I drove to my cousin Sharae's house. We reminisced of childhood days at Adventureland Amusement

Park, countless sleepovers, boy crushes, family moments, and our days of high school together. Before I left, our seemingly endless hug sealed our memories in a tiny box we'd keep forever. She was like a little sister to me. I could always count on a good laugh with her.

Geez, it had been an emotional day.

When I got back home, a parade of Power Rangers underwear, socks, t-shirts, and toy figurines were scattered down the hallway leading to my room. Sedrick was in my room watching TV, lying on my bed with his little backpack on, and using his pillow and blanket from his toddler bed.

I giggled. "Sedi, what are you doing?"

"Waiting for you."

"I mean, why did you make a mess in the hallway? What are all your clothes doing on my bed?"

"Mama said you're not going to the bigger girl school. She said you're going to the school where there are airplanes, so I got my clothes and stuff, too. I'm going with you."

I picked him up, hugged him tight. "Aw, Sedi, you can't go with me this time, but I'll be back."

His little bottom lip poked out.

"Hey, no crying. I'm coming back, okay?"

"Okay." He wrapped his little arms around me and laid his head on my shoulder.

"Okay, so let's go pick up this stuff in the hallway." It was incredibly hard to hold back my tears.

The morning I prepared to leave for basic training, Sam came by. We sat on the front porch and talked. He reiterated how proud he was of me and encouraged me to keep climbing to reach my goals.

He grabbed my hand. His voice was low and raspy. "In life, you may not get everything you think you should. Your dreams can come true if you really believe in yourself. Don't give up on yourself. You can still go to college; be sure to look into it when you get time. Got it?" He kept turning his head away. I wasn't sure if he was hiding his tears or what. Sam worked for the government. He had gone to college and played college basketball, too.

I believed he and Mom were connected solely for Sedrick; they weren't like they used to be. Not together. But he still came over to hang out and for holidays and celebrations. I thanked him for his advice and waved at him as we pulled away.

The journey had begun.

We were headed to Des Moines, Iowa. I would be transitioning into the mysterious journey bright and early the next morning. The time went by so fast. Mom, Aunt Bernice, Jordan, and Sedrick and I stayed in a hotel for the night. I couldn't sleep, thinking about what was to come of the next day and the days after. My recruiter told me to repeat to myself: It's only a mind game. Don't let anything or anyone get under your skin. I wondered if that would help.

Mom examined my face almost all night, like she was trying to memorize it. I knew she was worried and probably a bit scared, but I kept smiling at her, hoping to give her comfort.

The alarm went off at 4:00 a.m. sharp. I was already awake because I just couldn't sleep. The speedy process went smoothly and my family stood behind me as I took the oath to serve this country. I lifted my hand in the air, stood in front of a sergeant, and repeated the words verbatim. It was done. The limited list of items to take didn't allow me to pack much in my bag, which meant no music for over ten hours, which was going to be torture. The parking lot was full of people preparing for basic training and embracing their families with their farewells and goodbyes.

Jordan grabbed my hand. "Sis, you can always back out. You don't have to go."

"No, Brother, I can't. I took an oath. I can't renege now." We hugged. Jordan was taller than me now, about six foot one. We held each other for quite some time, and then we lost it. It had always been him and me, no matter what. Our emotions swirled into a furious whirlwind. I couldn't let him go. He couldn't let me go.

He whispered, "Please stay. Please don't leave me." He sobbed on my shoulder.

"I don't want to, Brother, but I have to do something. I have to go try. This might be a good thing." My heart was breaking into pieces. God, it hurt so much.

"Will you come back?"

"Yes, I promise. I'll call you when I can, I promise. I love you."

"I love you, too." I kissed him on both cheeks, and he walked away. He sat on a bench with his hand on his head. I wasn't trying to intentionally hurt him. It tore me to pieces watching him sitting there crying because of me. One day, I prayed he would understand. I prayed maybe me taking this step would encourage him to do the same.

Aunt Bernice held both of my hands, her face full of tears as she bowed her head and prayed over me for my safety. She kissed my cheek then walked to sit next to Jordan. I bent down to pick up Sedrick, and his little face was so red. I squeezed him in my arms and rocked him from side to side, planting kisses all over his face. I held him so tight because letting him go was harder than I ever thought. Mom attempted to take him. He kicked and cried, screaming my name at the top of his lungs. Jordan came to get him. I covered my face with my hands as he continued to scream my name, over and over again.

"Mom," I managed to say. She grabbed me, wrapped her arms around me, and held me as she hummed. For the first time, I felt her true presence, her heart beating in sync with mine, and it felt so damn good soaking in all of her love.

She whispered in my ear, "Baby girl, I'm sorry. I'm so sorry if I pushed too hard. I'm sorry you had to grow up so fast . . . so quickly."

"Mom, it's not your fault."

"I love you so much."

"I love you, too." I cradled the moment and all its essence as it capsized under the magnitude of emotions. I didn't want it to end, yet I knew it had to.

And soon it did.

A sergeant stood on the platform with a bullhorn, commanding everyone to wrap up their goodbyes and line up to board the bus.

Mama continued to hold me, repeating, "Oh, God, please. Please watch over her."

"Mom, I'll call you when I can. I don't know when that will be, but don't worry. Can you do me a favor?"

"What is it?"

"When you see Tori, will you give her a hug for me? Tell her I love her. And tell her I'm sorry. She'll know what it means."

She smiled. "Sure, I will. Be strong, pay attention. You better call me. Don't have me come looking for you."

I chuckled. "Really, Mom. What are you, an undercover FBI agent or something? You can't come on a military base." I just wanted her to stop crying.

She kissed my cheek and I kissed hers. It still took a minute or two for her to let go of my hand. Once I found a seat on the bus, I attempted to get situated, but looking out the window and watching my family walk away, I choked up again. I was confident in my decision, and deep down I was amped. Back home, I had a tarnished homecoming tiara on my dresser that spoke volumes about my place in the world. And along with a high school diploma hanging on my wall, they commemorated the moments where, against all odds, I'd succeeded. I didn't give up, though at times I wanted to. So, this was me trying yet again. Trying to do better. Trying to be better.

I wanted to experience new places, new people, and learn as much as humanly possible. I wanted to be free to be me, to figure out *my* life, finally. Everything from the past happened for a reason, good or bad, but this . . . this was my chance, my opportunity to have whatever life I chose. I would not fail, under any circumstance, regardless of the situation at hand. I would not fail.

The bus hiccupped and started to roll, and as I leaned my head against the window, my mind began to trail down memory lane. I closed my eyes and exhaled.

Although I didn't know what the journey would bring, I prayed it would help me figure out who I was.

AUTHOR'S NOTE

WHEN THE GROUND underneath your feet begins to crumble, do you stand still or do you attempt to run to solid ground? The clock is ticking. Life's uncertainties have a tendency to completely shake up what once was, transforming your life to the here and now, forcing sudden changes that you never thought would or could happen. I was just a girl when life slapped me in the face—innocent and clueless about the altering dynamics my family endured on a regular day. The mental photo album of my mother's countless health battles, stuck in my head, are daily reminders as to why I continue to strive for the best in life.

People all over the world unfortunately fight various health challenges on a daily basis; a plethora of heart-wrenching stories captivate us during the morning, afternoon, and nightly news. This story settled in my heart and mind for years as I toggled with the *Should I?* and *Could I?* and finally became comfortable with unveiling it to the world. This book contains various journal entries from my perspective as a young girl, as I watched life around me change, shape, and challenge my family, as well as myself. Through life's constantly changing paths, we learn to maneuver, accept, and push through the face of adversity.

Do you ever feel like you're standing center stage in the spotlight and life just keeps throwing tomatoes at you? Do you stand your ground waiting for it to stop throwing them, or do you run off the stage in defeat, hiding? Deep down, no one likes to lose. No one. Even when the most horrific, catastrophic events present themselves in your life, you have to find the strength to keep going. Giving up is the easy thing to do, but if you want the best out of your life, stand up, no matter what. Stand up and fight for the one life you've been given.